I0525607

The
SIGMA
CONSPIRACY

a J.T. Ryan Thriller

A Novel
By

Lee Gimenez

RRP
River Ridge Press

The SIGMA CONSPIRACY
by
Lee Gimenez

This is a work of fiction. The names, characters, places, incidents, and dialogues are products of the author's imagination and are not to be construed as real. Any resemblance to actual persons, living or dead, is entirely coincidental.

Printed in the United States of America.

Published by
River Ridge Press
P.O. Box 501173
Atlanta, Georgia 31150

Cover photos: Copyright by Mmaxer
used under license from Shutterstock, Inc.

Cover design: Judith Gimenez

ISBN-13: 978-0-578-63445-6

Novels by Lee Gimenez

The Sigma Conspiracy

Crossfire

Fireball

FBI Code Red

The Media Murders

Skyflash

Killing West

The Washington Ultimatum

Blacksnow Zero

The Nanotech Murders

Death on Zanath

Virtual Thoughtstream

Azul 7

Terralus 4

The Tomorrow Solution

Lee Gimenez

The
SIGMA
CONSPIRACY

a J.T. Ryan Thriller

Lee Gimenez

Chapter 1

November 3
Atlanta, Georgia

J.T. Ryan, his feet propped up on his desk, glanced out of his office window at the city skyline and sipped coffee. Yesterday he had finished a big case and was savoring the down time.

There was a knock at his door and a good-looking woman walked in, sat on one of his client chairs.

"You Ryan?" she asked.

"That's what it says on the door," he replied, dropping his feet to the floor and giving the woman an appraising look. In her mid-thirties, she was dressed in a tailored black suit with a white blouse. Her blonde hair was shoulder length, straight, and parted in the middle. A looker, but her expression was all business.

Reaching in her jacket, she pulled a badge and held it up for him to read. "I'm Erin Welch. Special Agent with the Secret Service."

"How special are you?"

She shook her head. "Steve Nichols told me you were good. But also a pain in the ass."

Ryan chuckled. "That would be me, alright." He turned serious. "Steve sent you? You're working on something with the FBI?"

Erin leaned forward in the chair. "The Secret Service and the FBI have set up a joint task force on a counterfeiting case. The Service has been working on it for a while, but the scope of the investigation has gotten too big for us to handle alone. We spend most of our time doing protection duty for government officials."

Ryan took a sip of coffee, put the cup down. "Would you like some? I just brewed a new pot. It's pretty awful, but it hasn't killed me yet."

She frowned – it was clear the woman didn't have a sense of humor. "No, thanks."

"Okay. You say it's a counterfeiting case. How do I fit in?"

"Nichols said he's hired you in the past as an FBI consultant."

"That's a fact. He and I go way back – we served together in the Army."

Erin nodded. "He told me about that. You guys were both in Special Forces – covert ops. After that he went in the Bureau and you became a private investigator."

He smiled. "I have to make a living, and regular police work is – a little constraining. Too many rules."

"Yeah. You don't seem the Bureau type."

"Not by a long shot. Now, tell me about the case."

A stern look crossed her face. "Tell me your fees first."

He told her.

"Okay," she said. "You're expensive, but we'll be sharing the cost with the Bureau."

"So, I'd have two bosses on this?"

"Got a problem with that?"

He thought about that for a moment. The paperwork was a bitch, but government agencies always paid on time. "No problem," he said.

She reached in her jacket, took out a folded sheet of paper and placed it on the desk. "Sign this so we can get started."

Ryan grinned. "Mind if I read it first?"

Erin frowned. She *was* the serious type, he mused. He scanned the letter – it was a standard non-disclosure form and he scrawled his signature at the bottom. "There you go. Now. About the case?"

"Sure. By the way, when I read your FBI file, it referred to you as J.T. Ryan. What's the J.T. stand for?"

"John Taylor. But call me Ryan. Everybody does."

She leaned back in the chair and folded her arms in front of her. "Okay. About six months ago, we noticed some new, counterfeit U.S. dollars turning up. Mostly twenties, but also fifties and hundreds. They showed up in the Southwest – Arizona, New Mexico, a couple of other states. Then a month ago they turned up here in Atlanta."

"I'm with you so far," he replied. "But you must see forged bills all the time."

Erin shook her head. "These are different. Most of the counterfeit money we see is crap – stuff cranked out on color copiers, using regular paper. To the naked eye, this new stuff is indistinguishable from the real thing. It takes sophisticated lab equipment to tell the difference."

He nodded.

She pulled a small manila envelope from a pocket and put it on the desk. "Take a look."

Ryan opened the envelope, took out four twenty-dollar bills. He examined them carefully, felt the weight of the paper, and looked closely at the printed seals.

Pulling out his own wallet, he selected a twenty from there and placed it on the desk next to the counterfeits. The fakes looked and felt identical.

"I'm no expert," he said as he looked up from the desk, "but I can't tell them apart."

"Now you see our problem."

"You got any leads so far?" he asked.

"One," she replied. "And this is where you come in."

"I'm listening."

"You still offering the coffee?" she asked.

Standing, he went to the coffee machine sitting on top of the file drawer. He poured her a cup. "Cream and sugar?"

"I take it black."

"Me too," he said, handing her the cup.

He sat back down and watched her as she took a sip.

The woman shook her head. "This *is* awful."

"I told you. But it's hot."

She shrugged. "We've had agents working on this since we first spotted the bills, and we've added resources as more and more of them turned up. You can imagine the impact on our economy if people can't trust their money. Eventually, we turned to the FBI – they have a lot more agents. So we set up a joint task force to work on it. Nichols and I head it up."

Ryan listened intently, said nothing.

"Anyway," she continued, "two weeks ago an FBI agent based in Rome, Italy called his supervisor in Washington. Told him he'd found a lead on the counterfeit currency case. Something called 'sigma'. He didn't have much else, but was continuing to work on it."

"Sigma?" Ryan said. "What the hell is that?"

A frown crossed her face. "We don't know. They found the agent's body in his Rome apartment the next day. Dead. Two rounds to the forehead."

Ryan rubbed his jaw. "Any leads on who did it?"

"None. The apartment had been wiped clean of prints. No DNA, or any other trace evidence. No shell casings left behind. The rounds were 9 mil, but were fragmented inside his skull."

"A pro did it," he said.

"Yeah. No doubt."

Ryan got up, refilled his coffee and sat back down.

Erin sipped from her cup, grimaced, and put it on the desk. "This is where you come in, Ryan. At first, we thought this problem originated in the U.S. But now we're thinking it's international. We need someone who's used to working overseas, speaks multiple languages, and who's not afraid to get his hands dirty."

He nodded. "The last part is what makes me useful to you government types. I don't mind breaking some china when it needs to be broken."

"Yeah. We do have a lot of regulations to follow. And more every day, it seems. Okay, Ryan, I'll call you tomorrow, after I have your consulting contract written up. You can come to my office downtown to sign it." She stood, pulled a business card from a pocket and handed it to him.

"Don't you want to finish your coffee before you go?" he asked.

She made a face and shook her head. Turning around, she left the office.

Ryan laughed at his own joke, then reached in his top right drawer and pulled out his Smith & Wesson .40 caliber automatic. Slipping the pistol in his hip holster, he stood and shrugged on his navy blazer. He left the office, locked up, and headed to the elevator of the high-rise building.

Half an hour later he was at the security checkpoint in the lobby of the FBI's downtown offices. After showing ID and surrendering the S&W, he was given a day-pass into the building. Skipping the elevator, he took the stairs to the third floor, and made his way to Steve Nichols's office. The door was open and Ryan stuck his head in. The FBI agent was sitting behind his desk, tapping away on a laptop.

"Hey, Steve," Ryan said as he stepped in and sat on one of the chairs that fronted the desk.

"Ryan," Nichols replied, a smile on his face. The man was tall and lean, with regulation-short sandy hair. "I figured you'd stop by, after you met Welch." The agent stuck out his hand and the men shook.

"Sorry I couldn't give you a heads-up on the case," Nichols said. "But she insisted on meeting you first."

"No problem, Steve. She's a looker, but all business."

Nichols nodded. "She filled you in?"

"You guys don't have much."

"Yeah. Not much at all," Nichols said. "We lost a good agent in Rome. I didn't know him personally, but he had several commendations in his file." Nichol's phone rang and he picked up the receiver.

While Ryan waited for the other man to finish the call, he glanced around the room. Nichols had recently been promoted, and now rated his own office – a big step up from the cubicle he had earlier. Ryan saw several pictures hanging on the left wall, and he got up and took a closer look at them. They were of Nichols and other men, wearing Army fatigues and carrying automatic weapons. One of the photos showed the agent and Ryan standing next to each other in front of a camouflaged Blackhawk helicopter.

Nichols ended his call and looked up.

Ryan tapped on the photo. "That was the covert ops in Iran, right?"

"Where I saved your life, remember?" Nichols said.

Ryan shook his head but smiled. "How can I forget? You remind me all the time."

The agent laughed and Ryan sat down again.

Nichols closed the lid on his computer. "Did Welch tell you about the lead we got? Sigma?"

"Yeah. What is it?"

"We don't know yet. We've checked everything with that name. The problem is, it's fairly common – there are a lot of businesses and products that use that name. We've interviewed people, checked databases, but they all come up clean. The only connection we have is that it's pertinent to the case and it's related to Rome somehow."

Ryan rubbed his jaw. "What else do you have?"

"Welch probably told you we've seen some of the forged currency show up here in Atlanta. We're on a stakeout tonight, a strip club. We traced the money there."

"That's a start," Ryan said. "I'll go with you."

"Sorry, buddy. I wish you could. But Welch has to write up that contract first."

"You got to go by the book, right?"

The agent sighed. "I'm afraid so."

"Okay, Steve. You have anything else you can tell me about the case?"

"Not yet. Maybe we'll have more after this stakeout."

Ryan stood. "I'll see you tomorrow then."

"Say hello to Lauren for me," Nichols said. "My wife and I want to have you both over for dinner one night."

"That'd be great."

Ryan left the office, took the elevator down to the lobby, and made his way to the multi-level parking garage next to the FBI building.

Getting in his Acura sedan, he pulled out of the garage and headed north on Peachtree. As usual, traffic was heavy in downtown and he weaved around the slower cars until he reached his gym on the north side.

The place wasn't much to look at, just a large room with bare, gray concrete walls. It catered to die-hard boxing and martial-arts enthusiasts. It had none of the flatscreen TVs and sushi-bar atmosphere most fitness centers sported these days. Which is why he liked the place. There was a boxing ring in the center of the room, with a variety of fitness equipment and boxing bags arranged around the walls. Only a few people were at the gym today – two guys boxing in the ring, and a young woman on a Stairmaster.

After changing into sweats, Ryan pounded the heavy bag for thirty minutes. He was a fit and rugged man and the bag thudded from his solid punches. Later, he pummeled the speed bag for another half hour. Drenched with perspiration, he headed for the showers.

Afterward, he called Lauren on his cell phone, asked her if she wanted him over for dinner. She said yes, and on his way over he stopped and picked up a bottle of Cabernet and a six-pack of Sam Adams.

Pulling into her driveway a while later, he got out of the car and walked to the front door of her home. It was a brick-front, two-story townhouse, located north of Atlanta. His own apartment was in a mid-town tower near his office.

She must have heard the car pull up, because she opened the door before he rang the bell.

"Hi, you," she said, a smile on her face. Lauren Chase had been Ryan's girlfriend a long time, but she still took his breath away. In her early thirties, she had sculpted good looks, long auburn hair, and hazel eyes. She was also highly intelligent, with a Stamford PhD. Now she was a full professor of computer science at Georgia Tech university.

Bending down, he gave her a kiss on the lips.

He held up the bottle of wine. "I hope this is okay."

She inspected the label. "You did well."

Taking the bottle, she went to the kitchen. He followed, pulled a beer from the six-pack, and put the rest in the fridge.

The appetizing aroma of garlic filled the room.

"What's for dinner?" he asked.

"Shrimp and pasta."

"Great. How was your day?"

"Just classes, nothing special," she replied, as she opened the bottle of wine. "How about you?"

"Picked up a new case."

"Really? Tell me about it."

"Counterfeiting. Consulting with the Secret Service and the FBI."

She stirred the pot of pasta. "You've never worked with the Secret Service before. Who's your contact?"

"An agent named Welch. She's on a joint task force with Steve."

Lauren looked up from her cooking. "What's she look like?"

"A typical, by-the-book government employee."

"Yeah, but what does she look like?"

"Not bad looking – but not nearly as good-looking as you."

A satisfied look crossed her face. "Good answer." She took a sip of wine and continued stirring.

"Steve and his wife want us over for dinner sometime. How's that sound?"

"Sure. Just set it up."

"Okay." He leaned against the kitchen counter and admired the way she filled out the blue blouse and black knee-length skirt. "You want me to spend the night?" he asked.

Lauren looked up from her cooking, a sparkle in her eyes. "Of course."

"Good. After dinner, let's skip dessert. You're all the sweet I need."

Lauren was somewhat shy and he noticed her blush slightly. She smiled, put down the wooden spoon and walked up to him. She went up on her tiptoes and gave him a quick kiss.

"What's that for?" he asked, chuckling.

"Because I love you."

Ryan bent down and returned her kiss, this time longer. They pulled apart a moment later and he looked into her eyes.

He wrapped his arms around her and they stayed like that for a while.

***

Ryan awoke with a start. His cell phone, which was resting on the nightstand, was buzzing.

He glanced at his watch – the luminous dial glowed the time in the darkened bedroom: 3:54 a.m.

Lauren, lying on the bed next to him, woke up and mumbled, "What?"

"Just the phone, hon. Go back to sleep."

She settled back in the bed as he pressed the cell to his ear.

"It's Erin Welch," he heard. "I've got bad news for you."

Ryan sat up and rubbed his eyes. "Tell me."

"During the stakeout tonight, Agent Nichols was shot."

"How bad is he, Erin?"

"He's dead."

Chapter 2

Rome, Italy

Vincento Amati crossed the wide courtyard of the Piazza Navona, oblivious to the Baroque facades, Bernini fountains and the tourists who gathered around them, snapping pictures. As usual, the piazza had a party-like atmosphere, something the Italian visitor's bureau encouraged, often staging festivals in the area.

It was a chilly night for November, and he buttoned the light jacket he was wearing. Making his way past the open-air restaurants that lined the piazza, he walked east on Via D. Sediari, the narrow street that wound its way through the upscale Roman neighborhood. In this part of the city, exclusive shops, businesses and tony trattorias were interspersed among high-end apartment buildings. The cobble-stone streets and historical facades of the area lent an air of charm that distinguished it from the rest of Rome, which was crowded and noisy.

Amati reached the unmarked two-story building, tapped his passcode on the keypad and unlocked the ornate wooden front door. Going inside, he crossed the marble floor foyer and walked down a long corridor. The hallway was lit by elaborate chandeliers and large oil paintings set in intricate gilt frames hung on the walls.

Reaching the end, he turned right, where he faced a wide double door. Unlocking that, he stepped inside the beautifully appointed room.

The two others were already seated around the highly-polished mahogany table.

"I'm sorry to be late," Amati said in English, as he sat down. "The meeting with the board took longer than expected." Amati was chairman of the board of a media empire based in Italy. To his left sat Dimitri Petrovich, a Russian oil tycoon, and to his right was Hector Sanchez, a 'businessman' who headed up Mexico's largest drug cartel. Since the three men were of different nationalities, they used English to communicate with each other.

At one side of the room, wearing a maid's uniform, stood a comely young woman with dark hair. Amati signaled her and the woman approached.

"Please serve us the scotch," he said. "Then you may leave."

From a side table she poured Glenlivet into hand-cut glass tumblers, served the men, curtsied, and left the room.

Amati stood, went to the door and locked it, and then sat back down.

"Now we can get down to business," he said. "Thank you both for flying in on such short notice. I thought we should meet to face-to-face this time, due to some recent developments. But before that, why don't you gentlemen fill me in on the progress in your sectors. Hector, why don't you begin."

Sanchez took a sip of his drink. The man was short and stocky, with a swarthy complexion. A wide scar ran down his left cheek. "Of course," he replied. His English was flawless, but he spoke with a heavy Spanish accent. "My operation is going quite well. As you know, we've set up the counterfeiting plant in Monterrey. From there we've been transporting the currency to a transit point in Ciudad Juarez, then across the border into El Paso, Texas. We're using the same...operatives and routes...we use for our cocaine, and meth, and fentanyl smuggling."

"Any problems with law enforcement in the area?" Amati asked.

Sanchez laughed. "The Mexican *Federales* are in our pocket...like we say... *'plata o plomo'*...silver or lead. As for the American Border Patrol, DEA, and other alphabet soup agencies, their staffing has been cut back by the gringos' budget problems."

"That's good to hear, Hector." Amati took a sip of the scotch, savored the burn of the liquor as it went down his throat. He turned to his Russian counterpart. "What about you, Dimitri? How are things in the frozen north?"

Petrovich was a tall, lean man in his fifties. He had a hooked nose, thinning gray hair and intense blue eyes. "It is not so cold in Moscow yet, my friend. In January, that will be another matter."

Amati waved a hand in the air. "That is why I prefer Italy. The weather...and the women...are warmer."

Petrovich shrugged. "That may be, Vincento." He spread his hands flat on the table in front of him. "The operation in Russia is proceeding as planned. My plant in Moscow, using the sigma machines you supplied, are producing Swiss francs, British pounds, Russian rubles, and other European currencies in large quantities. We are using our network of oil brokers to distribute the product to cities in Europe. So far, everything is going quite well."

"Excellent news, Dimitri." The Italian took another pull from his drink, knowing his own summary would be difficult. He paused a moment, looked at the two men in turn, and began. "Our counterfeiting operation here in Italy is also going well. Production and distribution has been running smooth. However, several issues have arisen. I am sure you are not aware of them, as they happened quite recently."

Sanchez glared at him. "Issues? You mean problems?"

"Yes," Amati replied. "Problems may be a more accurate word for them." He took another sip of scotch. "Two and half weeks ago, an American FBI agent somehow stumbled onto a connection to the sigma machines. Luckily for us, we have listening devices located at their office here in Rome. Since our operation began, we have been monitoring them."

"But how did this FBI agent learn of sigma in the first place?" Petrovich demanded.

"That I do not know," Amati replied. "My people are working around the clock. I can assure you, we will find out."

"What about the American agent?" Sanchez asked.

"The situation has been contained," the Italian responded. "He was eliminated later that day. He will no longer be a problem."

Petrovich frowned. "But still, we do not need the scrutiny."

Amati nodded. "I agree. We have a mole at the FBI office here and we have increased our surveillance – if they learn anything else, we will know immediately." The man paused a moment. "However, one other matter has cropped up."

The Russian and Mexican leaned forward in their chairs, but said nothing.

"A few days ago," Amati continued, "there was shootout in the American city of Atlanta – one of our low-level operatives was involved. Unfortunately, another FBI agent was killed."

"The Americans will be very suspicious," Sanchez groused. "Two dead in a matter of weeks."

"True," Amati answered. "The timing is bad. But, sometimes these things happen. My people in the States are monitoring the situation closely. We will contain any further issues."

Petrovich shook his head. "They better. I have lot to lose if this operation is compromised."

Sanchez nodded. "We all have a lot riding on this."

Amati held up his hands, palms out. "Don't worry, my friends. As the leader of the Alliance, I will make certain nothing derails us. We have come too far to fail now." He dropped his hands, placed them flat on the table. "Now that I've told you the unpleasant news, I have some good news to share." He took the last sip of his drink, and stood.

He walked to the far side of the room and input a series of numbers on a keypad attached to the wall. A portion of the wall slid open, revealing a darkened interior.

Amati motioned the two men to join him. "Come see." As soon as they stood next to him, he said, "As you know, we have been using advanced technology to produce the forged currencies. However, there has been a new breakthrough. Alliance engineers have developed equipment that is even more sophisticated. I present the second generation of the sigma machine." He turned on a light switch and the darkened interior of the wall cavity was bathed in light. Sitting on the marble floor was a machine about the size of a large desk. Constructed of heavy-gauge metal, the machine was painted a gloss black.

"It's smaller than the ones we've been using," Petrovich said.

"That's the beauty of this new technology," Amati continued, pride in his voice. "The forged currency is just as accurate, but the machines are smaller and much faster. We'll be able increase production."

Sanchez nodded. "Excellent. I'm impressed."

"Good," Amati said. "I'll be supplying each of you ten of the new machines in a matter of days. More will follow in the coming weeks."

"Very good, Vincento," Petrovich said. "I look forward to receiving them. But you have never told us where the machines come from. Perhaps you will enlighten us now."

Amati laughed as he turned off the light and closed the panel. "That is not important, my friend. The important thing is that you and Sanchez will become even more wealthy and powerful than you are now."

Petrovich shrugged. "You are right, as usual."

Amati went to the side table, poured fresh drinks for the three of them and motioned for the others to join him. Picking up his glass, he held it up in the air. "To the continued success of Alliance. Our operation is now entering its second phase, and soon, we will be at the third and final stage. *Salute!*"

The three clinked glasses and drank.

Chapter 3

Atlanta, Georgia

Ryan drove his Acura into the parking lot of the strip club, found an empty slot and shut off the engine. It was past midnight and the lot was almost full.

After checking the load in his S&W, he climbed out of the car and looked closely at the seedy, warehouse-like building with the garish neon sign. The sign described the place as a *'gentlemen's club'* but to him it looked no different than the other sleazy strip joints in this part of town.

He waited in line at the front door, paid his cover and went inside, where he was assaulted by the pounding beat of earsplitting music. Strobe lights blended with cigarette smoke and cast a hazy sheen over the high-ceilinged area. The place smelled of stale beer and other rancid odors he couldn't identify.

Nude women gyrated on the stage, and a long bar ran across the left wall. Small tables fronted the stage, most of those taken by men in jeans, T-shirts, and dirty work-boots. Topless waitresses circulated among the tables, pushing overpriced drinks.

Shoving his way past the throng of customers, he found an empty table and sat down. Glancing around, he was glad he'd dissuaded Erin Welch from accompanying him tonight. He convinced her he'd make more headway on his own.

A statuesque waitress wearing only short-shorts and six-inch heels walked up, gave him a tired smile.

"My name's Candy. What's your pleasure, sweetheart?" she asked loudly, trying to be heard over the din in the place. The young woman had short dark hair and a face marred by acne scars. She was probably in her early twenties, but her eyes were weary, like she'd been around the track too many times.

"I'll have a beer," he replied, trying not to stare at her large breasts.

"See something you like?" she asked with a laugh.

"I like your twins, but I'm working."

"Working? You a cop?"

"Nope. Just looking for information." He reached in his blazer's inside pocket, pulled out a fifty-dollar bill. He handed it to her, said, "Bring me a beer, and keep the change. I've got more where that came from."

Candy perked up when she heard that, turned and sashayed to the bar, balancing her tray on her hip.

She was back a moment later and placed a bottle of Budweiser on the small table.

Ryan handed her another fifty and took a sip of beer.

"You're not a regular around here, are you?" she asked.

"What makes you say that?"

"Mostly we get construction workers and low-lifes – you look too respectable for this dump."

He laughed. "Listen, a couple of days ago, there was a shooting in the parking lot of this club. I'm sure you heard about it."

Candy frowned. "You said you weren't a cop."

"I'm not. The guy who was shot was a good friend of mine. I'm just looking to settle the score."

"Okay. I was working that night. I heard stuff."

"Tell me."

"Not now. I get off at 2 a.m. Meet me in the parking lot – I've got a green Corolla. But the info's going to cost you."

"How much?"

"Four hundred."

"It better be good."

"It is, hon."

Candy gave him a quick smile and moved away.

He glanced at his watch and realized he had time to kill.

Picking up the Bud, he took a sip and began to stare at the stage. He might as well enjoy the show.

But after a while, the throbbing music and meat-market atmosphere of gyrating strippers and leering men wore on him, and he decided to wait in his car.

She came out of the place an hour later, wearing a zip-up white sweater and gray slacks. Crossing the parking lot, she got in her Corolla, parked a few rows over from him. He waited a moment to make sure no one followed her, then climbed out, walked over and slipped in the passenger side of her car.

"Thanks for waiting," she said, her voice hoarse. "I wasn't sure you'd be here."

"Like I told you, it's important."

She nodded. "Got the money?"

He pulled bills from his pocket, handed them over.

The woman counted them and tucked them in between her ample cleavage. She glanced out the windows of the car, saw no one around and turned to Ryan. "Sure you're not a cop?"

Ryan chuckled. "Scout's honor."

"Funny, you don't strike me as the boy scout type. What's your name?"

"Ryan. How about you? Candy your real name?"

She grinned. "It's Nancy – but after I started going by Candy, my tips got bigger. Anyway, about the shooting. I've been hearing some strange stuff over the last couple of days."

"Like what?"

"About a month ago a new guy started showing up at the club, a real showy guy. Spreading lots of cash around. Big tips, getting private lap dances in the back rooms, buying rounds for everybody."

"What's the guy's name?"

"I don't know for sure, but he's Italian, you could tell that by looking at him. Had an Italian accent, too. Some of the girls started calling him Guido. He thought that was funny, and it kind of stuck."

Ryan rubbed his jaw. "What does this have to do with the shooting?"

"Slow your horses. I'm getting to that. Anyway, this Guido guy, when I was serving him drinks one day, told me he'd give me 500 for a BJ. I told him I didn't do that kind of thing. He said okay, said plenty of the other waitresses would oblige. Which is true. Half the women here are pros, at least on the side."

"But not you?"

She seemed offended and he said, "Sorry."

She shrugged. "This is a tough place to work. People here think we're all whores. I've got a baby to support, and I need the money. But I draw the line. All I do is serve drinks, smile, and shake my ass. Nothing else."

Ryan nodded. "Okay. Tell me more about this Guido character."

"Yeah. Like I said, he's spending money like a drunken sailor. A couple of nights ago, a guy gets shot. Later, the cops were all over the place, asking questions, even closed the club for a few hours. Everybody clammed up – nobody talks to the police."

"What happened after that?"

"I'm getting to that. One of the other girls who works here, Amber, told me the next day it was Guido who did the shooting."

"Did she see it?"

"No. But the guy was sweet on her – she was one of his special girls, willing to do…willing to do whatever he wanted. He gave her lots of cash. Anyway, he told her later, was bragging, that he'd shot the FBI agent. She got frightened, tried to break it off with him. He got rough, beat her up a little."

"I need to talk to her. What's her full name?"

"Amber's her stage name – I don't know her real one. But you're out of luck – she's been missing since it happened."

"Damn," Ryan said, slapping the dash with his hand. "What about the Italian guy?"

"Haven't seen him since. He hasn't been back to the club."

"That's not much to go on, Candy."

She frowned. "Please don't make me give the money back – I need every cent I make. My kid's sick half the time and I don't have medical insurance."

"Don't worry, the money's yours. But give me a description of the guy."

She thought about that for a moment. "He was big, over six feet, and heavy. He had a cross tattoo on his neck. And one time Amber referred to him as Tony, so maybe that was his real name. And one other thing – he drove a new Cadillac, an STS sedan."

Ryan nodded. "That's a big help. Thanks."

Her face relaxed. "So what are going to do now?"

"I go looking for him."

Candy looked at her watch. "It's pretty late, and I need to get home. But my place isn't far from here. You can crash there if you like. Unless you're married, or something."

"I appreciate the offer, but I'm with someone. Have been for a long time."

She gave him an appraising look. "Lucky lady."

"I'm the lucky one, actually."

She nodded. "If I think of anything else, how can I reach you?"

He pulled out one of his cards from his jacket and handed it to her. "Here. By the way, let's keep this conversation between us. This Guido or Tony, or whatever his name is, may come back, and he doesn't sound like a pleasant guy. I'd hate to see you get hurt."

"Don't worry. I may be young, but I know how the game's played."

"Take care of yourself," he said, and climbed out of the car.

He drove to his apartment, had a light snack and went to bed. He was asleep in minutes.

***

The next morning he called Erin and gave her the info on the Italian guy. With her resources, he was sure she'd be able to dig up something. Told her he'd stop by later in the day.

He went to his office, did paperwork on a couple of pending cases, then after a bite of lunch at a nearby diner, worked out at the gym for an hour.

Later he drove to the Secret Service offices in downtown, which were close to the FBI building. After going through several layers of security and obtaining a pass, he was escorted by a male agent past rows of cubicles, until they reached Erin Welch's office. Previously, the two had met in a conference room, and this was the first time Ryan had seen her work area. She rated a corner office, with a good view of the city. It was clear to him now the woman was higher-up than he'd suspected.

When he walked in, the two shook hands and she asked, "Coffee?"

"Sure, if it's as good as mine," he replied with a grin.

"Couldn't be worse."

She poured them cups and they sat down.

"Find anything on the Italian guy?" he asked, taking a sip. The stuff was Starbucks quality, a lot better than his.

"Yeah. His name is Tony Bianchi. He's from Italy, but he's been in the U.S. for years. Long rap-sheet. Mostly assault, loan-sharking, drugs, B&E. Did a nickel at Calhoun State Prison a while back."

"Good work. Where can I find him?"

She shrugged. "That's the bad news. He took an Alitalia flight to Rome yesterday morning. We lost track of him after that."

"Damn."

"Yeah."

Ryan took another sip of coffee, put the cup down on her desk. "I'll go after him. He's our only lead."

"We don't have any Secret Service staff there – usually we coordinate cases with the FBI office in Rome."

"I'm used to working with those guys. I just need money for expenses."

"You'll get it. Along with anything else you need. When are you planning on leaving?"

He looked at his watch. "Today."

Chapter 4

Moscow, Russia

Dimitri Petrovich turned up the collar of his fur coat and brushed snow from his face. Although it was only November, the first snowstorm of the year was already falling. He was crossing Red Square on foot, in a hurry to make his meeting with the Russian Prime Minister. To his left, the bulbous multi-colored onion domes of St. Basilius, flood-lit from below, shimmered through the sleet. It was past ten in the evening, and the lights illuminated a dark, turbulent sky.

As usual they were meeting in a suite at the Shekaroski Hotel, away from the prying eyes and ears of the Kremlin government buildings that bordered the Square. Their talks were in secret, as the prime minister's involvement in the Alliance was known to only a few of his trusted aides.

He crossed the wide, open expanse of the historic city Square, trudging over the snow-covered pavement. Only a few people were out, and they, bundled in heavy parkas, appeared to be government workers in a hurry to get home after a long day of work.

Reaching the end of the Square, Petrovich veered left onto Ulitsa LL'Inka and followed the street for another four blocks. He reached the hotel a few minutes later, entering the plain lobby of the industrial-looking building and made his way to the elevators. Unlike the luxury hotels near Red Square that catered to wealthy tourists and powerful oligarchs, the Shekaroski was favored by those wishing to keep a low profile.

Looking around to make sure no one was following, Petrovich took the elevator to the penthouse floor, where he was met by two of the PM's security detail. After the obligatory weapons search, they escorted him to the end of the corridor, where another two, bulky, blank-faced men stood by the double doors.

Entering the suite, he walked across the modest foyer into an unassuming sitting area. The functional décor always reminded Petrovich of the old-style, Soviet-era furnishings favored by Kremlin apparatchiks.

The prime minister, Ivan Chernov, was sitting alone on one of the couches. He was a thin, balding man with weathered Slavic features. He was watching news on a flatscreen TV mounted on one wall of the room.

Chernov looked away from the news and stood up. "Dimitri," he said, holding out his hand. "Good to see you again."

"Good to see you also, Ivan." They shook and sat down, Petrovich on the opposite couch.

Chernov picked up the glass that sat on the side table and raised it. "Vodka, my friend?"

"No, thank you, comrade."

The PM took a sip and set it down. "How was your trip?"

Petrovich shrugged. "Some good, some not so good."

A frown crossed Chernov's face. "Tell me the good first – it has been a difficult day, dealing with our esteemed President."

"How is our young friend?" the oil tycoon asked.

"President Lazarenko thinks he knows everything. Unfortunately, he is the elected leader of Russia, and I have to work for him for the next three years. But, maybe, if our plans materialize, all that can change." A smile spread across the PM's face, as if he were relishing the thought. "But enough of that. Tell me your news."

"Amati has some new sigma machines for us," Petrovich replied. "Much faster than the ones we're using now. We should be able ramp up distribution in a matter of weeks."

"Excellent news, Dimitri. The currency markets around the world are already being affected by the counterfeit money. Inflation is rising in Europe and the Americas at a fast rate."

Petrovich nodded. "Yes. I have been watching the news also. The central bank in the U.S. and several European countries are getting nervous."

"Soon," the prime minister added, "we will unveil our proposal to the world."

"Has the President signed off on it, Ivan?"

"Not yet, but he will. I just have to convince him it's his idea. The man has a huge ego, but a tiny brain." He laughed. "A bad combination. But something I can manipulate to suit our needs."

"He has no clue as to the existence of the Alliance?" Petrovich asked.

Chernov took another sip of vodka. "None. All he cares about is public opinion and being on TV all the time."

"He is much like an American politician," the oil man said, chuckling.

Chernov laughed, then his face turned serious. "You said some problems came up?"

"Yes, comrade. Two American FBI agents appeared to have found a connection to our operation. They have been terminated, and Amati believes the situation has been contained. His media company has several very competent wet-work operatives on retainer."

The PM's face flushed red. "It had better be contained. The Alliance cannot be compromised. If Amati needs help, offer him the services of the FSB. I have several agents there that I trust."

Petrovich knew the man was referring to the Federalnaya Sluzhba Bezopasnosti, Russia's federal security service and the successor to the Soviet Union's KGB. "Thank you, Ivan. I will offer it to him, if the situation worsens." However, he had no intention of doing so. The FSB was ruthless, but also messy in their methods. Petrovich preferred to use his own *grupperovka*, members of the Moscow mafia, to do his dirty work.

Chernov poured himself another vodka and downed it in one gulp. He leaned back on the couch. "What are your plans now?"

"Tomorrow I go back to my office to work, and later home to the wife. But tonight," he said, with a gleam in his eyes. "Tonight I relax. There is a new club that opened off Tverskaya Street. I've heard the young women who go there are *tyolkas*, bitches in heat. I plan to enjoy myself."

Chernov smiled wistfully. "We had a lot of good times in the old days, the two of us, chasing women and drinking vodka. Now that I am in the public eye, unfortunately, my options are limited." He poured himself another drink. "I envy you, Dimitri."

"Maybe, Ivan, after the operation is over and we have all the power, you too can relax."

"Maybe so, my friend. Maybe so."

Chapter 5

Rome, Italy

Ryan paid the fare and got out of the taxi, then joined the line of tourists waiting to get into the Colosseum. Probably the city's most prominent landmark, the ancient circular structure towered over the nearby Forum.

The Colosseum was an odd place to meet, Ryan had thought, when FBI agent Paul Adams suggested it. But obviously the man didn't want to meet at his office.

It was a sunny and cool day, and if the detective hadn't been in the city for business, he would be out enjoying the sights. He'd visited Rome several times before and had always liked the ambiance and energy of the historic city. As it was, he was tired and jet-lagged from the long flight. After checking into his hotel and calling Adams, he had come straight here.

Paying the entrance fee, he made his way under the arched entrance and climbed the massive stone staircase to the highest level of the Colosseum.

Stepping out into the bright sun, he stood on the overlook and gazed down at the crumbling stone interior of the vast structure, waiting for the agent to show up. Sightseers thronged around him, snapping photos.

Ten minutes later he spotted the FBI agent as the man came out from behind a column. Adams had described his own appearance during the phone conversation and it was easy to pick him out from the crowd. A tall, lean, African-American man, the agent had close-cropped hair and a thin mustache. He wore a gray suit and polished black shoes.

Adams approached him, said in a low voice, "You must be J.T. Ryan."

"That's me."

"Let's step over there," Adams said, as he pointed to a quiet area underneath an arch.

They walked over and the agent pulled out a badge, showed it to the detective.

"Can I see your passport?" Adams asked.

Ryan reached into his sports jacket and held up his passport for the other man to read.

"Erin Welch filled me in on you, Ryan. Told me you'd been assigned to the counterfeiting case."

"That's right. By the way, why didn't you want to meet at your office?"

Adams shook his head slowly. "We suspect there's a leak. Sensitive information keeps getting out. It may be why our guy got shot. We're working on the leak, but this is Italy. Security here isn't the same as in the States."

Ryan nodded.

"Are you carrying?" the FBI agent asked.

"I brought along a revolver. Welch gave me a special permit and I packed the gun in my luggage."

"Just be careful. The *carabinieri* aren't keen on foreigners with weapons. If you get in a tight spot and the cops show up later, you probably want to ditch it."

"I'll keep that in mind. You have anything on Tony Bianchi?"

Adams frowned. "We lost him after he landed in Rome, but we're still looking for him. I hope I'll have something later today. Where are you staying?"

"The Givani, on the Via Cicerone."

"I know that hotel."

Ryan handed the man his card. "My cell number is on there."

A crowd of tourists moved past them and the two men went quiet.

"Have you learned anything about 'sigma', whatever it is?" asked Ryan.

"Nothing yet."

"You FBI guys are really on top of the situation."

Adams glared. "They told me you were a smartass."

Ryan chuckled.

"Okay," Adams said. "I'll call you later, when I have more."

They shook hands and the agent turned and moved away. A moment later he had disappeared into the crowds.

Ryan descended the stone staircase and a few minutes later was outside the Colosseum complex. Crossing the car-clogged street in front of the structure, he found what he was looking for, Il Gladiatori. It was a favorite restaurant of his, one he had frequented several times on previous visits. Named in honor of the gladiators who had fought in the ancient Roman spectacles, the place offered a great view of the city, good pasta, and plenty of Peroni beer.

***

Ryan's cell phone buzzed, waking him from a deep sleep. Looking around the dimly-lit room, he groggily remembered where he was. The Givani Hotel. Glancing at his watch, he noted the local time: 1:13 a.m.

He picked up the cell, held it to his ear.

"It's Adams," he heard the man say. "We've got a lead on Bianchi. I'll pick you up in fifteen."

"See you soon," he replied, turning off the phone.

Ryan washed up, ran a comb through his close-cropped brown hair and dressed in his usual attire: gray slacks, a buttoned-down shirt, and a navy blazer. Checking the load in the snub-nosed .38 caliber Ruger revolver, he slipped it in his waistband. Then he headed out of his room.

As soon as he stepped out of the hotel's lobby, he spotted Adam pull up to the curb in a black Fiat sedan. The Givani was usually a busy hotel, with cars and vans double-parked in front of the place to pickup and deliver, but at this time of night the area was deserted.

Ryan got in the car, inspected the Spartan, cheap-plastic interior. "Adams, I figured you'd be driving a Beemer."

The agent gave him a hard look. "Cut the crap, will you?"

Ryan laughed and the car pulled away.

"Bianchi has an uncle in Mantana," Adams said, "a city north of here. We suspect he's holed up there."

They drove east and eventually merged unto the A24 highway out of Rome. Minutes later they were headed north on the A1. There was almost no traffic and they made good time.

An hour later they reached the outskirts of Mantana, got off the highway and went into the center of town. More a village than a city, the place had the typical cobblestone streets, wrought-iron gates, small gardens, and quaint look of Italian towns. Driving past the rustic facades of the town center, Ryan noticed that, outside of a few streetlamps, most of the town appeared dark and asleep.

They found the house minutes later, a two-story, stone-front home with a barrel-tile roof. Adams drove past it and parked on the street half a block away.

"How do you want to play this?" Ryan asked.

The agent frowned. "Not sure. I didn't call the local police ahead of time. Wasn't sure I could trust them." He paused. "Sometimes in Italy, the cops and local thugs…have an arrangement."

"So," Ryan said sarcastically, "you're planning on knocking on the door and asking if Tony wants to come out and play?"

"Something like that."

"I got a better idea, Adams. I'll go in alone and find Bianchi. Afterward I'll call you and you can help me get him in the car."

"I can think of at least three or four laws you'd be breaking, including B&E and kidnapping."

"You want to find out who killed two FBI agents, don't you?"

"Of course," Adams said.

"This way it's clean. If I get caught, you can drive off and your FBI record remains spotless."

Adams looked doubtful, but Ryan didn't wait for permission. Instead, he got out of the Fiat and began walking to the house. Going past it, he noticed the place was dark, much like the other houses on the street. But there was a full moon that night, providing enough illumination for him to find his way.

Ducking into the driveway next to the place, Ryan circled back and approached the back door. It was an arched, wooden affair with a small circular window at the top. Peeking inside, he saw only gloom.

Pulling a lock-pick tool set from a pocket, he fiddled with the brass lock for a moment. Hearing a click, he drew his gun, slowly turned the door knob and stepped inside.

Letting his eyesight adjust to the dark interior, he realized he was in the kitchen. The aroma of garlic filled the air.

Up ahead and to his right he noticed a staircase. With his gun trained in front of him, he moved toward it. Most likely, he thought, the bedrooms were upstairs. Gingerly, he began climbing the old wooden stairs. Like the rest of the house, the stairs were probably a hundred years old, and made a slight squeaking sound.

Reaching the top, he saw the corridor ran to his left. Turning that way, he was momentarily blinded when the overhead lights came on.

A heavy-set man wearing sleepwear was pointing a shotgun at his face.

"Stop right there!" the fat man yelled in Italian. The man was in his sixties, and was probably Bianchi's uncle.

Ryan froze, and with his adrenaline pumping, ran through his options quickly. "I'm Tony's friend," he replied in Italian.

The man looked confused a moment. "Friends don't break in – they knock. And they don't carry guns."

Ryan laughed. "A practical joke. This gun is a toy. Here, I'll put it down." Ryan slowly went to his knees and laid the Ruger on the tiled floor. Getting up he said, "I'm sorry I disturbed you. But Tony and I are always joking around. You must be his uncle. He told me all about you."

The man lowered the shotgun, but still held on to it tightly. "What's your name?"

"I'm Mike. Tony and I are friends back in the States."

"I can tell by your accent you're American," the uncle said, his eyes still wary. "Stay where you are. I'll wake Tony up."

Ryan waved a hand in the air. "Here he is now. Hi, Tony!"

The uncle turned, saw no one behind him and in the instant it took for him to turn back, Ryan lunged at him, knocking him down.

The shotgun clattered to the tile floor and Ryan grabbed it. Using the stock, he clubbed the fat man in the head. The man sagged, clearly unconscious.

Recovering his revolver, the detective began to open the other rooms along the corridor. They were empty, save the last, where he found a snoring Bianchi sleeping under the covers in a four-poster bed.

Ryan checked the room for weapons, found a Glock automatic in the nightstand. Pocketing that, he stood over the prone man. He placed the muzzle of the Ruger to Bianchi's cheek and said loudly, "Wake up, sleepyhead. Rise and shine."

Startled awake, Bianchi's eyes opened wide. "What? Who the hell are you?"

"Santa Claus. Here to give you an early Christmas present." Ryan flicked the gun across the man's temple, hitting him hard.

Bianchi yelped, but didn't pass out, and instead reached out with his meaty hands, trying to grab Ryan's throat.

The detective swung again, smashing the man's nose. An audible crunch. A spurt of blood. Bianchi slumped on the bed.

Satisfied the man was knocked out, Ryan went to the bathroom and rummaged through the cabinets. Finding a roll of bandaging tape, he returned to the bedroom and taped up the man's mouth and bound his hands behind his back.

He grabbed the inert man by the shoulders, dragged him out of the room and down the stairs. When he reached the kitchen, he took out his phone and made a call.

"Bring the car to the front of the house," Ryan said. "And keep the engine running."

Putting the phone away, he continued dragging the man out of the place, grunting as he did so. Although Ryan was and big and strong, Bianchi was also big but given to fat and was dead weight.

Adams was standing by the car.

"Help me get him into the back seat," Ryan said. "He's hurt." The detective smiled. "He's going to need some medical attention."

The FBI agent gave him a hard look, but remained quiet and the two loaded Bianchi into the car.

As the Fiat sped away, the agent asked, "What happened back there?"

"The less you know the better."

Adams nodded. "What next?"

"I've been thinking about that. You're FBI, but you don't have any jurisdiction in Italy. So you can't arrest him or even hold him for questioning for murdering someone in Atlanta." Ryan paused. "But, what if Bianchi broke into your car at the FBI parking area in Rome. And you saw him do it. Clear grounds for arrest."

Adams shook his head slowly, then smiled. "That'll work."

Two hours later they were in the basement level of the FBI offices, which were located in the Via Veneto area of Rome. The windowless, concrete walled room was bare, save for a metal table and metal folding chairs. Harsh fluorescent light glared down from the overhead lamps, casting a bluish pall over the room. The place smelled of mildew and cleaning solvents.

Tony Bianchi sat on one side of the table, his hands bound behind him. His long nose was bent at an odd angle and there was blood splattered on his pajamas.

Adams sat across from him, and Ryan stood at one side of the room, leaning against the wall.

"We know you shot an FBI agent in Atlanta," Adams said. "We also know you're involved with the counterfeiting operation. If you cooperate with us, tell us all you know, I'll talk to the D.A., try to get you a deal."

Bianchi stayed stoically silent.

Adams crossed his arms across his chest. "Talk and I'll get you a doctor to treat your nose, give you painkillers."

Bianchi grunted, but didn't reply.

Ryan glanced at his watch. "This guy's not going to talk, Adams. You've been at this for half an hour."

"I want lawyer," the Italian man finally blurted out in heavily accented English.

The FBI agent frowned. "You'll get one. Soon. But first, tell us about the currency forging."

"No lawyer, no talk," Bianchi said.

"Your method hasn't worked, Adams," Ryan said in a low voice. "Let's try it my way."

The agent turned toward the detective. "Your way? Okay, go ahead."

"You need to leave the room," Ryan responded.

Adams frowned again, slid his chair back and stood. Without saying another word, he left, closing the door behind him.

Bianchi sneered. "What this? Good cop, bad cop?"

"So. You're a killer *and* a comedian? No. I'm just mean cop."

Bianchi glared.

Ryan took a pocket-knife from his jacket and opened it. The stainless-steel blade glinted from the overhead lights.

"I want lawyer!" the man demanded. But his voice had a quaver that wasn't there before.

"You'll have to excuse me, Tony, but I'm hard of hearing."

Ryan went around the table and behind the seated man. Using the knife, he cut off the tape that was binding his hands. He walked back and sat across from Bianchi.

"That better?" Ryan asked.

The man seemed confused by the action, but obviously relieved. He rubbed his wrists, which were red from being bound.

"Okay, Bianchi. I just did you a favor. Now you have to return it. Who's your boss? Who hired you? Where did you get the counterfeit cash?"

Now that his hands were untied, the man's bravado returned. "Fuck you! Not talking."

Ryan shook his head slowly. "Now I'm insulted. I do you a favor and all you do is curse me? I'm not happy, Tony."

Bianchi must have thought that was funny, because he began cackling. A moment later he said, "Get me fucking lawyer. You not Italian police. You no FBI."

Ryan's hands clenched into fists. "You're right about that. I'm not in the Bureau, like my friend Adams. I have a different background. Where I work we don't have any rules. Now. I'm asking you one last time. Are you going to tell me what I want to know?"

"Fuck you. I want lawyer. I want doctor. Now!"

Ryan stood, walked around the table and said in a low voice, "Get up."

Bianchi grinned and stood. "Finally. You listen."

Ryan sized up the man. Bianchi was roughly the same height as himself, well over six feet. And they both weighed over 200 pounds. But where the Italian was flabby in the middle, Ryan was hard-packed muscle from years in the U.S. Army's Delta force.

"I just want you to know," Ryan said evenly, "I'm not carrying a piece right now. So this fight is going to be fair and square."

"Fight?"

"You don't think I'm going to let you walk out of here, do you?"

"You have to. It law."

"Fuck the law," Ryan said. He punched the man in the gut.

Bianchi groaned and doubled over.

A moment later the man caught his breath, and, his eyes full of hate, lunged at Ryan.

The detective side-stepped and the Italian went past him.

Bianchi turned around and swung a wild roundhouse punch. Ryan ducked and delivered a powerful left jab to the man's ribs, followed with a right uppercut, which landed on Bianchi's already broken nose. As the man staggered back, Ryan kicked the man savagely in the groin.

Bianchi cried out and crumpled to the concrete floor.

Groaning, the man lay doubled over on his side, clutching his groin.

"Want to talk now?" Ryan asked, as he squatted down next to him.

"Can't," Bianchi croaked hoarsely, still gasping for air. "They kill me."

Ryan laughed. "I'll kill you, if you don't."

"You with FBI. You can't," Bianchi cried out, but his eyes were wide and his voice had lost its bravado.

Using his thumb and index finger, Ryan grabbed the man's bloody and bent nose and wrenched it in the opposite direction.

The Italian howled in pain.

Ryan let go of the nose and wiped his now bloody hand on the man's pajama top. He formed his other hand into a fist and pulled it to his side, getting ready to strike another blow.

"Stop!" Bianchi whimpered. "Stop. I talk."

"You sure?"

"*Si. Si.*"

The detective took out a handkerchief and handed it to the man. "Here. It'll help with the bleeding."

Bianchi, his eyes wide with fear, took the cloth and pressed it to his face.

Standing up, Ryan went to the table, picked up the bottle of water that was sitting there, came back and handed it to the man. "Have a drink. You'll feel better."

Bianchi, relief showing on his face, grabbed the bottle and took a swig. He coughed, and after a moment, took another swallow.

"Sit up, Tony, so we can talk."

The man wiped his nose again and crabbed over to sit, his back against the wall.

Walking over, Ryan squatted to face him. "Now talk."

"My name Tony Bianchi," he said, in between groans. "Work in Atlanta. I broken laws. I got record —"

"Skip that part, we know all that. Tell me about the strip club and the counterfeit money."

"*Si, si,*" the man said, breathing heavily through his mouth. "I have crew. We do things – not legal…"

"Don't sugar coat it, friend, or I'll kick your ass some more."

"Okay." He paused, coughed again. "We rob. Run drugs. Cocaine, meth, fentanyl. We get supply from Mexico. Months ago, my distributor say he got new stuff. Counterfeit money. Twenties. Good shit. Can't tell it from real thing."

"What about the strip club?"

"My crew pass counterfeit cash in Atlanta. I find strip club." He took a deep breath through his mouth. "With that fake cash, I golden. Getting all whores I can handle. Haven't fucked that much in years. Come home tired."

"Yeah, I bet."

"One night, I was in parking lot, getting laid. This guy comes up to car, holds up badge."

"The FBI agent?"

"I guess. I pull chick off me, grab Glock, shoot out the window. I try scare him. The fucker points gun at me. I shoot again." Bianchi was pleading now. "You see? Self-defense!"

"I see you're the scumbag who shot my friend."

Bianchi held up his hands, palms out. "I no want kill him."

Ryan saw red, wanted desperately to reach out and strangle the bastard. Instead he took a couple of deep breaths. This wasn't the time or the place to exact revenge.

"Sure, Tony, whatever you say," Ryan said sarcastically. "The D.A. and the courts will sort all that out. Now tell me about your distributor. The one you got the currency from."

"He Mexican. Lives in Juarez."

"Name?"

"Manny. Manuel Rodriguez."

"You wouldn't be lying about any of this, would you, Tony?"

Ryan grabbed the man's nose and squeezed hard.

Bianchi yelped and held up his palms again. "No! All true!"

The detective let go and stood up. "It better be. Or I'll be back. And I won't be so gentle next time."

"What going to happen...to me?" the Italian asked.

"That's not my department. You're Adams's responsibility now. I'm sure he'll find you a nice prison cell back in the States."

"My nose hurt bad. Call doctor."

Ryan's thoughts flashed to his dead friend's face and rage filled him.

Stepping closer to Bianchi, he kicked the man in the stomach. The Italian gasped, folded over, and began to retch.

Ryan turned and walked out of the room.

***

Ryan was sitting across from Adams, in the FBI agent's office in Rome.

"Is it safe to talk in here?" the detective asked.

Adams placed his coffee cup on his desk. "It is now. We found the leak. One of the cleaning women."

"Good. So what's next with Bianchi?"

"Now that he's confessed, we'll work with the State Department, they'll talk with the Italian police to expedite his extradition to the U.S. What about you, Ryan? What are your plans?"

Ryan glanced at his watch. "Too late to get a flight out today. I'll leave for home tomorrow. I want to get started on the lead we got from Bianchi."

Adams nodded. "If I need you later, you'll be at the hotel?"

"Yeah," Ryan said, standing up and holding out his hand.

The men shook and Adams said, "Can't say I agree with your methods, but…"

Ryan laughed. "No need to thank me."

"I wasn't going to."

"I figured as much," Ryan said with a smile. "By the way, next time I'm in town, we'll have to get together, have a beer and trade war stories."

The agent frowned. "I can't socialize with contractors. It's against Bureau policy."

Ryan smiled and walked out of the office.

A couple of hours later, after dinner at a trattoria across from the Castel Sant' Angelo, he returned to his hotel. After booking a flight to Atlanta, he called Lauren and went to bed.

He was asleep in minutes.

Ryan was startled awake by a knock on his hotel room door. Rubbing his eyes, he saw the time on the nightstand clock: 1:43 a.m.

There was a second knock and he climbed out of bed, pulled on a robe, and took the revolver from underneath his pillow.

Glancing through the door's peephole, he saw a young brunette in a hotel staff uniform, standing behind a food cart.

"*Si?*" he said in Italian, without opening the door.

"*Signore* Ryan," he heard the woman say, "room service. Dinner and wine, compliments of Paul Adams."

"At this hour of night?"

"I apologize, *signore*. There was a mix-up. It should have been delivered hours ago."

"All right." He fastened the robe sash and put the revolver in the pocket. Flicking on the overhead light, he opened the door and the maid rolled in the cart.

The savory aroma of veal piccata filled the room.

She began to lift the ornate chrome lids from the platters of food and he said, "Just leave it. I'll take care of that."

Everything happened in an instant.

A tall, broad man dressed in black rushed into the room, brandishing a Sig Sauer automatic. Leveling the pistol at Ryan's face, the man said, "Get out, Anna. And close the door behind you."

The woman did as she was told, but not before giving Ryan a frightened look.

The detective held up his hands. "If this is a robbery, my wallet's in the nightstand."

The man smirked, but said nothing.

Ryan noticed the Sig Sauer had a silencer attached to the barrel and realized he was in serious trouble. This was no robbery. He had only seconds to react.

Spinning his body into a roundhouse kick, Ryan landed the blow to the man's chest, knocking him backward, the pistol flying off.

But the man, obviously a trained pro, quickly recovered. He lunged forward, landing a solid punch to Ryan's solar plexus.

The wind knocked out of him, Ryan went to one knee, and he tried pulling out his revolver, but the man was on him in an instant, punching him in the face and sending the detective to the floor.

Dazed and bleeding from the blows, Ryan was now on his back, and the man saw the opening.

He kicked Ryan in the groin, and the detective bellowed in pain. The man jumped on top of him, his bulky hands gripping Ryan's throat.

Ryan could feel the thick fingers choking him, his windpipe being crushed. The light in the room began to fade.

Willing aside the excruciating pain, Ryan reached out with both hands and slapped the man hard on his ears.

Startled, the man let go of Ryan's throat. The detective grasped the man's head and twisted it violently, first one way, then the other, until he heard a loud crack.

The man's eyes rolled up in his head and his body sagged.

Pushing the body off, Ryan got on his knees.

Still gasping for air, he checked the man's pulse, found none. He was dead.

After a moment, Ryan stood, went to the bathroom and washed the blood from his face. Coming back to the bedroom, he picked up his cell phone and punched in a number.

The phone rang for a long time, but eventually Adam's groggy voice answered it.

"It's Ryan. Get over to my hotel now. I've just killed someone, in self-defense. And by the way – you may have found one of the leaks at your office, but there's at least another one still there."

He hung up.

Chapter 6

Atlanta, Georgia

Ryan was sitting across from Erin Welch in her office.

"Adams called me," Erin said, "filled me in on what happened. How do you feel?"

Ryan fingered the bandages on his forehead. "Not bad, considering. Better bruised than dead."

She shook her head slowly. "Always the wiseass."

"Humor is good for the soul."

"Yeah, so they say," she replied primly.

Turning serious, he said, "Adams tell you about the Mexican connection?"

"Yes. We've been checking on Manuel Rodriguez. Problem is, he's a Mexican national, and he lives there. We can't touch him, at least not yet. We have no evidence. Just hearsay, from a known felon."

"You checked with the *Federales*, Erin?"

She nodded. "Rodriguez has a police record a mile long, mostly drugs. But without specific evidence, the Mexican police won't arrest him or deport him."

"Figures."

"You sure Bianchi was telling the truth? Maybe he was feeding you crap."

Ryan grinned. "I doubt it. I'm a persuasive guy."

"I bet. So what do you propose we do next?"

Ryan rubbed his jaw. "Been thinking about that. Where's Bianchi now?"

"In the process of being extradited. We'll have him in custody in Atlanta in a couple of days."

"Good. I need him."

"For what, Ryan?"

"I need to get close to Rodriguez. And, since he's not here, I have to go to him in Mexico. I want Tony to set up a meet. The excuse will be he wants to triple his allotment of the fake cash, but needs to meet face-to-face first."

"Okay. Sounds plausible. We can work that out, have Bianchi make the call."

Ryan leaned forward in the chair. "It'll take more than a call. Bianchi will have to come with me. There's no way Rodriguez would meet with me unless Tony was there."

Erin shook her head. "No way. Bianchi killed an FBI agent. We can't take the chance of him getting away."

"He'll be my responsibility. I'll take the fall if the plan gets screwed up."

"I don't like it, Ryan. Too much risk."

"The only way we can solve this case is by finding the original source of the counterfeiting. Don't you want to solve this?"

"Yes. There's been a flood of the phony money streaming in. It's showing up everywhere in the U.S."

The detective crossed his arms across his chest. "Listen. Steve was my best friend. The only way I can make sure his death wasn't in vain is by catching the bastards who set this whole thing up. I'm sure my plan will work. Trust me." He knew the risks involved, knew the chances of success were probably only 50/50. But unless he presented a confident attitude, the woman wouldn't back him.

Erin still looked skeptical. Tucking her long blonde hair behind her ears, she was quiet for a long moment.

Eventually she spoke in a low voice. "Okay. We'll do it your way. But if this blows up, it's your ass that's on the line."

Ryan smiled. "I wouldn't have it any other way. Now. Let me tell you some of the items I'll need for the trip to Mexico."

***

Later, back at his own office, Ryan made calls and did paperwork on his other cases. He figured he had several days until the trip and he needed to make the most of that time.

He finished at seven in the evening and drove over to Lauren's for dinner. After bad airline and airport food, he was looking forward to it.

She met him at the door, gave him a big hug.

"Missed you," she said, as she let him in.

He tilted his head down, kissed her. "I missed you too." She tasted good – a salty-sweet flavor of marsala wine. And, as usual, she looked good. Today, she was wearing a form-fitting black cocktail dress.

Apparently the meal was ready, because she led him into the dining room, where she had set out lighted candles.

"What's the occasion?" he asked, worried he had forgotten some important date.

"Nothing. Just glad you're back and that you're in one piece."

He rubbed his bandaged forehead. "Just a scratch."

"You always say that, J.T."

He chuckled. "Yeah. I guess I do."

They had dinner and wine, a Bordeaux red he had picked out on the way over.

Afterwards, they lingered at the dining table, sipping espresso. She turned pensive and he could tell something was troubling her.

"What's wrong?" he asked.

"Nothing."

"Something's up."

She put her cup down. "I was really worried about you. When you were gone."

"You always worry about me, Lauren."

"You take too many chances."

He smiled, trying to lighten the mood. "Didn't you know I can leap over tall buildings?" he said, chuckling.

"Cut it out, J.T. Those bandages on your face prove you can get hurt. I worry one day you won't come back."

"Everything's going to be fine. Trust me."

Lauren took a sip of the espresso. "There's a job opening at Georgia Tech," she said, her voice hopeful. "The university's head of security is retiring. They're looking for a new one. You'd be perfect for the job, and the pay is great."

Ryan shrugged. "You think I'd be happy doing that?"

"Well…"

"See, even you know I'd hate it eventually. No. I like my job just fine."

She sighed. "I know we've had this conversation before. I know I'm probably not going to convince you. But at least I have to try." Changing the subject, she said, "How's your big case going?"

"Got a good lead – I'll be working it soon."

Laura frowned. "Another trip?"

"Afraid so. Mexico this time."

"What's down there?"

He grinned. "Bad guys."

She shook her head slowly. "There's always plenty of those, it seems."

Ryan nodded. "Job security."

She smiled at his joke. A good sign, he thought.

"How soon before you go?" she asked.

"Couple of days."

A sparkle lit up her pretty hazel eyes. "We better not waste any time." She stood. "You open another bottle of wine and I'll clear the dishes. Then I'll join you in the bedroom."

"I like the sound of that," he said.

It was long and satisfying night for both of them.

***

El Paso, Texas

Ryan slowed the gray Chevy Suburban as they approached the Mexican border crossing just south of El Paso. The southbound Customs checkpoint was a duplicate of the one that headed north — twenty lanes wide, all full with backed-up vehicle traffic. The massive area was illuminated with fluorescent lighting, which lit up the nighttime sky.

Two semis, their diesel engines idling loudly, were in line ahead of them, waiting to get into Ciudad Juarez, and points south.

Tony Bianchi dozed on the passenger side, his seat's angle raked back as far as possible. The man had slept most of the way down on the long drive, which was fine with Ryan. The less he had to communicate with Steve's killer, the better.

Up ahead, one of the semis moved through the checkpoint and Ryan drove forward so that he was only feet behind the other truck.

Slapping Bianchi on the shoulder, Ryan said, "Wake up. We're almost at Customs."

The man awoke and rubbed his eyes. "What time?"

"Nighttime," Ryan replied. "Now remember what I told you. I'll do the talking. Just give me your passport and shut up. And don't even think of running off, or I'll break your nose again."

"You grouchy," Bianchi said, handing over the passport. The man grabbed a half-empty bag of Lay's potato chips from the floor and began to loudly crunch away.

Ryan shook his head. "Jesus."

"What?" Bianchi asked, his mouth full of chips.

The semi in front moved past the customs point and the uniformed guard in the glass cubicle motioned for Ryan to pull up.

The Suburban stopped in front of the guard, who had one hand touching the butt of his holstered automatic.

The detective lowered the vehicle's window and the odor of diesel fuel filled the Suburban.

"*Pasaportes*," the guard said in Spanish.

Ryan handed them over. "A lot of traffic tonight, huh," he replied in the same language.

The guard had a bored look on his face. "It comes, it goes. It doesn't matter to me. I get paid the same." He scanned the passports, looked up at Ryan. "Why are you visiting Mexico?"

"Business convention. In Mexico City."

The guard nodded. "For how long?"

"A week."

"Okay. I need you to open the back. I have to inspect it."

"Sure. No problem," Ryan said, as he climbed out of the SUV. Walking to the rear, he opened the back doors.

The guard turned on a flashlight and gave the interior a cursory look. "It could be an hour, maybe more, if I flag your vehicle for a thorough inspection. But you look honest enough. For fifty dollars, American, you could be on your way right now."

Ryan knew how the game was played. And he didn't want the guards to find the items he'd carefully stored inside the bodywork. "A small price to pay, for the convenience."

The guard smiled, his crooked, stained teeth showing. He was in obvious need of serious dental work.

As the man handed Ryan back the passports, he slipped him the money.

"*Vaya con dios*," the guard said. "Hope to see you on the flip side."

Climbing back in, Ryan drove through the Customs area, took an on-ramp, and merged with the highway headed south.

Next to him, Bianchi had resumed eating the chips. He washed them down with a swig of Pepsi. "Want some?" the man asked, offering up the can.

Ryan gave him a hard look, shook his head.

"Okay," Bianchi said, with a belch.

An hour later they were south of the sprawling, sleazy metropolis of Juarez.

It was dawn and the pink and blue rays of early morning were beginning to brighten the dark gray sky.

"How far are we?" Ryan asked, turning to Bianchi.

"Ten mile more. Next exit."

Ryan scanned the horizon. On either side of the highway, the arid, flat landscape was empty save for scrub-grass and cactus. Opening his window, he let in the warm air. It smelled much fresher than the smog-choked Juarez they had driven through.

Seeing the exit sign, he took the off-ramp and stopped at the end, where it intersected with a two-lane asphalt road.

"Take left," Bianchi said. "The warehouse five miles."

Ryan nodded and drove west slowly, getting the lay of the land. But outside of a couple of gas stations and convenience stores, there was little else.

He spotted the sprawling warehouse soon after, the whole complex enclosed by tall, cyclone fencing. The main building, which had no signage of any type, was fronted by a parking lot. Truck loading bays lined the side of the building, with forty-foot containers parked in several of the bays.

As they approached the complex, Bianchi said, "I talk now?"

"Yes. Just remember to stay with the script. Or your deal with the D.A. is off the table."

Bianchi held up his hands. "I want this to work."

The Suburban pulled up to the security post at the entrance, which was guarded by two armed men. One carried an Uzi rifle, while the other toted an AK-47. Ryan noticed more men with AK's patrolling the area inside the fence.

"Tight security," Ryan said under his breath.

"*Si*," the other man whispered.

The guard with the AK-47 walked to the front of the vehicle, while the Uzi guy approached the driver's side.

"State your business," Uzi said in Spanish.

"Meeting with *Señor* Rodriguez," Bianchi replied in the same language. "My name Tony Bianchi."

Uzi went back to the guard post, used a phone and made a call. He was back a moment later. "Drive forward and park. You'll be searched, then you can go in."

"*Gracias.*"

The SUV parked and was quickly surrounded by four other armed guards. As soon as the two men had climbed out of the vehicle, they were frisked and scanned with metal detectors.

They were escorted inside and led into a simply-furnished conference room. Besides a long conference table and chairs, there was nothing else.

Moments later a tall, slender man with slicked-back black hair came into the room. He was dressed in a corduroy shirt and jeans.

"Manuel," Bianchi said. "Good see you."

The two shook hands and Rodriguez pointed to Ryan.

"Who's your friend, Tony?"

"Mike Peters. New partner."

Rodriguez extended his hand to the detective. "A partner, huh?"

They shook and the Mexican sat at the head of the table. The two others sat down also.

Rodriguez leaned forward in his chair. "So, Tony. How are things in Georgia? I just reviewed your numbers, and you're moving a lot of product. That's good. You're one of my best distributors."

"*Gracias*, Manuel. Things go well."

"You said on the phone you wanted to increase your allotment?"

"*Si*. That reason for my partner," Bianchi replied. "Mike from Alabama. He want distribute cash and drugs there."

Rodriguez grinned. "I see. Well, I don't have anybody in that state." He laughed. "It would be virgin territory for me. And you know, Tony, how much I like breaking in virgins."

Bianchi chortled at that, and the Mexican turned to Ryan. "Tell me about yourself, *amigo*. You have a large crew?"

Ryan nodded. "Yeah. About forty guys. We work out of Birmingham."

"What about the police there? A problem?"

"I have that under control," Ryan said. "We have an understanding with them."

Rodriguez leaned back in the chair. "Good. So, Tony, you want to triple your allotment?"

Bianchi nodded. "We blanket Georgia and Alabama."

"Okay, *amigo*. I'll work out the logistics with my supplier and start the increased quantity in a matter of weeks."

"You don't make the counterfeit cash here?" Ryan asked.

Rodriguez glared. "You are nosy, gringo. No. It comes from south of here. But that is not your concern. All you need to know is that you'll have the supplies when I tell you you'll have them."

Bianchi, obviously concerned the Mexican had become suspicious, quickly said, "I sorry for partner, Manuel. He not know you. I know you man of your word."

Rodriguez shrugged. "No problem. By the way, I am having a little party tonight, after work. Why don't you postpone your return trip a day and join me. I'm sure you and Mike will like it."

Bianchi beamed. "*Si. Claro.*"

The Mexican stood. "Excellent. I'll walk you back to your car."

He led the two men out of the room and through the adjacent warehouse. Ryan noticed several trucks being unloaded by the warehouse crew using forklifts.

There were several full pallets covered by green tarps next to a side door and Rodriguez stopped, pointed to them. "This is a new delivery. Let me show you." He pulled the tarp off one pallet, which revealed rows of stacked boxes underneath. Opening the top box, he pulled out a thick wad of crisp U.S. fifty-dollar bills. He handed the stack to Ryan.

"Take a look," Rodriguez said proudly. "Tell me what you think."

Ryan took the money, closely inspected Grant's picture and the other details. He whistled. "It looks perfect."

The Mexican laughed. "I agree. I've heard rumors that the American authorities are crapping in their pants."

Ryan handed back the money. "I can see why."

Rodriquez replaced the fake bills back in the box and pulled down the tarp. Then he escorted the two men outside and back to their vehicle.

After they left the complex, Ryan drove back to the two-lane road.

"Motel mile away," Bianchi said. "We check-in, wait until time to go to Manuel house."

Ryan found the place a few moments later. It was one of those generic, one-story, road-side motels, with a faded sign and peeling paint.

They checked in, grabbed some *huevoz rancheros* at the attached café and went to their rooms. It had been a long drive and Ryan was looking forward to a shower and a nap before night fell. Their rooms were next to each other and as he went in his, Ryan said, "If you try to make a run for it, Tony, you'll regret it. I'll catch you and kill you. Understood?"

A frown creased the other man's face. "I hear you."

Ryan, who was still holding Bianchi's passport and the SUV keys, knew the man wouldn't get far in the desert, even if he tried.

The detective went in the room, closed the blinds and lay down on the lumpy bed. He was asleep in seconds.

He awoke hours later, showered, changed into fresh clothes and knocked on Bianchi's door. The man opened it moments later, rubbing his eyes and yawning.

"Get ready," Ryan said. "We need to get going soon."

It was past seven in the evening when they reached Rodriguez's estate, which was located in a sparsely populated area of the desert. The walled, multi-story compound was set back from the road about half a mile, but it was so large it was visible from there.

The SUV's tires crunched over the gravel path that led from the road to the gated entrance. Ryan could see bright lights and hear loud music coming from the house. It was clear the party had already started.

Two armed men came out of the gate, searched them, and let them drive through the gate and up to the large, semi-circular driveway that fronted the house. There were BMWs, Mercedes, and Lexus cars parked in the driveway, along with several Land Rovers.

Climbing out of the Suburban, Ryan inspected the ostentatious, three-story, Tudor-style home. It looked out of place here, in the middle of the Mexican desert, but maybe that was the point.

They were searched again by the armed guards posted at the front portico. After, they were led to a large foyer by a young woman in a maid's uniform. Boisterous Mexican music was playing from somewhere in the house.

"Follow me, please," the maid said. "*Señor* Rodriguez and his guests are by the pool."

They went through the lavish house, which sported dark leather furniture and marble floors. It was clear to Ryan that Rodriguez's business was booming.

Exiting the rear of the house through tall French double-doors, they walked down the flagstone steps to the Olympic-size pool. Brightly colored lamps lit up the night sky and the aroma of rich food filled the air.

A mariachi band was playing to one side as Ryan surveyed the guests. Sitting on lounge chairs arranged around the well-lit pool were mostly older men, dressed in business suits, puffing large cigars and drinking. He noticed there was a large number of young women, girls really, chatting and playing volleyball in the pool. All the girls were either topless or completely nude.

Rodriguez, now in a sports jacket and slacks and with a drink in hand, came up to the two men. "There you are!" the Mexican said. "I'm glad you came."

The three shook hands and Bianchi said, "Good party."

Rodriguez pointed to the girls frolicking in the pool. "I got a new batch tonight. All good-looking and very special. They are only fifteen or sixteen years old. Very expensive, but well worth it."

Bianchi smirked. "You no disappoint, Manuel."

The Mexican pointed to a large buffet table. "Get yourself tequila, or whatever else you drink, and food. Later, pick out the girl you want. I have plenty of empty bedrooms, upstairs." The man grinned, downed his drink and headed to the bar for a refill.

"Is it always like this?" Ryan asked under his breath.

"*Si*," Bianchi whispered. "Great, huh? The old men are local politicians, judges, cops – the parties are part of payback for looking other way."

Ryan shook his head slowly. "Jesus. Those girls are so young."

"Sweet meat. Wait till you taste it."

"I don't do underage," Ryan said,

"Your loss," Bianchi responded, as he walked up to the edge of the pool and leered.

Ryan went to the bar, poured himself a scotch and sat on one of the lounges. He watched as several of the older men put out their cigars and escorted young girls back to the house.

Finishing his drink, Ryan got up and got another one. Downing it quickly, he mulled over what to do next. Knowing leaving the house would insult his host, he decided to find an empty bedroom and get some sleep.

He waited until Rodriguez was busy chatting with two girls – the man would never notice him slipping away now.

Turning away from the pool, Ryan climbed the flagstone steps.

***

A ray of sunshine crossed Ryan's face and he awoke. Glancing at his watch, he saw the time: 9:42 a.m.

He got up from the king-size bed and crossed the opulent bedroom to the window. Peering outside at the pool below, he noticed everything was quiet. Only a few maids were there, cleaning up from the night's festivities.

Going to the marble-floor bathroom, he washed up. He came back, shrugged on his blazer. He needed to find Bianchi and get out of there. They needed to focus on tracking where the counterfeit money was coming from.

But on the way out of the room he was stopped by two swarthy men pointing AK-47 assault rifles at him.

"Come with us," one of them said.

"What's wrong?" Ryan asked.

"Shut up and come with us. I won't repeat it."

Ryan frowned. It was clear something had drastically changed. The courteous behavior of last night was gone.

He was led down a wide corridor and down flights of stairs to a concrete basement level. The luxury of the rest of the house was absent here.

One of the men opened a metal door and said brusquely, "In there."

Ryan walked in the room, the door slamming shut behind him.

Glancing around quickly, he realized he was in deep trouble.

Tony Bianchi was tied to a chair, his clothes torn, his face bleeding. The man was groaning and his eyes were wide with fear.

Manuel Rodriguez was standing off to one side, and four armed men were in the room, their assault rifles pointed at Ryan's chest.

"I'm glad you could join us," Rodriguez spat out. He was dressed in a corduroy shirt and jeans.

"What's going on, Manuel?" Ryan asked, his voice low.

"Do you take me for a fool, *señor?* This morning, after I finished with my *putas*, I started checking on you and Tony." His voice was harsh and angry, the melodious sing-song inflection Mexicans have absent now. "I found some interesting things. First, my friend Tony was arrested in Italy and deported back to the U.S....there he went into FBI custody."

Ryan's face must have showed surprise, because Rodriguez said, "Yes. I have good sources of information too. I am not the stupid Mexican you take me for."

"Manuel," Ryan responded, "there must be some mistake. You've got it all wrong."

"Save it, *gringo*. I've been questioning Tony. He gave you up. I know you're connected to the FBI."

Ryan grimaced, his adrenaline pumping. There were four guards, their guns drawn and ready to fire. And Rodriguez was also armed. No matter how well trained he was, Ryan knew the odds against him were bad. A feeling of dread settled in the pit of his stomach.

Rodriguez chortled. "I've already decided what to do with Tony here." The Mexican stepped up to Bianchi, drew a large, gold-plated Colt revolver from his waistband and leveled it at the man, who was whimpering for his life.

"*Adios*, Tony," Rodriguez said, pulling the trigger.

A bloody hole appeared on Bianchi's forehead and the man, still strapped to the chair, toppled backward to the floor.

The echo from the blast and the smell of gunpowder filled the room.

Turning away from Bianchi, Rodriguez wiped blood and brain splatter from his cheeks. He faced Ryan, leveled the pistol at him.

His brain on overdrive as he furiously tried to figure out a way out, Ryan stared down the barrel of the revolver.

"The question is," Rodriguez spat out, "what should I do with you?"

The Mexican barked out a harsh laugh, as he pulled back on the trigger.

Chapter 7

Rome, Italy

Vincento Amati sat in the sumptuous office of his two-story building not far from the Piazza Navona.

Sipping Glenlivet and reclining in the leather executive chair, he thought about the upcoming video conference call. He wanted to share the good news with his partners, hoped they would have similar news of their own.

His hand-cut glass tumbler empty, he set it down on the teak-wood desk.

The maid, who stood by the serving table in a corner of the room, quickly approached and refilled his drink.

"Thank you, Maria," he said, admiring the way the young brunette filled out her maid's uniform.

"Would you like some coffee, *signore?*" she asked.

"No. Just clear the plates and you may go." He glanced at his Patek Philippe watch. "My conference call will begin in a few minutes."

Giving a slight bow first, the comely woman began to clear his dinner plates from the large desk. Although the building had a separate dining room, Amati usually preferred to eat in his office, while working.

As soon as she was gone, he stood and locked the office door. He turned on the large video screen that hung on the wall, next to the original Botticelli painting set in a gilt-edged frame.

Sitting in the leather chair, he set the video monitor to a split screen and waited for the two men to call in on the secure line.

At exactly 8 p.m. local time, the image of Dimitri Petrovich filled the left side of the screen. The Russian oil tycoon was wearing a gray suit and tie.

"Hello, Vincento," the oilman said. "I see our Mexican friend isn't here yet, as usual. He'll be late to his own funeral."

Amati shrugged. "He's a good man, but punctuality isn't his strong suit."

Petrovich smirked and the two men made small talk as they waited for Hector Sanchez to join them.

A minute later Sanchez's face filled the right side of the screen. Amati noticed the man's scar on his cheek was bright pink today, as if he'd been running.

"I'm sorry to be late, gentlemen," Sanchez said in his heavy accented English. "But my meeting with the President ran late."

"Good news, I hope?" Amati asked.

"*Si*," Sanchez responded. "The President, after much cajoling, has decided to back our plan."

Amati knew Sanchez had been lobbying the President of Mexico to support the secretive Alliance for weeks. It appeared the two-hundred million dollar bribe had worked. "Excellent, Hector. I know it hasn't been easy."

Sanchez grinned. "No, it hasn't. But with the President on board, my contribution to the Alliance is assured. And there is one other benefit. Now that he is on our side, my drug business can expand. The *Federales* will not impede my trade routes into the U.S., but rather go after my competitors."

Amati nodded. "Very good."

"I have more good news," the Mexican continued, as he rubbed his scar. "I got a call from one of my main distributors, Manuel Rodriguez. He distributes my products through El Paso. He uncovered an FBI surveillance operation that included that man you mentioned last week, Vincento. The dealer from Atlanta named Bianchi."

Amati leaned forward in his chair. "Yes, I remember him."

"Anyway, Bianchi and an undercover FBI operative were trying to trace the counterfeit cash. But Rodriguez did some checking and figured it out before any damage was done."

"Where's Bianchi now?"

"Rodriguez is holding him, along with the FBI guy."

Amati sat back in the leather chair. "Good work, Hector. I want to congratulate you. Two wins in one conference call."

Sanchez beamed. "Thank you, Vincento."

Amati turned to the left side of the screen. "Okay, Dimitri. Please fill us in on your situation."

The Russian nodded. "Of course. I also have progress to report. The Prime Minister feels his proposal to President Lazarenko will be accepted soon. And, on a separate front, my oil company is using its profits to continue buying gold. As you know, Russia is one of the largest producers of gold in the world, mining over 190 tons a year. My company is on track to purchase half of that amount, maybe more."

"That is music to my ears," Amati responded. "That part of the plan is as important as the rest. My own media company has also been busy purchasing gold. We've invested several billion dollars so far." Amati paused and smiled. "The additional quantities of the sigma machines have just arrived. You'll be receiving your share of them in a few days."

Both Petrovich and Sanchez grinned, obviously pleased with the news.

The Italian placed his hands flat on the desk in front of him. "Everything is proceeding on schedule. Any questions or other comments?"

There were none and Amati said goodbye and turned off the call.

He leaned back in the chair and sipped scotch.

Chapter 8

South of Juarez, Mexico

The Colt revolver had an external hammer and Rodriguez pulled it back to the first click. "So, *gringo*, what should I do with you?" the man spat out.

Ryan stared down the barrel of the gold-plated gun, knowing he needed to pick his words very carefully. His life depended on it. With his heart racing, he said, "I'm no good to you dead. And I have information that could help you."

Rodriguez sneered. "You're nothing to me. Less than nothing. I scrape shit like you off my boots every morning. I just killed Tony, one of my distributors. You think I'd hesitate to kill you?"

Ryan took a gamble, said, "I know about sigma."

The Mexican's face registered surprise. "Sigma? What do you know about that?"

"I know it's connected to the counterfeit money."

Rodriguez frowned and he took a step back. He motioned to the nearest of the four guards, said, "Beat the hell out of the *gringo*. We'll see what he knows."

The guard shifted his AK-47 so that the wood stock was up, and carrying the weapon like a baseball bat, he advanced toward Ryan.

Quickly shifting his body into a side-stance karate position, Ryan kicked the guard, toppling him backward. The rifle flew in the air and clattered to the floor.

Ryan spun around, landing a spin kick to the guard behind him. Groaning, the man staggered back, crashed against the concrete wall.

The detective heard a crack and felt a blinding pain in the back of his head.

Everything went black as he crumpled to his knees.

***

Ryan woke up staring at the gray ceiling of the same basement room. He was flat on his back and he turned his head, saw he was alone.

His head and ribs were sore as hell, and the recent events flashed back to him. Rodriguez's men had beaten him for days.

Sitting up painfully, he gingerly touched his ribs. Several must be broken, he thought. He felt the large lump on the back of his head and traced the cuts on his face. His shirt and pants were splattered with blood.

Then a welcome thought hit him. He hadn't talked. Besides telling them he knew the word 'sigma', he hadn't told them anything else. Not that he know much else, but the fact he hadn't broken made the pain more bearable.

Standing up, he inspected the room. Besides the locked, metal door and the fluorescent strip on the ceiling, there was nothing else. No windows, no vents, no way out, save the door.

The room smelled of mold, urine, and feces. It was clear Rodriguez used the place to torture competitors and people he couldn't bribe.

The guards had taken his cell phone, watch, and everything else he'd had on him. Luckily, they left him his clothes and shoes.

Taking off his left shoe, he turned the sole sideways and a couple of items dropped to the floor. A car key, a couple of folded $100 bills and his lock-pick tool set. Maybe, just maybe, he could get out of this mess.

Picking up the items, he pocketed the key and money, and approached the door. Using the lock-pick, he began fiddling with the lock. It had heavy tumblers and it took him several minutes before he heard a faint click.

Opening the door partway, he peered around the jam. To his right, on this side of the corridor, a man was sitting on a folding chair. It was one of Rodriguez's men, holding an AK-47 loosely on his lap. He wasn't moving and the detective heard a slight snore.

Ryan slipped out of the room, gingerly walked over and with the side of his hand, savagely struck the guard on the back of his neck.

There was a muffled cry, the man's body sagged, and Ryan grabbed the rifle before it fell to the ground.

Laying the guard on the floor, Ryan took off the man's belt and shirt and used them to tie his hands and gag his mouth. Lastly, he grabbed the man's keys and weapon and headed for the stairs.

Using the guard's keys, he unlocked the door at the top of the landing and slowly went out of the stairway and into one of the first floor corridors. Scanning the passageway, he saw no one there.

Loud mariachi music was playing from the rear of the estate. It was clear Rodriguez was having another of his night-time parties.

Sprinting down the corridor with the weapon in front of him, he went past a massive den and a couple of other sitting rooms, all unoccupied.

Just ahead was a side entrance and he stopped and peered out the windows of the French double-doors. He saw a moonlit sky, the landscaped grounds, but no one moving about. Unlocking the door, he stepped outside.

The music was louder here and he crouched, crabbing forward to the front of the house, avoiding the bright floodlights that lit the grounds.

When he reached the front, he scanned the driveway, which once again was filled with BMWs, Ferraris, and even a Rolls-Royce. His own Suburban was still there, where he had parked it a few days earlier.

Hiding behind the landscaping, Ryan checked out the grounds inside the seven-foot walls. Two armed guards patrolled by the closed gate. And there were probably more outside the walls. Should he take the SUV and try to crash through the gate? Or climb the wall and try to sneak away on foot? Both were risky, but he had no other options. Crashing the gate would alert everybody – and a damaged Suburban would never outrace the high-end cars chasing him. At least on foot he'd have a couple of hours head start before they realized he was gone.

Weaving his way slowly around the lush bushes and plants to avoid the lights, he reached a section of the wall away from the gate.

Slipping his arm through the sling of the AK-47, he lunged with both hands to the top edge of the wall. He caught the edge, but not before his ribs struck the wall. Ignoring the sharp pain, he pulled himself up and awkwardly lay down on the edge at the top.

Ryan spotted an armed guard, his eyes fixed out toward the desert, making a circuit of the outside perimeter. He waited quietly until the man was well past him, and dropped to the other side, hitting the ground with a thud. Another stab of pain shot through him as he landed.

He began crawling away on his hands and knees, keeping a watchful eye for Rodriguez's men.

When he reached the two-lane road a long while later, he stood and got his bearings. From the position of the moon, he estimated it was between one and two a.m.

The road was deserted at this time of night and began jogging toward his motel.

A half-hour later he was within sight of the place. But then it struck him – Rodriguez was surely well connected in this area, with snitches everywhere, including the motel staff.

Spotting a 24-hour gas station/convenience store close by, he decided to head there. The place looked deserted, with only one car in the lot, probably the clerk's.

Hiding the weapon behind a trash dumpster, he went in the store.

Finding the bathroom, he washed the blood from his face, tried combing his hair as best he could.

He searched the aisles of the store, picked up a handful of Snickers Bars, a bottle of aspirin and a can of Coke. Most importantly, he selected a pre-paid cell phone from the small selection they had.

Plopping the items on the counter, he said in Spanish, "How much?"

The clerk, a short, wiry man, gave him an odd look, told him the total.

Ryan paid, took the filled paper bag, and gave the man a $20 tip, trying to buy some goodwill.

The clerk grinned, his crooked teeth showing. "*Gracias, señor.*"

"*De nada.*"

Leaving the store, Ryan scanned the area to make sure there was no one around. He retrieved the AK-47 and began walking away from the road, deep into the dark and barren desert.

He found a large stand of sage bushes and dropped behind them.

Sitting on the hard-packed dirt, he unwrapped the Snickers and wolfed them down, then swallowed a fistful of aspirin and washed it down with the soda.

Tearing open the package containing the cell phone, he turned it on. The cell reception was weak here, but would have to do. He dialed a number, waited for the pickup.

It rang for a long time, but was eventually answered by a sleepy female voice.

"Erin, is that you?"

"Who the hell is this?" Erin Welch responded.

"It's Ryan."

"Do you know what time it is? Jesus, Ryan."

He gave her a moment to calm down. "Listen. I need help. I'm in the Mexican desert, with no car, and I'm hurt."

"What? How badly are you hurt? Never mind. Where are you exactly?"

"South of Juarez, off state road 52. About a mile north of a convenience store called '*La Chiripa*'."

"Okay, okay. I'll get you help. I've worked with an FBI agent based in El Paso. I'll call him. He'll get to you."

"Good."

"Give me your number, Ryan. When he gets close, he'll call you."

He gave her the number. "Do me another favor. Call Lauren Chase for me, tell her I'm okay. I haven't talked to her in a while."

"So, I'm your social secretary too?" she said, her voice hard.

"I'd call her myself, but this cell phone is a piece of crap and the reception is kicking in and out."

"Okay, Ryan. Now, how badly are you hurt?"

Ryan was about to make a joke, but his ribs began aching again and he simply said, "Not too bad."

"Glad to hear it. Where's Bianchi?"

"Dead. Rodriguez shot him."

"At least he didn't run off," she replied. By the tone of her voice, he could tell the woman was relieved. Ever the political animal, Erin desperately didn't want to lose Bianchi on her watch.

"I'll call the FBI agent now," she continued. "His name is Hank Mitchell."

"Okay."

"And Ryan?"

Yeah?"

"Try not to get killed before he gets there. We still have a case to solve."

He laughed. "And here I thought you liked me because of my charm and good looks."

Ryan heard her sighing on the other end and he disconnected the call.

Stretching out behind the bushes to wait, Ryan gazed up at the stars in the still dark sky. He was asleep a minute later.

The ringing of the cell phone woke him. It was daytime and already hot, though it was late November.

Picking up the phone, he held it to his ear.

"This is Hank Mitchell," he heard. "Is this J.T. Ryan?"

"That's me. Where are you?"

"Parked in front of *'La Chiripa'*."

"What kind of vehicle you driving, Mitchell?"

"A Buick sedan."

"This desert is rough terrain. You'll never get to me in that thing. Wait there and I'll come to you."

Hanging up the phone, Ryan stood, ditched the AK-47 and began jogging south, holding his painful ribcage with one hand.

He spotted the Buick a while later, waved to the man inside, and climbed in the car. The air-conditioned interior felt refreshing.

"Thanks for picking me up," Ryan said as he stuck out his hand.

"No problem," Mitchell replied, shaking hands. "Always glad to help the Secret Service."

"Welch fill you in on the case?"

"Yeah. Told me about Bianchi and Rodriguez."

Ryan appraised the tall, rangy FBI agent in the blue suit. He had the clean-cut look so many of those guys had. Even his shoes had a gloss on them.

"So, Mitchell. What do you know about Rodriguez?"

"Call me Hank. Rodriguez is well known in southern Texas and northern Mexico. He's a drug dealer – been doing that for years. And now it appears he's branched out into counterfeit money. But he's like Teflon. We can never get anything to stick on him. The Mexican police treat him with kid gloves, probably well paid to look the other way."

"I figured as much," Ryan said. "I was at one of his parties recently and it looked like a lot of local politicos were there."

Mitchell nodded. "What's next for you? By the look of your face, I need to get you to a doctor."

Ryan warily touched his ribs. "That's a fact. But I want to get back home first. Just get me across the border and on a plane to Atlanta. I'll get treated there."

"Suit yourself," the agent said, cranking up the engine. Driving out of the parking area, the man got back on the state road, merging with the flow of pickups and semis that made up most of the traffic.

Chapter 9

Rome, Italy

Vincento Amati exited the black Mercedes limo, crossed the Piazza San Pietro and climbed the front steps of St. Peter's Cathedral. He showed his special pass to the uniformed policeman on duty at the gate and waited for the man to inspect it. Amati's power and influence had secured the pass from the Vatican, which gave him unrestricted access to the historic building.

The officer opened the gate and let him through, to the grumbles of the tourists and local residents who were waiting in line. The line stretched half-a-mile, and wrapped around the immense elliptical piazza fronting the church.

Reaching the top step, Amati stepped through the massive double doors and into the marble-floored, football-field size interior of the cathedral. Even thought he had been there countless times before, the majesty of the place still amazed him. The ornate, stained-glassed windows, opulent religious icons, and large crosses gleamed in the semi-gloom inside. The visual impact of the room was breathtaking, due in part to the massive height of the five-story vaulted ceilings.

Ignoring the hushed crowds that headed toward the basilica at the front end of the church, he instead went toward the small chapel to his right. It was his special place. The place he always went when he wanted to pray and seek wisdom.

Crossing himself and dabbing holy water on his forehead, he stepped inside the chapel. Finding an empty pew, he knelt and began praying. Although the chapel was not that small, it was intimate compared with the vastness of the other rooms in the cathedral.

Finished, he sat on the wooden bench, breathed in the strong scent of the lit candles and incense. Around him, nuns in habits, robed priests, and simply-dressed locals prayed. As usual, there were no tourists here. They, cameras in hand, all flocked to the basilica and the Vatican museums.

Whenever Amati felt uneasy or uncertain, he came here, this special place with the heavy wooden cross over the altar. Although he always prayed for forgiveness for his sins, for his involvement in murder and other crimes, he also sought clarity in this holy place.

Today he had learned from his Mexican partner, Hector Sanchez, that the FBI operative held by Rodriguez had escaped.

A bad omen. It appeared the FBI was investigating the Mexican connection of the sigma operation. The deaths of the FBI agents, Bianchi's arrest in Italy, and now this. The American authorities were still far from piecing together the scope of the Alliance plan, but still. He was worried.

So concerned, that he was considering contacting the fourth, silent partner of the conspiracy. Up to now, Amati had kept the man in the dark about any miscues in the operation, preferring to handle problems on his own. Then again, his silent partner could be of help. He had resources that were not available to Amati.

Bowing his head, the Italian said a silent prayer. When he was done, he crossed himself and stood. He would make the call today.

Chapter 10

Mexico City, Mexico

Hector Sanchez was worried. As he sat by the pool of his sprawling villa outside the city, he mulled over the events of the last few days. He had spent a large portion of his drug profits on bribing the President of Mexico, and buying significant quantities of gold.

"You seem preoccupied," said his wife, who was sitting next to him on a lounge chair. Inez Sanchez had been his spouse for over twenty years, and was not only the mother of his two children, but also a close confidant.

"It's nothing," he replied, turning to face her. As usual when they were by the pool, the woman was a wearing a sleek, one-piece swimsuit. Inez had the dusky good looks of a faded TV star. She had been an actress for many years, a veteran of Mexican *novelas*.

"I've known you a long time, Hector. I know when something is wrong."

Sanchez idly scratched the scar on his cheek. "The Alliance plan," he replied, his voice low so that the servants who were in the massive back yard of the estate wouldn't hear. "I've pumped a lot of money into it. I hope it all pays off in the end."

She patted his arm with one hand. "You worry too much, Hector. I told you before, it's going to be very good for us, and for our children. You are in a nasty business, this drug cartel of yours. Killing, kidnapping, all of it. But once the plan is in place, you'll be able to hold your head up high, be a respected business leader in Mexico. Already you are seeing benefits. The president is now in your pocket. That's a hell of an accomplishment."

Sanchez nodded, seeing the wisdom of her words.

"Yes, I know. But I've spent so much money, it worries me."

Inez grinned. "Money you can replace easily over time. Remember, your drug routes are expanding. And now that you are distributing cocaine, and meth, *and* the counterfeit cash, your income flow is increasing. Do not worry, Hector. It is all going to work out. Trust me."

When Amati had come to him originally and told him about the sigma operation, Sanchez had been reluctant at first. But Inez had convinced him that it would give him the respectability and power he could never achieve running a criminal enterprise, no matter how much money it made.

He picked up the glass from the side table and took a sip of the tequila. He savored the familiar sweet-salty flavor as it burned down his throat.

"Thank you, Inez. Sometimes I have doubts, but talking it out with you always helps. You're right, as usual."

She smiled, took a sip of her martini and went back to reading on her iPad.

Chapter 11

Atlanta, Georgia

Ryan sat on the edge of the hospital bed while the intern finished cleaning and dressing the cuts on his face. The ER cubicle they were in smelled of antiseptics and that peculiar odor all hospitals shared.

"That should do it," the young doctor said when he was done. He stood back and handed Ryan a bottle of pills. "These are pain-killers. Oxycontin. It's strong, so don't take more than two a day."

The detective slipped the bottle in his pants pocket. "How long before the ribs heal, doc?"

"Hard to say. Broken ribs are funny. Each person is different."

Ryan nodded. "Okay."

The intern left the cubicle and disappeared into the crowded corridors of Grady Memorial.

Ryan awkwardly put on his shirt, signed himself out of the hospital, and walked out of the building to hail a cab.

Hearing a car honk, he spotted Erin Welch in a double-parked Ford Crown Vic. The woman waved and he walked over and climbed in.

"Thanks for picking me up," he said.

She fired up the car. "Lauren called me, told me she brought you here, but said she had to go out of town for some conference."

"Yeah. She's giving a speech at a robotics convention in LA."

Welch merged into traffic and got on I-75. Turning her head his way, she said, "You look like hell, Ryan."

He touched the bandages on his face.

"Yeah. But you should see the other guy."

She shook her head slowly, obviously not amused by his attempt at humor.

Turning serious, he said, "Rodriguez's men beat me up, but I was able to escape during one of his parties."

Welch passed a slow-moving semi. "So. What's his connection to the counterfeit money?"

"Rodriguez is only a middle-man. He warehouses the stuff in Juarez, but it's not made there. He gets it from a supplier."

The agent nodded. "Okay. I'll check my sources again, see if I can dig something up. What about you?"

He warily rubbed his ribcage. "I'll rest up for a couple of days, then head back to Mexico. I'm going to trace the fake cash. But I'll need help."

"Sure. I'll come with you, and bring a couple of my men."

He gave her a sidewise glance. The attractive blonde would stand out during undercover work – no way was he bringing her along. "I got a better idea. Why don't you work the case from here? I just need agent Mitchell to help me. He's familiar with Mexico."

Suddenly a red Corvette cut in front of them and she leaned on the horn.

"Bastard," she muttered. "Traffic in this city sucks. Okay, I'll call Mitchell. Set it up."

"Good. Can you drop me off at my place?"

"Sure. What's the address?"

He told her and she dropped him off.

When he got in his simply-furnished apartment, he took one of the pain-killers and stretched out on the sofa of his living room.

Grabbing the remote, he turned on the TV and surfed the channels, finally settling on a cable news station. They were running a story on the sudden high rate of inflation in the U.S.

The anchor, a bookish-looking man with graying hair, went on to explain that part of the reason for the inflation was the large influx of counterfeit money that was turning up in the country.

Ryan's interest perked up and he listened closely, but the Oxycontin must have kicked in, because he felt a mellow drowsiness and he drifted off to sleep.

Chapter 12

El Paso, Texas

Ryan walked out of baggage claim and out to the parking area of the airport.

He spotted Hank Mitchell right away, sitting in a gray Jeep Cherokee.

Walking over, he put his bag in the back seat and climbed in the vehicle.

"I'm glad you got the four-wheel drive," Ryan said as the two men shook hands.

"Yeah," the FBI agent replied. "I also got the other gear you wanted."

"Good – we'll need it. Let's get going."

Mitchell got on the highway heading south, went through the Mexican border crossing and two hours later they were on state road 52 south of Juarez.

As the barren, arid landscape rolled past them, Ryan began to recognize the few landmarks along the way, mostly cheap motels and gas stations by the road. Traffic was light, and it was all dusty pickups and semis.

When they were a few miles from the warehouse turnoff, Mitchell turned toward Ryan. "So, what's the plan?"

"Like I told you," Ryan said. "We need to stake-out Rodriguez's warehouse and watch them unload the cash. Then follow the truck back to the source."

"You make it sound simple."

Ryan chuckled. "It is. We just have to make sure we don't get shot while we're doing it."

"There is that."

The detective spotted the turnoff and pointed toward it.

"Keep going past it, and go a mile further. Take a right into the desert – we'll loop back and set up there."

The agent followed the directions and a few minutes later the Jeep was bouncing over the rocky terrain.

Ryan held up a hand. "Stop here, Hank. Let's take a look."

They climbed out of the vehicle and both men gazed out at the flat, almost empty horizon.

Ryan shielded his eyes from the strong midday sun, straining to see the warehouse. Pinpointing a dirty smudge in the far distance, he said, "Get the scope."

The agent pulled a thick telescope from the Jeep's back hatch, and using the scope's attached tripod, set it on the ground.

Ryan looked through it as he began to focus the instrument. He saw blurry images at first, but eventually the large warehouse came into view. Focusing again to get a tighter image of the loading bays, he spotted three trucks being unloaded. Using forklifts, the warehouse crew was taking off fully-loaded pallets. He inspected the tarps that covered each pallet. They were all white or brown in color. He remembered from his past visit to the warehouse that the fake cash pallets were covered with green tarps. At the time, Ryan had surmised that it was easy way for Rodriguez's men to segregate the types of products they stored and distributed.

"The stuff they're unloading now isn't cash," Ryan said, as he stepped away from the scope. "It's probably coke or fentanyl."

"You sure?"

"Yeah."

"So what now?"

"Now we wait and watch." Ryan motioned toward the Jeep. "You brought food and water for a couple of days?"

Mitchell nodded.

"Good," Ryan said. "I'll take the first watch." He brushed the perspiration from his forehead. "And if I were you, I'd rest in the car. No sense for both of us to fry out here."

The agent got in the Jeep, while Ryan went back to the scope.

A parade of semis continued to stream in and out of the parking area for the next five hours, their loads fork-lifted out, but none had pallets with green tarps.

The two men took turns every hour, but by early evening, the trucks stopped coming and the warehouse's bay doors rolled closed.

"Must be Miller time," Ryan quipped. "The truckers are done for the day."

"Or probably Corona time," the agent said.

"That's good, Hank." Ryan flashed a smile, glad the buttoned-down agent had a sense of humor. It looked like it was going to be a long stake-out and a little joking always helped pass the time.

As soon as the sun went down, the hot desert turned frigid and the men donned the jackets stored in the Jeep.

They had a cold meal of Spam and baked beans and turned in early, using the sleeping bags the agent had brought.

The next day was hot and monotonous, and to their disappointment, revealed no deliveries of counterfeit cash.

But on the third day, early in the morning, they caught a break. Two semis pulled up, both unmarked save for a rig number on the sides, and began unloading pallets with green tarps.

"We're in luck," Ryan said as he focused the telescope to inspect the pallets carefully. "These trucks are it." Pulling a pad from his pocket, he wrote down the rig numbers and a description of the vehicles, which were both Mack trucks.

"It's about time," Mitchell responded.

Ryan picked up the scope and folded the tripod legs. "Let's pack up quickly, so we can be on the road when the rigs pull out of the warehouse."

They stored their gear and minutes later were back on the road.

Fifteen minutes later they saw the two Mack trucks pull out of the turnoff and unto the state road, heading east.

"Drop back," Ryan said, "let some of the other traffic get behind the semis. They're tall, we won't have a problem spotting them."

Agent Mitchell slowed the Jeep and a couple of pickups passed them.

The flat, ugly desert of northern Mexico flowed past – mostly brown dirt, scrub brush, cacti, and rocks.

Ryan rolled down the window, breathed in the dry, dusty heat. It smelled of dried vegetation and death. He remembered something he'd read recently about the severe drought in northern Mexico. Cattle were dying from the lack of water, the local ranchers barely surviving. Some had turned to other cash crops, like running drugs or illegals from Central America to the U.S. border.

Ryan closed the window, focusing on the semis ahead.

"Okay," he said. "You're good. Follow them at this distance."

Mitchell nodded, picked up a little speed. The Mack trucks were clearly visible, followed by the pickups. Periodically, Ryan used the binoculars the agent had brought, checking the rig numbers printed on the back door of the second truck.

Time passed and the state road fed into the main highway going south, all while the Jeep kept its distance.

The desert turned hilly and eventually the hills gave way to mountains – Ryan realized they were getting close to the northern Mexico city of Monterrey. An hour later the semis took the first exit into Monterrey and they followed, giving the trucks enough distance so there were at least several cars between them.

An hour later the trucks took a side road and moments later pulled off unto a wide paved driveway leading to a high-walled, multi-story building complex that fronted a cliff.

"Keep going," Ryan said, "let them go in."

It was late afternoon and the hot sun was giving way to a cool November breeze.

The two semis disappeared into the complex and the Jeep drove past it on the local road.

Using the binos, Ryan spotted a small sign on the side of the building that read *INDUSTRIAS SPXE*.

Mitchell stepped on the gas and a minute later pulled off the single-lane road, well away from the building.

"I'll check on this company," Ryan said. "Let's find a local place to stay."

"You got it," Mitchell replied, as he sped away.

They found a cheap motel not far away, a no-name place with an attached restaurant that smelled of stale tortillas. The motel's shabby lobby was full of sad-looking coke whores. The women wore low-cut blouses and short skirts, their leering smiles showing stained teeth. The whores tried picking up the two men, but Ryan waved them away.

When he got to his room, he placed the overnight bag on the lumpy bed, washed up in the grimy bathroom, and pulled out his cell phone.

The motel room smelled of vomit, urine, and sex, and he tried not to think about any of that as he dialed the number.

It rang for a long time but eventually he heard Erin Welch's voice on the other end.

"It's Ryan," he said.

"Jesus, J.T., don't you ever call at a normal time? You caught me at a bad time. I'm on a date, having dinner."

"Sorry to disturb you. Someone from your office?"

"Yes."

"Bad idea, Erin. Those things usually don't end well."

"You're a piece of work," she replied, anger in her voice. "It's none of your business who I go out with. You need something, or are just trying to spoil my day?"

Ryan laughed. "Just saying."

He turned serious. "I'm in northern Mexico. I got a lead on Rodriguez. His source for the fake cash is a company here in Monterrey called *Industrias SPXE*. I need you to check it out."

"Good work, J.T. I'll check on the company. Now can I get back to my steak tartar?"

"You'll call me back with the info?"

There was a pause from the other end. "Yeah. I'll call you. But it won't be tonight."

He heard a click and realized she'd hung up.

Ryan put the phone away and peered out the blinds of the motel window. It seemed quiet in the parking lot of the place.

He put the S&W under his pillow, turned off the overhead light, and sprawled out on the bed, trying to avoid the suspicious stains covering parts of it. Pulling his cell phone from his pocket, he laid it on the dented, cheap nightstand and closed his eyes.

A minute later he was asleep.

Chapter 13

Monterrey, Mexico

Ryan's phone buzzed and he reached for his gun. Light was streaking in through the dusty blinds and he let go of the weapon as he became fully awake.

He picked up the cell from the nightstand, held it to his ear.

"It's Erin. I've been working on that Mexican company, SPXE. At first I couldn't get a handle on the ownership, since the proprietor set up the company through a couple of dummy corporations. But I have good sources. The owner is a Mexican national by the name of Hector Sanchez."

Ryan rubbed his eyes. "Never heard of him. Who is he?"

"That's a surprise," she said sarcastically. "I thought you knew everything. Anyway, Sanchez is well known to the DEA. He runs one of Mexico's largest drug cartels."

"That makes sense, Erin. Rodriguez has probably been a drug distributor for Sanchez, and later expanded his business to include the cash."

"That's what my DEA contact thinks too."

Ryan sat up on the bed.

"Does Sanchez work out of Monterrey?"

"He travels there frequently, but he lives on an estate outside of Mexico City."

"Give me his home address."

"What do you plan to do?"

"Not sure yet. I've got to work that out. But I may need some things. What's that address?"

She told him, then said, "Don't do anything stupid, J.T. This Sanchez is a major player down there, has a lot of soldiers."

"Do you want to get to the bottom of this?"

"Of course."

"Give me what I want, when I want it. Then stay out of my way."

"You're fucking insufferable, sometimes."

He chuckled. "Is that a compliment? People tell me I'm insufferable all the time."

He heard a sigh from the other end, but she said nothing.

"By the way, how was your date last night, Erin?"

There was a click and he realized she'd hung up on him again. Served him right, he mused. *Sometimes I am a pain in the ass.*

Stripping off his clothes, he went to the bathroom and tried taking a hot shower, but the water that came from the rusty showerhead was lukewarm at best.

Afterwards he toweled off and dressed in fresh clothes. Stepping out of his room, he knocked on Mitchell's door, which was a couple of rooms down from his.

The agent opened it, said, "Let's get something to eat. I'm starved."

Ryan nodded and glanced in the direction of the restaurant that was attached to the motel. "Why don't we find some other place for breakfast? Some of Sanchez's men may eat here and we need to talk without being overheard."

Mitchell agreed and they took the Jeep a few miles west, to a more upscale area with tony shops and restaurants. They found a brick-front café and went inside.

A slender waitress with dark hair pulled into a ponytail showed them to a booth and they ordered coffee.

Ryan gazed around the café, which reminded him of a 50's style diner, only classier. There were few customers, and they all looked like business people, getting breakfast before heading to work. The savory aroma of eggs and sausage filled the air.

The waitress served them coffee and the detective took a sip, relished the strong flavor. She took their order and moved away.

"Erin called me," Ryan said, keeping his voice low.

Mitchell leaned forward in his seat. "She found out about that company?"

"Yeah. SPXE is owned by a drug dealer. Guy by the name of Hector Sanchez. Apparently a big player in Mexico."

The agent nodded. "I've heard of him. He runs a couple of legitimate businesses — a large trucking firm and a chain of gas stations. But the word is he's dirty, uses the legit companies to launder his drug cash."

Ryan rubbed his jaw. "I'm trying to sort out the best way to go after this guy."

"It won't be easy," Mitchell said with a frown. "He's well connected. From what I've heard, he has bodyguards and his office and home have extensive security."

"That's what Erin said too."

"What do you plan to do?"

Ryan took another sip of coffee and leaned back in the seat, thinking over the options.

The waitress returned with heaping platters of food.

The fried eggs and side dishes smelled delicious and the two men dug in, savoring the first hot meal they'd had in days.

When they were done, the waitress cleared the plates, refilled their cups, and left the check on the table.

"We need to stake-out his home," Ryan said, "see the best way to get in there."

The agent held up a hand. "No problem. I can help you with that. But that's as much as I can do, without getting clearance from my regional office. I'm sure they won't let me get involved with anything beyond surveillance, unless they get authorization from the Mexican police."

"I figured as much. Don't worry, Hank. Just help me scout out the place and I'll take it from there."

"You're only one guy. Even if you are ex-Special Forces, this Sanchez character is going to have a lot of guns on his side. Maybe you should just report what you find to Welch, let her take it from there."

Ryan shook his head slowly. "It'll never work. She'll have to get approval from her boss, who in turn will have to get approval from the head office in D.C., and they'll have to coordinate with the State Department and the *Federales*. It'll be six months before anything gets done, if ever. Like you said, Sanchez is well connected. He probably spreads bribe money all over Mexico – they'll never touch him – that's my guess."

"You're pretty cocky, Ryan, to think you can flush this guy out by yourself and get him to talk."

The detective leaned forward in his seat. "My best friend was killed over this damn conspiracy. A guy who saved my life. I'm going to make sure he didn't die in vain."

"Okay. I can see that. And I'll help you as much as I can."

"Good. How is long is the drive to Mexico City?"

"About ten hours."

Ryan took a last sip of his coffee. "Let's check out of the motel, and get going. The sooner we get there the better."

Chapter 14

Moscow, Russia

Dimitri Petrovich was in a sour mood. He was in his oil company office and had just finished a video call with Vincento Amati. On the call he had learned that the FBI operative who Rodriguez captured had escaped. To make matters worse, it had happened days ago, and he was only learning about it now.

A control freak, Petrovich hated it when he didn't have total control, all of the time. It was the one thing he despised about being in the Alliance. He wasn't in charge. Amati was, by the mere fact he was the architect of the conspiracy and also controlled the sigma machines. Granted, the Italian was brilliant and cunning, but there were times, such as now, when Petrovich realized Amati didn't share all the information with him. After all this time, the oil tycoon still didn't know where Amati got the sigma machines, where they were made, and by whom.

Pushing the negative thoughts aside, he glanced out the floor-to-ceiling windows of his spacious penthouse office. The Moscow skyline stared back at him, now covered by a deep blanket of December snow. An ugly, gray sky hung over the city, typical for this time of year.

Taking a pull from his vodka, he mused that once the Alliance plan was complete, he, Amati and Sanchez would go their own ways, each richer than God, and very powerful. In effect, each man would control the economies of Russia, Italy and Mexico, with the capability to influence Europe, Asia and the Americas.

A thin smile crossed his lips as he visualized all this. Born of dirt-poor parents who had migrated from the Ukraine to Moscow when he was an infant, Petrovich had scratched and clawed his way out of the ghettos. In his teens he had dropped out of school and become a drug courier for a neighborhood gang. By the time he was in his twenties, he had set up his own crew, shaking down businesses for 'protection' money.

Using the money from this operation, he turned to the oil business, buying a small drilling and refining company and later branching out into ship transports. Now his oil business spanned continents, with countless refineries, oil fields, and shipping companies. His friendship with Ivan Chernov had helped immensely, greasing the way to ever bigger and more profitable ventures. The two men had met when they were in their thirties. Chernov had graduated from the University of Moscow with a law degree, and began representing criminals like Petrovich. Then the lawyer, in a move to clean up his background, began representing legitimate Russian businessmen. Eventually Chernov turned to politics, rising through the ranks of councilman, mayor of the capital city, and now prime minister.

As the two men grew in power, they helped each other. And when Amati came to Petrovich years ago with the Alliance plan, the oil tycoon realized having his friend Chernov in the conspiracy would be a perfect fit. Chernov would eventually become the new face of Russia and Petrovich, a man that shunned the public spotlight, would be the power behind the scenes.

Finishing his drink, he made a snap decision. Pressing the intercom on his desk, he said, "Karina, call Markov. Tell him I need to see him immediately."

"Yes, sir," his secretary replied. "Is there anything else you need?"

Petrovich visualized the shapely young woman who sat in the front office. Karina was an efficient secretary, but was also very proficient at taking care of his other needs. A mental image of her nude, voluptuous body filled his thoughts and he felt himself getting aroused. Suppressing his sexual urge, he said, "No, not now. I have to take care of business first. Let me know when Markov gets here."

"Yes, sir."

Pouring himself another vodka, he leaned back in his executive chair and gazed out the windows. It had started to snow again, a heavy, wet snow that was snarling the early evening traffic on the streets below. His thoughts turned to his upcoming meeting with Markov. Part of the *grupperovka*, the Moscow Mafia, Markov was Petrovich's fixer, his go-to-guy for resolving thorny problems. Markov was an expert assassin, but unlike many in the *grupperovka*, he was highly intelligent.

The oil tycoon took a sip of the vodka, and a small smile spread on his face. Since Amati was holding back information, Petrovich had decided he would take matters into his own hands.

***

The blond, crew-cut man stood ramrod straight in front of Petrovich's desk. Markov was a tall, muscular man, a laconic individual in his thirties who favored dark clothing.

"You did well," Petrovich said, leaning back in his chair, "on the last assignment I gave you. I'll be wiring you an extra bonus."

Markov nodded, but there was no change in his stony facial expression.

"I have something new," the oil man continued, sliding a manila envelope across the desk toward the other man. "This is a little different. I don't need anyone terminated. This time it's surveillance."

The blond man picked up the envelope, opened it, and quickly scanned the contents. Without a word he looked back at Petrovich.

Petrovich leaned forward in his chair. "I want you to trace the shipments of the sigma machines to the original source. As you know, we get them from Italy, but I want to find where they are made and who makes them."

Markov nodded again, but said nothing.

"Do you have any questions?" the oil man asked.

"My usual fee?"

"Yes, of course. Any other questions?"

"No."

"Very well. Keep me informed."

Markov once again nodded, and without another word, left the office.

Standing, Petrovich walked to the windows and drew the blinds closed. He went back to his desk and pressed the intercom. "Karina," he said, "you can come in now."

Chapter 15

Rome, Italy

Vincento Amati stood at the rear of the vast amphitheatre, the production room of his media corporation. At the far end of the room one hundred large TV screens, ten across and ten high, covered the wall, all showing different news images from across the world. A crew of operators manned the rows of consoles in front of the screens and behind them his three producers conferred, sorting out which stories to run for this evening's news broadcast.

Years ago, Amati himself would have picked the stories, but his business had grown too large for him to handle such tasks personally. His news operation was now as large as CNN or Fox News, supplying video feeds to thousands of local outlets in Europe and Asia. He now came into the production studio to observe the frenzied activity, and to relive his younger days. It was a pleasant diversion from the endless company meetings. Discussing budgets, staffing, and other mundane topics was the boring aspect of running a multi-national company.

Amati's cell phone rang, its tone barely audible in the din of the large room. Reaching into his suit pocket, he pulled out the phone and held it to his ear.

"*Signore* Amati, I have information about the leak." He recognized the voice immediately – it was his chief of security, a man he trusted implicitly.

For months, Amati's security people had been trying to find the person who had leaked information about sigma to the FBI. And until now, they had come up empty.

Amati listened closely as the man spoke, going into detail about what they had learned. When the security chief was done, Amati thanked him and hung up the call.

Shaken from the revelation, he decided to take action immediately.

***

Amati entered his building located close to the Piazza Navona and went to his sumptuous office on the second floor. Lifting the receiver from the ornate, French-style phone that was on his desk, he spoke into it briefly and replaced it.

He sat behind his desk to wait, and sort out his thoughts.

A minute later his maid Maria stepped in the room. The young woman curtsied. "You wanted to see me, *signore*? Would you like your meal served now?"

He waved a hand toward the wingback chair fronting his desk.

"Have a seat, Maria."

The comely brunette perched herself on the seat, her hands folded primly on her lap.

"Maria, how long have you worked for me?"

"Two years, *Signore* Amati."

"And in those two years, have I not treated you fairly?"

A frown crossed her face, as if she didn't know where the conversation was headed. "Of course. You have been a very good employer."

He stared into her dark eyes.

"Haven't I paid you well? In fact, much better than others in your position?"

"Yes, *signore*."

"Have I ever asked you to do anything you did not wish to do?"

Maria shook her head empathically. Amati was a man with a hearty sexual appetite, but had recognized that Maria was a demure, shy woman and therefore never asked her for sex, preferring to fish in other ponds.

Amati steepled his hands on the desk.

"I'm at a loss, Maria. I learned disturbing news earlier today. Very disturbing."

"What, *signore?*"

"My chief of security has irrefutable evidence. You have sold information about my operation."

She gasped, and a shocked expression crossed her face.

"There must be some mistake, *Signore* Amati. I would never betray your trust."

He slapped a hand on the desk.

"Don't lie to me. I also learned about your sick mother, and the expensive treatments she requires."

After a moment, she nodded. "*Si, signore.* I was trapped. I didn't know what else to do. But I promise, it will never happen again."

"You should have come to me, Maria. I would have lent you the money. We could have worked out a re-payment schedule. But now, how can I ever trust you again?"

"Please," she said, her voice pleading. "I made a horrible mistake. I swear, you *can* trust me!"

He slapped his hand on the desk again. "Stop it!"

Reaching into a desk drawer, he withdrew a Beretta 9 mm automatic and pointed it at the woman.

Color drained from her face and she gripped the chair's armrests.

"If you were one of my mortal enemies," he said, his voice low and harsh. "I would make you pay. Kill you in a slow and painful way. However, as I am a devout Catholic and you have served me faithfully for *most* of your time with me, I will spare you that."

Her eyes were wide with fear and she cringed in her seat.

"It is only fair," he continued, "that you die quickly."

Amati pulled the trigger and her head snapped back, blood splatter flying across the office.

As her body slumped to the floor, the sound of the blast echoed in the room. The pungent odor of gunpowder hung in the air.

He stuck the Beretta in his suit pocket, stood, and came around the desk.

Maria lay face up, her lifeless eyes staring up at him. There was a ragged, bloody hole on her forehead.

Glancing around the office, he noticed the splatter of red that covered some of the walls.

With alarm he realized his prized Botticelli, a one-of-a-kind priceless painting, had several red smudges on the lower half.

Quickly crossing the room, he took out a handkerchief and gingerly dabbed the blood away.

Enraged by what the woman had caused, he pulled out the Beretta and pumped three shots into her abdomen.

Feeling better, he put the gun away. He took out his cell phone and punched in the number for his security chief.

When the man answered, Amati barked out, "Come to my office now, and bring some men with you. I have some trash that needs to be taken out."

Chapter 16

Mexico City, Mexico

J.T. Ryan gazed through the binoculars, surveying the high walls that enclosed Hector Sanchez's estate outside the city.

Ryan and Mitchell were in the Jeep, parked a block away from the home. It was early evening and traffic was light in the exclusive neighborhood, comprised of other large, similarly walled homes.

An imposing solid metal gate fronted the estate, and earlier in the day, as vehicles had gone in and out, the momentarily open gate revealed a group of heavily-armed men patrolling the grounds.

"We've been at this for hours," Mitchell said. "See anything new?"

Ryan put down the binos, turned toward the FBI agent. "Sanchez has lots of security. It's going to be tough."

Mitchell grimaced. "I could have told you that, before we got here."

The detective scanned the house again with the binoculars, noticed the security cameras mounted everywhere. He was sure motion detectors were mounted on the walls and across the grounds.

"I need to get to Sanchez when he's most vulnerable," Ryan said. "Asleep in the middle of the night, or when he's in transit from his office to his home."

"Yeah, that's a fact. I told you I'd help you monitor his place, but I can't do much more."

Ryan stared at the other man. "What are you saying?"

"I'm saying it's time for me to get off the Ryan train."

"You cutting out on me?"

The agent nodded. "Got to. I'd be breaking too many laws, Mexican and otherwise, if I went any further."

"Okay, I knew it was coming. Look, I understand. But can you at least leave me the equipment you brought?"

Mitchell was quiet a moment. "Tell you what. I'll leave you the equipment and the Jeep. Just drive me to the airport and I'll catch a flight back home to El Paso."

Ryan grinned. "You're okay, Hank. For a Fed."

After a last look at the house, Ryan drove out of the area and got on the highway leading to Benito Juarez International, Mexico City's biggest airport.

He fought the congested traffic for over an hour, and finally pulled into the airport's departures on-ramp. The drop-off area was packed with vehicles and he double-parked in front of the AeroMéxico entrance door.

Mitchell grabbed his bag from the back seat and stuck out his hand. "Good luck."

The men shook.

"Thanks, Hank. I'll need it."

"Try not to get arrested," Mitchell said with a smile. "But if you do, you have my number."

Ryan grinned. "Getting arrested is the least of my worries."

The agent climbed out and disappeared into the throng of people entering the airport.

Not having a well thought-out plan of action, Ryan drove out of the sprawling airport complex and cruised aimlessly around the city, his mind churning. He had been to Mexico City many times and was familiar with the main streets.

Realizing he had to get some rest, he found a Florencia Hotel and checked in.

He was asleep a minute after his head hit the pillow.

***

It came to him just as he was finishing breakfast the next morning. It wouldn't be easy, but considering his other options, this one seemed the cleanest.

Paying the bill, Ryan left the hotel's restaurant and located the Jeep in the parking lot.

Doing a Google search on his cell phone, he located a tall men's clothing store close by and drove there. He needed a few things to make his plan work.

He picked out jeans, a turtleneck, watch cap and gloves, all in black. Lastly he needed a light jacket. It was hot in Mexico City, even in December, but he needed the pockets to carry supplies. Finding a black windbreaker his size, he paid for the items and drove to the upscale grocery market one mile from Sanchez's estate.

During the surveillance yesterday, Ryan had seen the market's truck make a delivery to the home at mid-afternoon. If his hunch was right, the family called in an order every day to insure getting the freshest meats and vegetables. Of course, if he was wrong, he'd be wasting a day.

Parking in the lot in front of the grocery store, he turned off the vehicle and dialed Erin Welch's number on his cell.

The woman answered a moment later. "This is Welch."

"Hey, it's Ryan."

"J.T. How are things down there? Mitchell called me, told me he'd bowed out,"

"Yeah. Listen, Erin. I need you to find out something."

"Before I agree, tell me if I have to break laws to get the info."

He laughed. "Probably. Hector Sanchez. I need to know if he's in Mexico City right now, or if he's out of the country."

"Okay. I can do that. It might take me a little time."

"Call me back." He disconnected the call, stretched out his legs, and leaned back in the seat.

It was a bright, sunny day and he watched idly as BMWs and Mercedes came into and left the lot. Rolling down his window, a warm breeze blew in, the air tinged with the scent of smog that pervaded the second-largest city in the continent.

Half-an-hour later Erin called back. "Yeah, J.T. He's there. Apparently his usual routine is he leaves his office at around seven p.m., goes home, then leaves the next morning by eight. What's your plan?"

"I'll let you know when it's done."

"Fair enough. Do you need anything else?"

"I may need you to wire me some more money soon, but I'm okay for now."

Hanging up, he grabbed the bag with his new clothes and headed to the store to change in the men's room.

Moments later he was back in the Jeep and he loaded his pockets with weapons and supplies. Then he strode around the perimeter of the store to the rear of the place.

He spotted the delivery truck parked by the loading dock, the cab empty.

Glancing around to make sure no one was watching, he crouched down and rolled under the truck. Lying face-up, he inspected the undercarriage. Grabbing the suspension, he pulled himself up and nestled his body against the underside. It was uncomfortable, but would work.

He lowered his body to the ground and waited.

Hours later he saw feet shuffling toward the truck and heard the vehicle being loaded. He grabbed the suspension and hoisted himself up, careful to avoid the muffler and the exhaust pipe. The undercarriage smelled of road tar.

The delivery truck exited the parking lot and merged with other traffic. From his limited vantage point, Ryan could still make out the stops the truck was making. First was a gas station to fill up, and then several expensive, but not walled homes in the area.

Eventually the truck stopped in front of a walled estate and Ryan breathed a sigh of relief. His muscles ached from the effort of holding himself off the ground.

"*Viveres para la familia Sanchez*," Ryan heard the driver say into the speaker by the gate. "Groceries for the Sanchez family."

The metal gate creaked open and Ryan saw boots approach the driver's side. He gripped the butt of his Glock, praying he wouldn't have to blast away so soon.

"*Pase*," he heard the guard say and the truck lurched forward, driving along a long, curved driveway. He could make out the manicured lawns, fountains, and extensive landscaping that covered the grounds.

The vehicle pulled to the rear of the sprawling home and stopped on a flagstone driveway.

He heard voices in Spanish, the maid and the delivery driver conversing – it was obvious they knew each other well.

Ryan, his heart pounding, stared out from underneath the truck, desperately trying to find the best place to hide. He heard the vehicle's cargo door open and boxes being unloaded – he had no time to waste.

He saw it. A row of ornate bushes a few feet from the vehicle.

Dropping to the ground, he quickly rolled his body from under the truck and kept rolling until he reached the vegetation. Grabbing a branch, he pulled himself between the shrubs, his body concealed. Lying face up, he looked through the branches and could make out the azure blue sky above.

Ryan heard the truck's cargo door slam shut. A moment later its motor started up and the vehicle sounds receded. He listened closely for other sounds, footsteps or voices, but all he heard was the chirping of birds and the distant sound of water splashing in a fountain.

He closed his eyes, knowing it would be a long wait until nightfall.

***

Stiff from being prone so long, he stretched his muscles as best he could. The sky was dark now, only stars overhead. Listening for voices, he heard none.

Carefully sitting up, he peered through the bushes at the house. Lights were on in several of the rooms on the first floor. Behind him, in the distance, he could make out the high walls that enclosed the property, floodlit and patrolled by armed men.

Turning back to the house, he spotted what looked like a service area at the rear of the home with trash cans lined in a neat row. It was past dinnertime, and Ryan watched and waited. A short while later, a maid came out of a side door and added a bag of garbage to one of the trash cans. Then she went back in the house.

Betting she wouldn't turn on the house alarm on until later, after all her chores were done, he pulled his watch cap so it covered most of his face and removed the Glock 9mm from his jacket pocket. Glancing back to the grounds, he saw one of the guards by the wall, but he was facing away from him.

Ryan stood and sprinted the fifteen feet to the house. Crouching by the side door, he peered in through the small window. He saw a wide corridor, which led on the left to a well-lit, immense kitchen. Two women, both wearing maid's uniforms, were at the sink cleaning pots. But to his right the hallway was dimly lit.

Slowly, he twisted the knob. The door opened and he crept inside, closing it behind him.

Turning away from the kitchen, he followed the dimly-lit corridor past several darkened rooms. He spotted what looked like a study with floor-to-ceiling bookcases and decided it was as good a place to hide as any. The only light in the room came in through the window, from the outside floodlights.

Stepping inside, he crossed a sitting area and noticed what was probably a closet door. Opening it, he went inside. The small, stuffy room was dark and full of boxes. Finding an empty corner, he sat on the floor, his back to the wall.

He placed the Glock on the floor next to him and glanced at the luminous dial of his watch. 8:13 p.m. Four hours to wait, he thought. *I'll strike at midnight.*

Ryan realized he must have dozed off, because the next time he looked at his watch it read 12:42 a.m.

He removed the night-vision goggles from his jacket and slid them over his eyes. The closet went from pitch black to a dimly-lit ghostly green.

Picking up the Glock, he stood, stretched his arms and back. After pulling down his watch cap, he turned the door knob and peered into the study. Like before, the room was dim and quiet, as was the hallway.

Crossing the study, he crouched by the doorway and listened for sounds. Other than a clock ticking somewhere, he heard nothing.

He stepped into the corridor, turned toward the kitchen area, which was also dark. When he reached that room, he glanced through the windows. The guards were still on sentry duty by the walls. Taking another hallway, he crept forward, the pistol in front of him.

After passing more unoccupied and darkened sitting rooms on the first floor, he reached a wide, marble-step staircase. Hanging from the ceiling at the top landing was an unlit crystal chandelier that must have cost a small fortune.

Careful to tread as quietly as possible, he climbed up the steps slowly.

At the top, the corridor went both ways. Crouching, he scanned the hallway. To his left was a row of closed doors, five on each side, probably bedrooms.

To his right the corridor led to a closed, large double-door – most likely the master bedroom.

But along the wall, close to the door, a large man sat on a wingback chair, loosely cradling a sub-machinegun. The man was not moving, probably dozed off.

Ryan's heart began to pound. He hadn't counted on Sanchez having a guard posted outside his bedroom. The detective's mind raced through his options, finally selected one.

Removing a small, marble-like object from his pants pocket, he activated the device and rolled it down the hallway toward the guard.

A moment later the marble stopped a foot from the guard, split in two, releasing a small puff of dust. The guard's head sagged to his chest and Ryan held his breath, hoping the sub-machinegun wouldn't clatter to the marble floor. His luck held and he sprinted down the corridor, took the weapon and leaned it on the wall. Grabbing the guard by the shoulders, he laid the body on the floor.

Ryan placed his ear against the double-door, heard nothing. Gripping the Glock tightly, he turned the knob with his other hand. To his relief the door opened and he peered into the ghostly-green room.

The bedroom was enormous and filled with heavy, ornate wooden furniture. At the far end was a massive, four-poster bed. Under the covers he could make out a man and a woman, both asleep. The man was lying on his back, snoring loudly.

Stepping in the room, he crouched by the door and glanced around to make sure there was no one else there. Erin had told him earlier that the couple had children, and Ryan wanted to make sure they weren't in the room.

Satisfied the couple was alone, he took several more of the 'marbles', turned them on and rolled them toward the bed. The devices went off and he waited a moment to let the gas take effect. While he waited, he inspected the bedroom's double door – it was thick and heavy, and most likely sound-proof.

Going outside to the corridor, he dragged the guard's unconscious body into the bedroom, gagged him and tied up his hands and feet.

Turning toward the bed, he searched the nightstands for weapons. Finding a Colt automatic handgun in the nightstand, he pocketed it. Then he began to tie up the unconscious couple. Afterward, he propped Sanchez so that the man was sitting up in bed, his back against the headboard.

Pulling up a chair so it was only feet from the Mexican, Ryan waited for the effects of the gas to wear off. Ten minutes later he heard Sanchez groan and the man's eyes snapped open.

Obviously disoriented and confused, he tried to free himself from the bonds.

To increase the man's level of fear, Ryan had kept the lights off in the room. To the detective, Sanchez was clearly visible, even if he was a green color. But the room was dark and to the Mexican, Ryan would only be a shadow with strange looking goggles on his face.

"*Que es esto?*" Sanchez demanded in Spanish, his voice shrill. "*What's going on?*"

"Don't worry," Ryan responded calmly in the same language. "I have everything under control. Just do what I say and nobody gets hurt."

"Damn it! Untie me. Who the hell are you? I can't see anything. Turn on the lights!"

"Lower your voice, Sanchez. We're just having a conversation here. I'd hate to have to hurt your wife."

The man, obviously remembering she was at his side, turned to her. The woman was wearing a negligee and was still unconscious. "Please," Sanchez said, his voice lower this time. "Let her go. You want money? I'll give it to you, whoever you are. Just leave my wife and children alone."

Ryan adjusted the focus on the goggles, looked closely at the heavy-set man in the striped pajamas. He had a wide scar on his cheek and had the imperious look of someone who always gets his way.

"I don't want your money, Sanchez. I want information."

Sanchez's eyebrows arched. "Information? What are you talking about? This isn't a ransom for money?"

"No."

The man struggled against the straps again, but eventually his shoulders slumped as if resigned.

"By your accent," Sanchez said, "I can tell you're not Mexican. You sound American."

Ryan nodded, but realized the other man couldn't see him. "Yes. But that's not important."

"I'm a rich man. One of the richest in Mexico. I can pay you in cash or gold, if you let me and my family go."

"Like I said, I don't want your money. Tell me about sigma."

A deep frown crossed the other man's face. "Sigma? What's that?"

Ryan stood, went over to a lamp and turned it on. Momentarily blinded by the bright light, he took off the goggles. He sat back down, faced Sanchez. "Maybe you need to see me," he said, "see I'm a serious man. Now tell me about sigma!"

Sanchez eyes blinked rapidly as he glanced around the room, saw the guard tied and gagged on the floor. The man also noticed Ryan was by himself.

"One man?" Sanchez said, derision in his voice. "I have twenty men here, all armed. You think you're just going to walk out of here? Harm my family and they'll cut you down like raw hamburger meat."

"You let me worry about that. Now talk."

"Like I said, I don't know what this sigma is."

Ryan leaned forward in the chair. "You have a distributor in Juarez. His name is Rodriguez. He handles your drugs and counterfeit cash. He gets the fake cash from your plant in Monterrey."

"Monterrey? I don't have an operation there."

"SPXE. Remember?"

Another frown spread on Sanchez's face and the man went quiet. His eyes darted around the room, as if trying to figure a way out.

"What do you know of SPXE, *gringo*?"

"I know you own it. I know you make counterfeit U.S. dollars there."

"You're a crazy American. But if you leave now, I'll give you one million U.S. dollars."

Ryan stood, took out a switchblade from his pocket and clicked it open. The stainless-steel blade glinted from the light.

Sanchez's eyes went wide.

But instead of approaching the man, Ryan walked around the bed to the wife's side. He placed the blade against the unconscious woman's cheek and caressed her skin with it. Ryan had no intention of hurting her, but had to make it look good.

"Stop!" Sanchez said, "Don't hurt her."

Ryan pulled the blade away from her face.

"Okay. Tell me about the counterfeit money."

"I can't," Sanchez pleaded. "I'm in too deep."

The detective flicked the blade, cut off one the spaghetti straps that held up the woman's nightgown.

"I told you Sanchez, I don't want to hurt her. But I will if I have to."

"I can't talk about sigma. The group is too powerful. They'll hunt me down, torture and kill me and my family if I do."

Ryan ran the tip of the blade from the woman's neck across her chest to between her partially exposed breasts, applying light pressure to avoid cutting her skin.

He noticed Sanchez shutting his eyes and turning his head away.

It was clear he wasn't going to talk. Ryan realized the man loved his wife, but was willing to sacrifice her to keep his secrets, so he decided to take a different tactic.

"You leave me no choice," Ryan said, moving back to Sanchez's side of the bed. "Talk now or I'll have my men kill your children."

Sanchez's eyes snapped open.

"You thought I was doing this by myself?" Ryan lied. "Are you crazy? I've got two men in your children's bedrooms now. If I give the order, they're dead."

Sanchez's eyes showed true terror.

"No! Not my children! Anything but that. Kill me, just leave them alone."

"I'm sorry, Sanchez. You've left me no choice." He put the switchblade away and pulled out his cell phone, began to punch in a number.

"Okay, *gringo*. I'll talk."

"You sure?"

"Yes. Yes!"

Ryan put the phone in his pocket.

"Tell me about sigma."

The Mexican, his shoulders slumped, began talking. "It's a machine. A machine that produces counterfeit money. We use it to make U.S. dollars and ship them across the border."

"Why? What do you get out of it?"

"I sell the stuff ten to one to my distributors. Ten fake dollars for every real one. It's a good profit margin. As good as drugs."

Ryan nodded. "The fake currency is very good quality. Some of the best ever. How did you develop the technology? You're a drug dealer, not a scientist."

Sanchez stared back at him, said nothing. It was clear the man was reluctant to say more.

The detective pulled out the phone, began dialing.

"No, stop," Sanchez pleaded. "I'll tell you. I have a partner in Italy. I get the machines from him."

Ryan surmised the man was telling the truth. It was an FBI agent in Rome that had first learned about sigma.

"Tell me the rest."

"That's it, *gringo*. I get the machines, I make fake dollars, I make a profit. It's that simple."

"Who's your Italian connection? What's his name?"

"I don't know his name."

"You're lying, Sanchez!"

"I'm not. I swear!"

Ryan took out the switchblade, flicked it open and walked around to the other side of the bed. He leaned over the woman's unconscious body and said, "Where shall I cut her, Sanchez? Her face? Her breasts? Tell me."

"No. Please don't do it," Sanchez whispered.

Feeling sick from having to cut the woman, Ryan nevertheless pricked her shoulder, cutting a small gash. A trickle of blood ran down her arm.

"Her pretty face is next," Ryan said. "But it won't be pretty when I get done with her." He knew he couldn't do it, prayed the man would talk.

"His name is Amati," the Mexican said. "Vincento Amati."

"Now we're getting somewhere. Who is he? Where does he live?"

"He runs a media company. He lives in Rome."

Ryan had never heard of this Amati. Was Sanchez lying?

"How do I know you're telling the truth?"

"I swear *gringo*. I swear to God, it's the truth."

Ryan nodded. Maybe he was telling the truth, maybe he wasn't. He planned to keep questioning the Mexican until he broke down completely. But he needed more time. Glancing at his watch, he realized he had to get out of this house, and soon. It was 2:15 a.m. Anytime now, one of the children could wake up, and all hell would break loose. Ryan would be in the firefight of his life. Sanchez said he had twenty armed men at the home, and he believed him. Those were odds he couldn't overcome.

Closing the switchblade, the detective put it away. He took out his cell phone and held it up in the air.

"Listen closely, Sanchez. I'm going to tell you this only once. If you don't do exactly what I say, I'll have your kids terminated. Understood?"

The Mexican nodded vigorously.

"Okay. I'm going to untie you. You're going to call your driver. Tell him to get your car and park it in front of the house and have him wait for you. Tell him you have a business meeting to attend in Monterrey. Then you and I are going downstairs and get in the car and leave. I want you to act natural, as if I were your best friend. If you set off an alarm, or call for help, I'll kill you and have your children killed. Understood?"

"Yes, yes, I understand."

"Good. After we're well away from here, I'll let you go. I'll call my men and have them leave the house. You and your family will not be hurt."

The detective took out his Glock, and with his free hand he used the knife to cut off the binds on the man's hands and feet.

Holding the pistol to Sanchez's temple, he pointed to the phone on the nightstand

"Do it."

Sanchez picked up the receiver, pressed the number 3, and spoke a moment.

"Okay, Sanchez. Now get dressed."

The man went to the closet, quickly picked out clothes and dressed. Keeping an eye on him, the detective took out another of the marbles, activated it and placed it next to the unconscious woman. He moved away from the bed and a moment later the device went off.

Ryan took off his cap and dropped it to the floor. With his weapon still trained on the Mexican, he opened the bedroom door partway and peered out.

The corridor was dim and quiet.

Opening the door all the way, he whispered. "You lead the way, Sanchez. One false move and you're history."

The man nodded and walked out into the hallway, the detective following, his gun in the jacket.

They descended the stairs, walked the long main corridor of the house to the front door.

Stepping in front of his captive, Ryan cracked the door open, looked outside. A white Rolls-Royce Phantom sedan was parked at the foot of the steps, the engine running.

The portico was dark, the only lights coming from the floodlights on the grounds. The guards were still patrolling the perimeter.

Ryan stepped outside, motioned for Sanchez to do the same.

"Get in the car," the detective whispered.

With Ryan right behind, Sanchez walked down the steps, opened the rear door and climbed inside, sliding across to the far side of the plush seat. Ryan followed him in, closed the door behind him.

The rich smell of the leather seats filled the spacious cabin, which was separated from the driver in the front by a glass partition.

The partition whirred down partway.

"*Señor* Sanchez," the driver said, "you want to go to SPXE in Monterrey?"

"That's right, Julio. We can leave now."

"*Si, señor.*" The glass partition whirred closed.

The large sedan glided away from the house and made its way on the long driveway to the closed gate. As soon as the car approached it, the guards came to attention and the gate swung open. The Rolls drove through, turned unto the deserted street, and headed north to connect with the highway.

Ryan faced Sanchez, held his finger to his lips, and the other man nodded.

As soon as they reached the freeway the detective settled back on the plush seat, his hand gripping the Glock inside the jacket.

They drove in silence for hours.

Sanchez was fidgety the whole way, surreptitiously looking at Ryan, then back out the window, as if searching for something.

The Mexican's mood changed abruptly when they reached the remote mountainous area south of Monterrey. There was almost no traffic on this part of the highway.

Sanchez pressed a button on his armrest and the glass divider separating the front and rear cabins whirred down.

"Pull off road," he told the driver.

"What the hell are you doing?" Ryan whispered.

"See those mountains out there?" Sanchez responded, pointing out the window. "There's no cell phone reception here. My family is safe now."

The Rolls-Royce slowed, veered off the freeway, and came to a stop on the shoulder.

Ryan quickly pulled the Glock from his pocket, pointed it at Sanchez.

"I can still kill you."

A thin smile came over the drug dealer's face. "Maybe not, *gringo*."

Sanchez must have set off a silent alarm, because the driver, without saying a word, turned around in the front seat and pointed a Ruger revolver at the detective.

His heart racing, Ryan said, "Your driver's holding a revolver. He may be able to squeeze off one shot, but by that time I'll have pumped five rounds into you, Sanchez." As he furiously thought through his options, he added. "I guess we have a Mexican standoff."

Sanchez grunted. "Whoever you are, *gringo*, you have a good sense of humor for somebody who is about to die."

"But you'll die first, Sanchez."

The drug dealer frowned. "A risk I do not want to take. Put your gun away, and I'll tell Julio to do the same. You can leave the car unharmed and I'll return to Mexico City."

Ryan shook his head. "No way. As soon as I start walking you'll drive until there's phone reception and call your goons. They'll be here soon enough and hunt me down."

"So. It looks like we do have a 'Mexican standoff', as you put it. What do you suggest, *gringo*?"

Ryan glanced at the driver, then back at Sanchez.

"You and Julio give me the car, and I'll let you guys walk away, unharmed."

A pained expression crossed Sanchez's face.

"This is an expensive automobile – I'd hate to part with it."

"Those are my terms," Ryan snapped. "You said you had plenty of money. Buy yourself another one."

"How do I know you won't shoot both of us?" Sanchez asked.

"I give you my word. And I'm a man who keeps his word."

Sanchez studied Ryan's face a moment.

"I accept. Julio, put your gun down."

The driver lowered the revolver.

"Okay," Ryan said, "here's how we do this. Julio will throw his gun out the window. Sanchez, you'll climb out of the car and wait. Then Julio will get out and wait. After that, I get out, get in the driver's seat and take off. Understood?"

Sanchez nodded. "Julio, do what he says."

The driver whirred down his window and pitched the revolver to the shoulder of the road.

The drug dealer opened the back door of the Rolls and climbed out, while Ryan tracked him with the Glock the whole way. The driver got out next.

The detective slid across the leather seat and climbed out, pointing the gun at the two men, whose hands were raised in the air.

Ryan crouched by the revolver lying on the ground, picked it up and pitched it into the deep ravine that sloped down from the shoulder.

Standing, he got in the Rolls-Royce and started the engine. He glanced at the two men, who were still holding their hands up.

Gunning the motor, he steered the large sedan back on the highway. Through the rear-view mirror, he could make out the driver scurrying down the ravine, obviously trying to find the gun.

Ryan buried the gas pedal with his foot and the engine roared, hurtling the Rolls to near one-hundred mph. He glanced at the rear-view mirror again, and the men were no more than tiny dots in the distance.

Chapter 17

Rome, Italy

Vincento Amati was in his sumptuous office on the phone with his broker.

He had just instructed the man to buy another fifty million dollars worth of gold bullion. A large sum, but necessary, for the Alliance plan to succeed. A good investment, Amati thought, as he concluded the call and hung up the phone.

Leaning back in his executive chair, he stared at the empty space on the front wall, previously occupied by his beloved Botticelli. The painting was now being cleaned by the city's best restorer, Maria's blood stains being painstakingly removed from the masterpiece.

Pushing aside the thoughts of that traitorous woman, he glanced at his Patek Philippe watch. He had ten minutes to spare before the video conference with his partners.

Pouring himself a scotch, he took a sip and mulled over the upcoming video call. It had been hastily initiated by Hector Sanchez. The Mexican had said there was an urgent problem the three men needed to address.

Amati drummed his fingers on the teak-wood desk. The group didn't need any urgent problems, not now. They were getting close, very close, and Amati could almost taste the sweet flavor of success.

On the side wall of the office hung an intricately carved gold cross, a religious icon dating back to the 13th century. Inlaid with genuine diamonds, emeralds and rubies, the priceless cross had been a present from the Vatican. The previous Pope had given it to Amati years ago, in exchange for positive news stories about the Church on his TV network.

Amati stared at the cross now, said a silent prayer. He strongly believed in the power of prayer, and even more so when the stakes were high.

Concluding the prayer, he knocked back the rest of the scotch and turned on the video screen.

To his surprise, both men were already on the line. The usually tardy Sanchez was right on time today.

Sanchez's swarthy complexion stared back at him on the left. On the right was Dimitri Petrovich, his piercing blue eyes as intense as ever.

"Gentlemen," Amati said. "Good to see you both again. Hector, since you asked for this meeting, why don't you begin."

Sanchez rubbed the wide scar on his cheek. "Of course, Vincento. As I mentioned in my email, we have a problem."

"I don't like the sound of that," Petrovich interjected, his voice agitated.

"Please, Dimitri," Amati said, "let's hear the man out."

The Russian grimaced, but went quiet.

Sanchez rubbed his cheek again. "I'm sure you remember that a few weeks ago there was an FBI probe into the operation of one of my distributors. Rodriguez in Juarez. Rodriguez captured an FBI operative, but the man subsequently escaped."

Amati leaned forward in his chair. "Yes, I remember."

"Well," Sanchez said, "a man, an American, broke into my house in Mexico City and held me and my wife at gunpoint. Going by the description Rodriguez gave me, the operative who escaped is the same man who broke into my home. This operative, whoever he is, somehow traced the shipment of counterfeit dollars from the Juarez warehouse to my SPXE plant in Monterrey. Then traced it all back to me."

Amati's heart began to pound. "How could this happen, Hector? How could he get in your house? You have excellent security, as do I. And an FBI agent? The American FBI usually doesn't operate outside their country and they don't hold people hostage. And they coordinate with the host country and its police."

Sanchez held up his palms in front of him. "I agree. I suspect this man was a paid contractor, an operative of some kind. Certainly the methods he used were not typical U.S. law enforcement. I've talked with the President of Mexico and he assured me that no one in our government coordinated with the FBI on the raid on my home. In fact, the President is filing a formal protest with the American State Department."

Petrovich's pale face had turned red. "Enough with the details, Hector," he demanded. "What did this man find out about our operation?"

Sanchez's shoulders slumped. "The man was ruthless. He threatened to kill me, my wife, and my children. I tried to throw him off as best I could, but he learned some key information."

"Like what?" Amati barked out. A feeling of dread settled in the pit of his stomach.

"He knows about the sigma machines," the drug dealer said. "He knows they make the fake currency."

Petrovich leaned forward in his seat. "What else?"

Sanchez frowned. "He knows they come from you, Vincento. I had to tell him that they come from you."

The Italian's stomach churned, the scotch mixing with the bile from the bad news. "Damn you, Hector! Damn you to hell. I can't believe you told him."

"I'm sorry, my friend," Sanchez said, his eyes downcast. "I had no choice."

"The man got away after learning all this?" Petrovich asked.

Sanchez nodded. "Yes. Luckily, the information he got was limited. He knows about me, obviously, and he knows that Vincento is involved, but fortunately he doesn't know about the overall Alliance plan."

"Did you tell him about me?" the Russian asked.

"No."

Petrovich nodded, and his expression relaxed somewhat.

The three men went quiet for a long time, lost in their own thoughts.

Amati took a couple of deep breaths, trying to calm himself. Finally he said, "Okay. Let's think through our options carefully. We don't want to panic and make things worse. What's done is done, we can't change the past. Hector, you said the Mexican President is going to file a complaint with the U.S. government?"

"Yes, that's correct."

"In that case, you are protected. The Americans will be careful how they deal with you. Even if you are charged with a crime and try to extradite you, your friend the President will likely prevent that."

"Yes, Vincento, I believe you're right."

Amati turned toward the Russian. "As for you, Dimitri, they don't know about you, so you can relax for now."

Petrovich nodded, but said nothing.

Amati poured himself two fingers of scotch and took a sip. "As for myself, I have to come up with a plan for my protection."

"What do think you'll do?" Sanchez asked.

Amati shook his head. "I don't know yet. I'll consult with my security chief. Hector, you have description of this American?"

"Yes. I had an artist do a sketch of his face and I wrote down a detailed physical description. After this call I'll email you both the information."

"That's a start," Amati said. "I need to find this man, before he learns anything more. He needs to be terminated."

"I have a specialist," Petrovich said. "An expert assassin. A man I trust implicitly. He could be very useful, Vincento, in solving this problem."

Amati thought about this a moment. "I'll talk to my people, Dimitri, and get back to you. If he's as good as you say, I may take you up on the offer." He took another sip of scotch. "Unless there's something else, let's end this call. I know we all have pressing matters to attend to."

The two others agreed and he turned off the connection.

The large screen went dark, matching his mood.

Chapter 18

Moscow, Russia

Dimitri Petrovich opened the blinds of his office window to let in the hazy daylight. Ominous clouds hung over the city's skyline and a heavy, wet snow continued to fall.

Turning away from the window, he shrugged on his suit jacket and watched as his secretary smoothed down her dress and reapplied her lipstick.

The encounter with Karina had satiated his sexual appetite. For now.

"Will there be anything else?" she asked, her pretty face still flushed from the recent exertion.

Petrovich sat down behind his desk. "Yes. Contact Markov. I need to see him immediately."

"Yes, sir." The young woman turned and left the room.

An hour later the tall, blond man stood ramrod straight in front of the oil tycoon's desk.

"Your assignment," Petrovich said. "How is it going?"

Markov placed an envelope on the desk. "It is all in my report."

Petrovich knew his operative was a man of few words, but he still wanted a verbal description. "I'm sure the report is very detailed, as usual. Give me a summary."

Markov nodded. "Yes, Mr. Petrovich. I did surveillance on Amati's operation. It took some time, but I was able to determine that the sigma machines come into Italy by ship."

Petrovich raised a brow. "They're not made in Italy?"

"No, sir. They come from the United States."

"What? Are you sure, Markov?"

"Absolutely. I traced them through a couple of dummy corporations, but they come from the U.S."

The oil man shook his head, amazed by the revelation. What connection did Amati have in America?

"Tell me more," Petrovich demanded.

"I have a subcontractor in the U.S., a person who works for me there. He says the cargo containers with the machines are shipped from the port of Baltimore to the port in Fiumicino, Italy. He was able to trace the original source of the machines to a company in Arlington, Virginia."

Petrovich leaned forward in his chair. "What is the name of the company?"

"Tarniski Exports."

"Never heard of them."

Markov nodded. "Neither had I. I believe it is also a dummy corporation, a front that is owned by another company."

"I see. You're still researching this?"

"Yes."

"Excellent work, Markov. I'll wire a payment to your account today." He swiveled his chair to face the window, gathering his thoughts as the snow continued to fall.

A minute later, the oil man swiveled his chair to face the other man.

Markov was still standing, silent and unmoving, his facial expression stony as always.

"Put that assignment on hold," Petrovich said, his voice low. "I have something more urgent for you to work on."

Markov nodded, said nothing.

Petrovich took a folded sheet of paper from his jacket pocket and handed it to the other man. "There is a threat to the Alliance. An American, who appears to be connected to the FBI, has found out certain information about the sigma operation. He is a threat to Amati, which makes him a threat to me." He paused a moment and leaned back in his chair. "All the information that we have about this man is on this sheet. A sketch of his face, a physical description and a few other things. It's not a lot to go on. But you're a resourceful man. I know you can find him. Any questions?"

"My usual fee?"

"Yes."

Markov nodded. "And when I find him?"

"You kill him, of course."

Chapter 19

Atlanta, Georgia

Ryan parked the Rolls-Royce in the Secret Service's underground parking lot and turned off the engine.

Climbing out, he stretched his arms, which were stiff from the long drive. Then he took out his cell phone, called Erin Welch, and leaned against the car to wait.

Hearing the clicking of heels on concrete a while later, he turned, saw the agent coming his way. Wearing a stylish pants suit, the blonde woman stopped in front of him. She gave him a thin smile and folded her arms across her chest.

"I was beginning to think you wouldn't make it back," Erin said.

"Hope springs eternal," he replied, chuckling.

"Not true, J.T. I still need your help solving this damn case."

"And, once again, I thought you wanted me for my body."

She ignored his attempt at humor, nodded toward the Rolls. "Nice wheels."

Ryan looked at the car. The luxury sedan was dusty and had a few scratches from the trip, but its pearlescent white paint still gleamed from the garage's florescent lights. "Yeah. It's Sanchez's car. Or it was, until I borrowed it." He tossed her the keys. "Now it's yours."

Erin caught the keys, stuck them in her pocket. "Thanks. I'll have the forensics guys check it out. They may come up with something that'll help."

Ryan stifled a yawn. "You got any fresh coffee? It was a long drive and I could use some."

"Sure. Let's go up to my office. We can talk there."

They took the elevator to her floor and soon after they were in her corner office overlooking downtown. It was a cold but sunny day, and the bright sunshine reflected off the city's skyscrapers.

Erin poured him a cup of coffee, handed it to him, and sat down behind her desk.

"Have a seat," she said.

"I've been sitting for days. I'll stand." He took a sip of the hot, strong brew, appreciated the robust flavor.

"Suit yourself." She picked up a newspaper and slid it across the desk. "It's today's paper. Read the top story."

Picking up the Atlanta Journal Constitution, he scanned the blaring headline above the fold. *U.S. and Europe in crisis*, it said. He quickly read the lead paragraph, which summarized the panic embroiling the world's financial markets. Global inflation was rampant, food prices were soaring, and the value of the U.S. dollar and European currencies was plummeting. Finance ministers from around the world were holding an emergency meeting today to discuss the crisis.

He let out a low whistle. "This is really bad."

Erin tucked her long hair behind her ears. "It's actually worse than the paper says. Government officials have been downplaying the crisis, to prevent a panic. But it's becoming more difficult. Inflation is at an all-time high. Gasoline prices are through the roof. A food riot broke out in Detroit yesterday. Staples like milk and bread are no longer affordable."

Ryan slumped on one of the visitor chairs. "Jesus. Is this connected to the fake currency?"

Erin nodded. "Absolutely. The stuff has flooded into the country, making the real money worth less."

"In Europe too?"

"Yeah. It's widespread. Europe, Asia, India. It's a disaster."

Ryan leaned forward in the chair. "The progress I made on the case will help. Hector Sanchez is definitely involved, as is an Italian by the name of Amati."

She began taking notes on a legal pad. "You're sure about Sanchez?"

"No doubt about it. He admitted the counterfeit money is produced using equipment called sigma. The money is made in the SPXE plant in Monterrey. He transports it from there to his distributors in northern Mexico. Rodriguez is one of them."

"How can you be sure Sanchez wasn't lying?"

He smiled. "Trust me. It's all true. I asked him politely and he answered politely."

She gave him a hard look. "I won't ask how you got him to talk."

"Good. You don't need to know."

Erin continued writing. "Tell me about the Italian connection."

"His name is Amati. Vincento Amati. He must be one of the ringleaders because Sanchez gets the sigma machines from him."

She looked up. "What else did you learn about this Amati?"

"He lives in Rome. He runs a media company there."

"What else?"

Ryan gave her a word-by-word description of what the drug dealer had said.

"Anything else, J.T.?"

"That's about it. I wanted to question Sanchez more, but I was in a tight spot. I had to get out before Sanchez's thugs found out what the hell was going on."

Erin nodded. "I talked to agent Mitchell, when he got back to El Paso. He told me he thought you were crazy to go in there alone."

Ryan grinned. "Yeah. I probably was."

She shook her head slowly, but eventually a brief smile crossed her lips. "J.T., you're a piece of work. But Nichols did warn me about you."

At the mention of his dead friend's name, Ryan's levity vanished. He grimaced and went quiet.

"Sorry," she said, picking up her pen again. "I'll contact all my sources, get as much information as possible on Sanchez and Amati. Between the Secret Service, FBI and DEA, I'm sure we'll get a detailed workup on those two."

Ryan finished his coffee and set it down on the desk. "You should go after Sanchez immediately."

"I will. But I need evidence. Something we lack."

"Work with the D.A, Erin. Indict the son-of-a-bitch. Extradite him and lock him up. He'll crack. I know he will."

"Listen, I want this as much as you do. But I've got to follow procedure. These people aren't Americans. I have to get their governments to cooperate. You've been around the block. You know how it works."

His face turned red and he gripped the armrests of the chair. "Screw that, Erin! Just get it done."

She glared, but said nothing.

Ryan took a deep breath and let it out slowly. "Look, I know it's not going to be easy."

"I'll meet with the Federal District Attorney this afternoon, J.T. Believe me, we'll nail those bastards."

***

Ryan unlocked his apartment door and went inside. The place was cold and smelled musty.

Turning on the lights, he adjusted the thermostat and called Lauren, leaving her a message.

He went in the small kitchen and rummaged in the thinly-stocked refrigerator. Besides a six-pack of Sam Adams, some cold-cuts, a carton of eggs and one lonely tomato, there wasn't much else.

Grabbing one of the beers, he got a can of tuna from the cabinet and made himself a sandwich with stale bread.

He ate it standing up, washed it down with the lager. After, he headed to the bedroom and changed into a sweatshirt and sweatpants.

Snatching another beer, he plopped down on his living room couch. Turning on the TV, he surfed the channels, finally settled on ESPN. The Lakers were playing the Knicks, and LA was up by four points.

He tried to follow the game, but he was sound asleep in minutes.

It must have been hours later when he was startled awake by a touch to his shoulder.

Instantly he closed one fist and coiled his arm to throw a punch, only to find Lauren standing over him, her eyes wide.

"J.T., wake up. It's just me."

Now fully awake, he gave her a wide smile. "God, it's good to see you again."

Her face relaxed and she returned the smile. "Remind me to be careful when I wake you."

"Sorry," he said, opening his fist and caressing her face with his palm. Her silky skin felt soft and warm, and her perfume had a hint of lavender.

Her hazel eyes sparkling, she bent down and gave him a kiss on the mouth. She tasted sweet and salty at the same time.

He returned the kiss hungrily, then pulled her down beside him and enveloped her with his muscular arms. They held each other like that for a long time, not saying anything, content to be with each other after being separated for weeks.

Realizing the TV was still on, he grabbed the remote and turned off the set.

"I'm glad you're back," she whispered. "I love you. I missed you terribly."

"I love you, too." He studied her face, noticed the slight black smudges under her eyes. "You look tired, Lauren. Are you okay?"

"I haven't been sleeping well. I was worried about you. I kept calling that bitch Erin, trying to find when you were coming home."

"Sorry I couldn't call more. Things were...hectic...in Mexico."

"I'm sure they were. But don't tell me what happened there. I'm just glad you're back."

Ryan caressed her face, noticed she was wearing her hair differently – she'd pulled her long, auburn tresses into a ponytail. "I like the way you did your hair. It looks good."

She made a face. "I want to cut it – it's way too long. But I know you hate women with short hair." She played with the ponytail. "This is a compromise."

He kissed her again and she kissed him back, hard, their tongues exploring each other. As they kissed, she pressed her body against him, and the sexual tension he'd felt from the moment she'd walked in had boiled over into a raw, physical hunger.

Pulling away from her, he studied her eyes, saw she needed him as much he needed her.   "Let's go to the bedroom," he said.

She smiled coyly, hit him playfully on his chest. "Not before you take a shower. I want to do naughty things to you, but I want you clean first."

Ryan smiled. "Join me?"

"Sure," she said, standing up.

Holding his eyes with hers, she very slowly and deliberately unbuttoned her blouse and unzipped her skirt, letting them drop to the floor. To his amazement, he saw she wasn't wearing anything underneath.

By now he was fully aroused, his breathing labored.

She blushed, as if she'd just realized she had performed a seductive striptease, something totally out of character for her.

With a shy smile, she turned and pranced into the bathroom.

Quickly taking off his own clothes, he followed.

***

Ryan woke up before she did the next morning, and as quietly as possible, slipped out of bed, threw on a robe and left the bedroom, closing the door behind him.

Going to the kitchen, he made a pot of strong coffee and began scrambling eggs. Reminiscing about last night's last night's lovemaking with Lauren, he began to hum contentedly.

He put up some toast and set the silverware on the dinette table.

"Hey, you," he heard her say from behind him.

Turning around, he saw her approach, wearing one of his long-sleeve dress shirts, the long tails covering her to above the knees.

She went up on her tiptoes, gave him a quick kiss. Then she inspected the skillet with the almost done scrambled eggs.

"You're cooking," she said with a chuckle. "That's a scary thought."

He playfully slapped her behind. "Quiet, you. This is my specialty."

Lauren poured herself a cup of coffee. "Try not to burn them. They'll taste better that way."

Turning off the gas burner, he pulled the skillet from the stovetop. "Smartass."

She sat at the table and sipped coffee as he scooped the eggs from the skillet and filled two plates. Handing her one, he took his and sat down across from her.

Carefully taking a dainty bite, she chewed thoughtfully.

"Not bad, J.T."

"That was a compliment, right?"

"Maybe."

She gave him a rueful smile. "But I better do all the cooking from now on."

"Ouch," he replied.

She covered his hand with hers. "It was a nice thought, and I appreciate it."

He grinned. "Okay. I'll stick to detecting."

"Talking about detecting. What happens now, J.T.?"

"Now we finish our breakfast and we climb back into bed."

"Frisky this morning, aren't you? Didn't you get enough last night?"

He held her gaze. "Not by a long shot."

"Good. I like to hear that." Her face turned serious. "What I meant was, what's next on the case?"

He nodded. "I know what you meant. I keep working it. I got some good leads, and I'll be working with Erin on them."

She made a face. "I don't like her."

Ryan shrugged. "She's a government employee. A by-the-book agent, like most of them are."

"Bullshit. She's got the looks of a model. I don't like you spending so much time with that bitch."

He raised his palms in front of him. "You don't have anything to worry about. I only have eyes for you."

She crossed her arms in front of her, studied him for a long moment. Her face relaxed a bit. "I know. You could've stepped out on me years ago. But you haven't. Have you?"

"No. I love you. And only you."

Lauren uncrossed her arms and took his hand with hers. "I love you too. I know I can trust you. I just don't like being apart so much."

He squeezed her hand. "Neither do I. I promise, after this thing is all over, we'll go on vacation somewhere. You name the place, I'll book it."

A wistful smile crossed her face. "Paris? I've never been there."

"Absolutely."

"Okay, J.T. It's a deal." She finished her coffee, stood, and refilled both their cups. Sitting back down, she said, "Tell me about the case."

"I thought you didn't want to know."

"Spare me the details. Give me the Cliff notes version."

Ryan rubbed his jaw. "Okay. I'm sure you've been watching the news lately. The rampant inflation rate, the financial crisis?"

"Sure. Every time I go to the supermarket or fill-up with gas. Prices are going through the roof. I've got a good-paying job, but a lot of folks are struggling right now. Really struggling."

"This case, Lauren, the counterfeit money, it's tied to that."

She shook her head slowly. "I didn't know."

"The U.S. and other governments are playing it down, but there's a real crisis."

"And you've got a lead on who's behind it?"

"Yeah. I won't tell you the details. It's safer if you don't know. But we have a pretty good idea who the source is."

"You're going after them?"

"Erin is going to work with the D.A. first." He shrugged. "We'll see how far she gets. The people involved are not in this country, so she has to work with the State Department, get their help with extradition."

"I see. And if that doesn't work?"

"Let's see what happens."

"So. You may have to go after these people?"

Ryan saw the frown on her face and he said, "Let's not worry about that right now." He squeezed her hand again. "Let's just focus on you and me."

She gave him a mischievous smile. "I see where this is going."

"You catch on fast, Ms. Chase."

"So formal. If I remember correctly, you weren't very formal last night."

Ryan smiled back. "Neither were you."

He stood, took her hand and led her back into the bedroom.

Chapter 20

Rome, Italy

Vincento Amati peered through the wire mesh of his fencing mask at his instructor and waited for the man to attack.

Amati, dressed head-to-toe in a body-hugging fencing uniform, was tired, hot, and in a sour mood. The last thing he wanted to do was take this class, but he'd wanted to placate his wife. She kept reminding him that he was overweight and that the fencing helped him stay fit. True enough, he thought, but with everything going on in his life right now, it was hard to focus on today's practice match.

His instructor lunged forward with his foil, the pointed tip targeting Amati's chest.

Amati parried with his own foil, but the instructor was relentless, slashing left, then right, in rapid succession. Backpedaling and parrying as best he could, Amati was able to beat off the furious attack, but not before tripping over his feet and falling backwards unto the rubberized floor of the fencing hall.

Dazed from the fall, he lay there on his back, staring at the ceiling through the mask. "*Basta!*" he said. "Enough! Enough for today."

"*Perdono, Signore Amati,*" his instructor said as he reached down and helped Amati to his feet. "I am truly sorry."

"No harm done," Amati responded, taking off his mask and brushing the sweat from his forehead. "My mind is not in it today. We'll continue this next week."

"Of course, *signore*. Until next time." The instructor gave him a quick bow and turned toward the locker room.

Amati glanced toward the wooden bleachers that ran along the wall of the large, high-ceilinged building, located on the grounds of his gated villa in Rome.

Livia, his wife and the only spectator, got up from the bleachers and walked towards him.

"You're better than that, Vincento," she said primly.

He shrugged. "You're right. I have a lot on my mind."

Livia frowned. "Thinking about your whores, I'm sure."

Amati studied his wife closely. A thin, bony woman with a pinched face and a hooked nose, Livia was no beauty queen. Far from it. But her family was wealthy and their money had provided the seed capital that helped his business grow to the media powerhouse it was today. Out of loyalty to that, he had remained married to her for over thirty years. That, and the fact she ignored his numerous affairs with young Italian starlets.

He gave her a gentle smile. "You are my wife, Livia. You will always be my wife. As God is my witness."

She grunted, but her expression softened a bit, and he could tell his answer mollified her.

"Let's sit down," he said, touching her arm and leading her back to the bleachers. "We need to talk."

Glancing around the room first to make sure there were no servants about, he sat down across from her on the wooden bench.

"What is it, Vincento?"

"A problem has come up."

"Problem? You need more money?"

He shook his head. "No. Not that kind of problem."

"What then?"

"It has to do with business."

"You never tell me about your business. Unless you need money, that is," she sniffed, her pinched face scrunching up into another frown.

He covered her hand with his, felt her bony, cold fingers. Staring into her stony eyes, he said, "Livia, I have a problem. A serious problem. And I need your help in solving it."

Amati rarely asked his wife for help; it was only when he needed an infusion of cash. But she must have sensed the urgency of his tone, because the hardness of her expression softened, as if the countless years of infidelity were forgotten, if only for a moment.

"What is it?" she whispered, her voice tender.

"The American authorities are investigating one of my business dealings. There is no basis for their accusations, but they are asking questions, making false charges."

"The Americans? What are you involved in, Vincento? You run a TV company. What would they want with you?"

He shrugged. "Their FBI claims I'm involved with counterfeit money and the death of one of their agents. Total fabrications."

"Why do they think that?"

"You know Americans...they are crazy sometimes. They want to question me, but I have refused. It is beneath me – I'm not a criminal. But they have requested that the Italian government compel me to answer their questions. If I refuse, the Americans may indict me and try to extradite me to the U.S."

"That's outrageous!"

"Of course it is. My attorneys will fight it. But remember that during the last election, my news stations endorsed the losing candidate. Prime Minister Bertoli has never forgiven me for that. He would love to see me tried in an American court."

She patted his hand. "You poor dear. I'll help you in any way I can. Just tell me what you need."

"Talk to your father. He knows Bertoli. Have him intercede. It may help."

"Of course, Vincento. I'll talk to him immediately."

There were tears in her eyes and he realized that deep down, the woman was still deeply in love with him. He made a silent vow to himself that from now on he would be totally discreet with his extramarital affairs. He owed her that much. "Thank you, Livia."

She brushed a tear away from her face. "But what if my father can't convince Bertoli? What then?"

Amati mulled that over, his thoughts racing over his options. Finally he said, "I go see the Cardinal."

Chapter 21

Atlanta, Georgia

Ryan was in his office doing paperwork on several cases when he heard a knock at his door. Glancing up, he saw Erin Welch walk in and sit down on one of the client chairs.

"Morning, J.T.," she said tersely. She was wearing a stylish black business suit with a white silk blouse.

"My favorite Secret Service agent," he replied with a smile. "Here to brighten my day." He dropped the report he was reading on his desk.

"Cut the bullshit, J.T."

"Testy, aren't we? Didn't get enough coffee this morning? I just brewed a fresh pot if you want some."

She shook her head. "No way I'll drink that swill you call coffee."

Ryan laughed, leaned back in his chair and studied the blonde. It was clear she wasn't in the mood for humor. "Bad day at the office?"

"I didn't get the promotion I was expecting."

"Sorry to hear that."

"Yeah. The Director gave it to somebody else."

He nodded. Erin was a very competent agent, but he knew office politics could be byzantine – a reason he never wanted to join the FBI, like Steve Nichols had.

"Look on the bright side, Erin. You were able to get the indictments on Sanchez and Amati. That was a win."

"True. And getting your testimony at the grand jury was an important part of that."

"How is that going, by the way?"

Erin tucked her hair behind her ears. "The D.A. is working with the State Department. Both Sanchez and Amati are powerful men in their countries, but since we can tie them to the worldwide financial crisis, the Mexican and Italian governments may cave."

"We need that extradition. I want those bastards to burn."

"Don't worry. If we get them into the U.S., I'll make sure they go on trial and do serious jail time."

He grimaced. "They need to pay with their lives for Steve's murder, but I guess I'll have to settle for your solution."

Erin leaned forward in her chair and lowered her voice. "There's a reason I came to see you today."

"You finally realized you weren't paying me enough on the case," he said with a grin, "and you want to give me a raise."

She rolled her eyes. "Enough with the jokes. This is serious."

Ryan held up his palms. "Alright. I know I get carried away. Lauren tells me that all the time."

"Your girlfriend is a saint, to put up with your bullshit."

"She is that." He went quiet and waited for the agent to continue.

Erin crossed her arms in front of her. "When you testified at the grand jury, we kept it quiet. Your name was never released to the press, and the only people who knew about your testimony were the jurors and the court personnel. And, of course, they're sworn to secrecy."

"There's a but in there, somewhere."

She frowned. "This is a big case. Dangerous people are involved, people with lots of money."

"I know. So?"

"Your name could leak out."

"I'm a big boy. I know the risks."

"There's more," she said, taking a folded piece of paper from her jacket pocket. She slid it across the desk. "This looks a lot like you."

Picking up the sheet, he unfolded it and scanned it. It was a sketch of Ryan's face. Not exact of course, but close enough. There was a phone number written underneath the drawing.

"Where'd you get this, Erin?"

"A man was handing these out on a block close to the FBI building here in Atlanta. Said he was looking for the man in the sketch, would pay big for information. A clerk who works at the Bureau got one of the flyers and turned it in."

"The Bureau call the number?"

"Yeah. A man answered, but he must have gotten suspicious because he got cagy and hung up."

"They trace the phone?"

She nodded. "It was a burner cell. No lead there."

"They get a description of the man?"

"The FBI clerk said he had a thick mustache, a beard and bushy hair. All fake, I'm sure."

Ryan frowned, went quiet.

"Watch your back, J.T. It's obvious they don't know your name. But someone's out there, gunning for you."

"Looks like it. Could be Sanchez's men, or maybe Amati's."

"Or maybe both. You packing?"

"Every day," he replied, opening his desk drawer and lifting up the S & W automatic.

"Keep it handy, J.T."

Chapter 22

Mexico City, Mexico

Hector Sanchez was in his bedroom, looking at his reflection in the full-length mirror. Not happy with the folds of his tie, he retied it. He adjusted the length of his cuffs and buttoned the center button of his Armani tuxedo. Finally, he was pleased with his appearance.

Turning, he watched as his wife Inez finished applying her makeup. The aging beauty was wearing a sleek, ankle-length Dior gown. She looked elegantly regal in the dress.

"I should have never let you talk me into having this party," he said, irritation in his voice.

Inez looked up from her make-up table. "But Hector, it's your birthday. You're an important man. You have to celebrate it."

He grimaced. "The timing is all wrong. Unless you've forgotten, I've been indicted by the damn Americans. The bastards!"

She stood, gracefully crossed the room and caressed his cheek with her palm.

"You worry too much, Hector. I told you before, we're going to beat this."

He breathed in her perfume, a musky scent that always reminded him of flowers and sex. "I wish I had your confidence."

"You'll see. I'm always right." She smiled and took a step back from him. "Now, let me look at you." She studied his attire, then took a silk handkerchief from the nightstand drawer and tucked it in the chest pocket of the tuxedo. The red cloth added a splash of color to his all black-and-white ensemble. "Now you look perfect, my husband."

Sighing, he said, "All right. Shall be we go downstairs?"

Inez nodded and held out her arm. She had a gleam in her eyes. "I'm going to give you a special birthday gift. After the dinner is over and when all the guests have left. Something extra special for you tonight." She smiled seductively and his mind raced, wondering what new sex trick she had in store for him.

Sanchez smiled back, his anticipation palpable. Linking his arm with hers, they left the bedroom.

***

The ornate dining room was massive, easily accommodating the one-hundred guests. Murano glass chandeliers hung from the twenty-foot ceilings and priceless Goyas and Picassos decorated the walls.

A live band was playing classical music in a corner of the room, but the music was overpowered by the boisterous guests. The Dom Perignon champagne had flowed freely and with every passing hour, the crowd became louder and more animated.

Sanchez was seated at the head of the long, marble-top dining table. To his left sat Inez, looking every-inch the former TV star she had once been. To his right was the mayor of Mexico City. Other important business and government leaders and their wives lined both sides of the table.

The dinner party had gone very smoothly.

Sanchez's only regret was that the President of Mexico had, at the last minute, cancelled his attendance. A worrisome sign, Sanchez thought when he'd learned of it, but after his fifth glass of champagne, this concern was forgotten.

Sanchez drained his glass and signaled the waiter to take away his empty dinner plates. The staff scurried and instantly the plates were removed and his drink refilled.

He heard a tinkling sound, turned to see Inez tapping a knife on her champagne glass.

The elegant woman stood.

The band stopped playing and the guests went quiet.

Picking up her champagne flute, she held it high in the air. Turning to face him, she said, "I'd like to propose a toast."

The guests raised their own glasses in the air.

"A toast," she continued, her voice proud and strong. "To Hector Sanchez. A shrewd businessman. A generous benefactor to countless charities. A leader in the community. A man of true character." She paused and smiled. "But most of all, a wonderful father to our children. And the best husband any woman could wish for."

As the crowd cheered and broke into applause, Inez leaned down and kissed him.

***

Back in their bedroom hours later, Sanchez took off his tie and tuxedo jacket and dropped them to the floor. Dizzy from all the Dom Perignon, he plopped on the edge of the bed and began to untie his shoes.

When he was done, he leaned back against the headboard and waited for Inez to finish in the bathroom.

Moments later she came out, wearing an alluring negligee that barely covered her ample curves. Despite all the drinks, he became aroused.

"Come here, Inez. I've waited long enough."

"Don't worry, my dear husband. I'll take care of you. Like I always do. But first, I have something else you'll like."

The woman turned and went into one of the walk-in closets. She came out a moment later, pushing a silver food cart. On the cart was a birthday cake with one lit candle on top.

"Chocolate!" he said. "My favorite."

"Godiva chocolate. Nothing but the best for you." She rolled the cart to the side of the bed, cut a piece of the cake and served it on a plate. After handing him the plate, she very slowly and seductively began to take off the negligee. As the nightgown fell to the floor, he hungered for her voluptuous curves and flawless skin. The numerous plastic surgeries she'd had were worth every penny, he mused.

"Eat the cake, Hector. Savor it. Then you can savor me."

Without taking his eyes off of her, he took a bite and swallowed. It tasted rich and sweet, but also oddly bitter.

Inez came closer, sat on the edge of the bed. Smiling provocatively, she placed one hand on his upper thigh. Tracing her fingers over his pants, she said, "Have some more cake. I made it myself."

Sanchez took another bite and swallowed. The subtle bitter taste was still there and he grimaced and put the plate on the nightstand.

He felt a sharp pain in his stomach. Bile rushed up his throat and his heart began to race. Doubling over, he clutched his churning stomach, which felt as if it were on fire.

He gagged, vomit filling his mouth.

Sanchez tried to stand up, but instead collapsed to the floor, landing on his back.

The last thing he saw was a nude Inez standing over him, hands on her hips, a sneer on her face.

Chapter 23

Moscow, Russia

Dimitri Petrovich entered the lobby of the Shekaroski Hotel, brushed the snow from his face and fur coat, and headed for the elevators.

Reaching the penthouse floor, the prime minister's bodyguards let him into the large suite. Petrovich was a well-known figure to the guards, having met secretly with their boss many times before.

As usual, Ivan Chernov was sitting on one of the couches, watching news on the wall-mounted TV. Seeing the oil tycoon, the PM stood, offered his hand. "Dimitri, good to see you again."

The men shook.

"Good to see you also, my friend."

Chernov turned off the TV and Petrovich took off his coat and sat down across from the other man.

"You said on the phone you had some good news, Ivan?"

"Excellent news." The prime minister rubbed his hands together. "Would you like something to drink first?"

"No thank you, comrade. I have something to attend to after we meet, and I want to have a clear head."

Chernov gave him a sly smile. "What's her name?"

Petrovich grinned. "I wish. Unfortunately it is a business matter."

"Too bad. So, let me tell you my news." He rubbed his hands together again, obviously anticipating the oil man's reaction. "Finally. After months and months of hand-holding and cajoling, our dear President Lazarenko has agreed to our plan!" A broad smile spread on his face. "And the best part is, he thinks it's all his idea."

Petrovich jumped up from the seat.

"You did it, Ivan. That's wonderful news!" He stuck out his hand to shake again, but instead Chernov rose to his feet and gave the other man a bear hug. Petrovich clasped him back heartily. He pulled away, said, "I will have that drink after all."

Chernov went to a side table, poured out two glasses of Stolichnaya. Handing one to the other man, he said, "To our plan. To the Alliance!"

"To the Alliance!"

They drank and sat back down.

"Tell me, Ivan, how did you finally convince him?"

"I told him the plan would put Russia back on center-stage economically. We would finally be on an equal footing, maybe surpass, the Americans and the Chinese. Told him he'd be compared to Russia's great leaders of the past – Stalin and Lenin."

"But you've told him that before."

"True. But this time I also appealed to something more basic. Greed."

Petrovich's eyebrows shot up. "Greed?"

"Yes, I told him I'd give him fifty percent of the profits from my share of the venture."

The oil man nodded. "I see. But that is substantial. I didn't know you were willing to share."

A cunning smile spread on the prime minister's face. "I will share. At first, when the deal is consummated and everything is in place. But later...let's just say I have contacts at the FSB who consider me the real power in Russia, and are willing to...dispense with any obstacles in my way."

Petrovich nodded again. "I like it. You are to be commended, my friend, for securing the last piece of the puzzle. And, on a related matter, I have continued to buy gold bullion – our stockpiles are growing according to schedule."

"Excellent, Dimitri. Nothing can stop us now."

***

Petrovich crossed the street in front of the hotel and walked two more blocks to his waiting limousine. He had been successful in keeping his clandestine meetings with Chernov a secret, and didn't want to jeopardize that now. If it required braving Moscow's bitter January cold, it was well worth it.

Climbing into the black S-Class Mercedes, he buzzed down the glass divider and gave instructions to his driver. He leaned back in the plush leather seat and thought about his upcoming meeting.

Petrovich watched the wet snow continue to fall as the driver left the center of Moscow and took the MKAD freeway and headed north. Called Ring Road by some, and the Road of Death by others because of its high rate of traffic fatalities, the MKAD circled the center of the city and provided one of the few high-speed highways for traffic-choked Moscow.

A half-hour later the Mercedes took an exit and followed surface streets until they reached an industrial area lined with warehouses. The car slowed and pulled into a parking lot. The lot fronted a two-story, windowless structure that must have dated back to the 1950's. It had concrete-block walls and a sagging roof. There was only one car in the lot, a blue Lada with scratched paint.

The driver lowered the glass partition. "This is the address, Mr. Petrovich."

"Wait for me here," the oil man replied, buttoning up his fur coat and putting on his hat. Climbing out of the car, the sting of frigid air felt like a slap to his face.

Pulling his hat lower, he inspected the building closely. An unlikely place to meet, Petrovich thought. Markov must have a good reason for wanting to meet here.

He walked to the front door and rang the buzzer.

Moments later Markov opened it and the two men walked to the back of the almost empty warehouse to a small office.

The simple office furnishings consisted of a dented, metal desk, a metal file drawer, and two folding chairs.

"Please, have a seat, sir," Markov said, waving the other man to one of the chairs.

The oil man took off his hat and coat and sat on the chair, while the blond, crew-cut man remained standing, ramrod straight as usual.

"An interesting place to meet," Petrovich said.

Markov glanced around the office. "I work out of here. I also live here, upstairs."

"That's convenient, but a bit Spartan, wouldn't you say?" Considering how much money the assassin made, it was amazing he lived in a dump like this. But then, Petrovich thought, some people were content with simple personal possessions. The room was ice-cold, as if it weren't heated. Incredibly, Markov was dressed in a short-sleeve shirt and black slacks.

The assassin said nothing in reply, his facial expression stony.

"I'm assuming you have a good reason to meet here, Markov?"

"Yes. During my investigations, I found you have a spy in your office."

"What? Are you sure?"

"Yes, Mr. Petrovich. I am certain."

"Who is it?"

"Your secretary. Karina."

"That's impossible," Petrovich scoffed. "She's been with me for years."

"Believe it."

"You have proof?"

Markov walked to the file cabinet, opened a drawer and took out a large manila envelope, which he handed to the other man. Petrovich took out photographs, which were of Karina and a man he recognized immediately. Ivan Chernov. The pictures were grainy, as if taken with a long lens, in a variety of locations, mostly restaurants.

Petrovich's face flushed and he threw the pictures to the floor. "That bitch! That lying bitch! She told me she'd never met the prime minister, had only seen him on TV."

Petrovich stood, began pacing the small office, his thoughts racing. It was clear she must be on his payroll, a way for Chernov to keep tabs on him. Some friend he was, the oil man thought.

He shook his head slowly and slumped back down on the chair. The prime minister was an intrinsic part of the Alliance plan – Petrovich knew he had to come to terms with the deception, accept it, and move on.

The oil man glanced up at the assassin, who was still standing, unmoving and silent.

"I agree, Markov. She is a spy."

The assassin nodded. "You want me to terminate her?"

"No. I'll handle her in my own way."

"Yes, sir."

"Tell me about your progress on the other matters I assigned you."

Markov went to the file cabinet again and took out a manila folder, which he handed to the other man. "It is all in my report."

Petrovich, still angry about Karina, dropped the folder on the desk and said brusquely, "I'll read it later. Tell me."

"As you'll remember from our last meeting, my subcontractor in the U.S. back-tracked the original source of the sigma machines. They were shipped to Amati through several dummy corporations, but he was able to track them to a company in Arlington, Virginia. Tarniski Exports."

"Yes, I remember."

"The trail went cold after that. The ownership of Tarniski was hard to trace, but he contacted me yesterday. He's found the owner. An American. A powerful American."

"Who is it?"

Markov told him and Petrovich's jaw dropped. "You're sure?"

"Yes. My man has verified it through several sources. It's all in the report."

Petrovich grabbed the folder on the desk and read through the contents quickly. Satisfied of the facts, he looked up at the assassin. "You are a resourceful man, Markov. I'll be wiring you a bonus later today. Continue with your report."

Markov nodded, but his face showed no expression. "Regarding the matter of the FBI investigation."

Petrovich's hands clenched into fists at the thought of the American indictments on Sanchez and Amati. Both men had assured him there was nothing to worry about, but he wasn't so sure. The Alliance didn't need any complications right now. They were so close to success. Luckily, Ivan Chernov hadn't learned of the indictments, and the oil man wasn't about to tell him. If Markov was successful, the problem would go away.

Petrovich leaned forward in the chair. "You have good news on that, I hope?"

"Yes, sir. I was able to track down the American who gave testimony to the grand jury. At first I thought he was an FBI agent, but now I believe he is a security contractor who works for the FBI and the Secret Service. The man is based in Atlanta."

"What's his name, Markov?"

"I don't know. Yet. But I will, soon."

"Find out, damn it! Eliminate him!"

Markov nodded, but said nothing.

Petrovich gave the other man a hard stare. "What are your plans now?"

"I go to the U.S."

"When?"

"Today."

Chapter 24

Atlanta, Georgia

The Brookstone Grill was one of their favorite restaurants, an upscale but cozy place with wood-beam ceilings and a stone-front fireplace. The fire was crackling now, giving off pleasant heat and that comforting scent of burning wood. They had a window table.

The early evening sky was a dull gray and light sleet was falling.

Ryan was finishing his dessert, a five-layer Napoleon, while Lauren nursed a black coffee. He looked up at her. "Sure you don't want some of this, hon?"

"I'm fine, J.T."

"So, how long is your trip?" he asked, after taking the last bite.

"Just overnight. I give my talk in the morning and catch the flight back from Miami tomorrow night."

He pushed his empty plate aside and took a sip of coffee. "What's the talk about?"

"Programming techniques for nano-technology in robotics."

"I don't even know what that means," he said, chuckling.

Lauren smiled. "You're good at detecting, I'm good at computing."

He gave her a sly grin. "That's not the only thing you're good at, Ms. Chase."

She blushed, gave him a shy smile.

Glancing at his watch, he noted the time. "We better get going, so you can make your flight." He signaled the waiter for the check.

Scanning the bill a moment later, he let out a whistle. "Jesus. The prices have almost doubled since we were here last."

She nodded, her expression somber now. "I filled my gas tank yesterday. You wouldn't believe what I paid."

Shaking his head slowly, he reached for his wallet.

***

Ryan saw the airport exit, slowed the Acura and got in the right hand lane.

A moment later they were on the loop leading to Hartsfield-Jackson. It was sleeting harder now, the street lights casting a shimmering glow on the near black-ice roads. Fortunately, traffic was light tonight, a rarity for the city.

He pulled up to the departure area, located the Delta gate and double-parked.

They climbed out, kissed and said their goodbyes. He watched as she headed into the building, rolling her small suitcase behind her. But before he lost sight of her, Lauren stopped and turned around. Smiling, she gave him a last wave. Then she was gone.

***

Ryan drove north on I-85, keeping his speed down because of the lousy weather. He was in the middle lane, his thoughts still on Lauren. I'm a lucky guy, he thought, as he kept track of the few cars that were on the highway.

Taking the mid-town exit minutes later, he noticed a white Range Rover right behind him. It looked no different than the other SUVs that cruised Atlanta, but Erin's warning had made him edgy.

Instead of taking Piedmont Avenue as he usually did on his way home, he turned left, merged onto Peachtree Street. The SUV followed on the four-lane road, its bright headlights filling his rear-view mirror.

He was about to pull the Smith & Wesson from his hip holster when he glanced back again.

The Range rover veered hard left, and, with its engine roaring, sped up so it was alongside the Acura.

Ryan saw a muzzle flash, heard a blast, and felt shards of glass hit his face as the side window imploded.

His heart pounding, he smashed the accelerator pedal. The Acura leapt forward, the tires spinning slightly on the ice. But the Range Rover stayed even, fired again. The round smashed through his front windshield, creating a spider web of cracks.

Oblivious to the gust of frigid air that now filled the car, Ryan pulled the S & W, pointed it at the other car.

But it was too late – the SUV side-swiped him, the howl of scraping metal deafening. It was obvious the assassin wanted to run him off the road to finish him off.

Making a split-second decision, Ryan slammed on the brakes. The Range Rover, still maintaining speed, went right past him.

Taking his foot off the brake, Ryan buried the gas pedal and his car shot forward. He spun the wheel hard left, smashing the tail-end of the SUV with the nose of his Acura.

The Range Rover fishtailed on the ice, then, with its tires spinning wildly, spun completely around as it crossed the two lanes of opposing traffic. Brakes squealed and horns blared.

Narrowly missing an oncoming truck, the SUV clipped a Toyota Camry parked on the street, kept rolling over the sidewalk, and smashed into the front of a theatre building.

Ryan, his adrenaline pumping, steered his car to the side of the road and turned it off. Climbing out, he held the pistol in front of him as he crossed the road to the other side.

Traffic was backing up on both sides of the street as cars slowed to watch the unfolding drama. He heard the wail of sirens in the distance.

The Range Rover had hit the building head-on.

The SUVs front-end was completely crumpled, but Ryan approached carefully, half-expecting the driver to jump out and start blasting. He crouched by the driver's side door, holding the automatic with both hands. The smell of leaking anti-freeze and motor oil hung in the air.

A large man was slumped over the steering wheel, his body still, his face bloody.

Opening the badly-damaged car door, he touched the man's neck and felt for a pulse.

He was dead.

***

Ryan sat on the back ledge of the EMT truck while the paramedic worked on the cuts on his face. The glass shards had left deep gouges. They had wanted to take him to the hospital, but he'd refused.

Instead he asked for a blanket, which was now draped over his shoulders. The adrenaline rush had worn off and he felt the cold of the freezing rain as much as the cuts.

Peachtree Street had been blocked off and there were police cars everywhere, parked haphazardly in the middle of the road, their lights flashing. The cops had set up barricades to keep the growing mid-town crowd from contaminating the crime scene. The coroner's wagon, painted a dull black, was parked close to the smashed-up Range Rover. It looked like the M.E. was done, because they were zipping up the body bag.

After it all took place, Erin Welch had been Ryan's first call. The agent was now conferring with a knot of plainclothes from Atlanta PD. Breaking away from the group, she strode over to him, waited for the paramedic to finish.

When the man was done, she stood in front of Ryan, her arms crossed over her chest. She was wearing a knee-length, Burberry trench coat. Stylish, like everything else she wore.

Shaking her head, she said, "J.T., I can't believe you caused this."

"I thought you'd be glad I made it out alive," he said with a chuckle.

"Of course I am, damn it. I'm not talking about that." She pointed to the facade of the building the Range Rover had crashed into. The ornate glass entrance was shattered. *"That's what I'm talking about!* Of all the places in town, you pick the Fox Theatre. A landmark in Atlanta. The mayor is going to be *so* pissed!"

Glancing at the famous marquee, he now realized what she meant.

He began laughing, but the motion hurt his face and he stopped. "Look, Erin. I didn't pick this fight. The D.B. did. Blame him."

"He's dead. You, on the other hand, are alive and you work for me. I'm going to catch hell for this."

"You're a big girl. You can handle the heat."

She glowered, but after a moment seemed to calm down.

"I'm glad you're okay," she said finally.

Ryan pointed to the body bag, now on a gurney being rolled toward the coroner's wagon. "Who was he?"

"He had an Italian passport on him. His name is, or was, Luigi Tattori. We ran a check on him. He's got a criminal record, in Italy and in the U.S. Owns a house in Rome, but keeps an apartment in Brooklyn, New York."

"How about the Range Rover?"

"Atlanta PD ran the plates. It was reported stolen earlier today."

Ryan nodded. "So this guy probably worked for Amati."

"I'm sure of it."

The gurney was loaded into the wagon and the cargo doors slammed shut.

The sleet was falling harder now, the icy-wet particles stinging his face. He pulled the wool blanket tighter against his shoulders.

Erin tucked her long hair behind her ears. "Watch your back, J.T. This guy's probably not the only one who's gunning for you."

Chapter 25

Rome, Italy

Vincento Amati sat in his office, sipping Glenlivet and counting the minutes to his upcoming video conference call. He dreaded facing his partners, since he had bad news to report. But the call was unavoidable – Petrovich had insisted, his email alluding to a big win.

Glancing at the bejeweled crucifix on the wall, Amati crossed himself and said a silent prayer. He downed the rest of the scotch and turned on the video screen.

Dimitri Petrovich was already on, his face filling the right side of the screen. The left side was dark. Sanchez, as usual, was late.

"Dimitri, good to see you again," Amati said, forcing a smile.

"And I you, Vincento. I see our Mexican friend is not on yet," Petrovich said with a grin. It was clear the Russian was in a festive mood.

"You have a positive report for us, Dimitri?"

"That I do. But let's wait until Sanchez gets on."

Suddenly the left side of the screen lit up and a woman's image appeared. She was middle-aged, with long, dark hair, high cheekbones and dusky good looks. The woman was wearing an elegant, black empire dress with a black chiffon scarf around her neck.

"Gentlemen," she declared, her voice strong and authoritative. "I am Inez Sanchez."

Although Amati had never met the woman, he remembered Sanchez talking about his wife many times, attributing much of his success to her business acumen. Amati had seen pictures of her in newspapers, but her appearance was even more attractive on the video screen.

"I have tragic news," she continued, "regarding my dear husband."

Amati leaned forward in his seat. "What is it, Mrs. Sanchez?"

"Hector has just passed away," she said, her voice breaking. Tears filled her eyes and she dabbed them away with a black handkerchief. "It's horrible. He died very suddenly. It's been a crippling blow to our children, to the community, and most of all, to me."

"Oh, my God," Amati said, "that is tragic news. My deepest sympathies are with you, Mrs. Sanchez."

Petrovich echoed his condolences, while Amati's brain went into overdrive, processing the implications of the drug lord's death.

"How did he die?" Amati asked.

"It was quite sudden," she replied. "Our family doctor, a good and dear friend of mine, has attributed it to a heart attack."

Amati leaned back in the seat. "I see. Mrs. Sanchez, as you know, Hector was an integral part of our group. I know this is a very difficult time for you right now, but have you thought about your husband's business? Who will run the operation?"

Inez straightened her shoulders and held her head up high. "Mr. Amati, I have been involved in Hector's business dealings for many years. Now, I will be taking over."

"I see. Will you also continue participation in the Alliance?"

"Absolutely. I, in fact, was the one who convinced Hector to join."

Amati nodded, relieved that the counterfeit money pipeline from Mexico to the U.S. would continue. "Very good, Mrs. Sanchez."

"And in fact," Inez continued, "there is one positive aspect to my husband's death. As you know, the FBI indicted Hector, and was trying to extradite him. With his passing, that problem has been eliminated."

"That is true," Amati replied, knowing his own problems regarding the FBI were far from over. "Well, Mrs. Sanchez, welcome to the Alliance!"

"Thank you, Mr. Amati. But please, call me Inez."

"Of course, Inez. Now I'd like to have Dimitri bring us up to date. I know he has information he wants to share."

Petrovich beamed. "That I do, Vincento. And I'd also like to welcome Inez to the Alliance. Now, on with the news. As you know, Vincento, the Russian Premier has been trying for some time to persuade President Lazarenko to back our plan." He paused, steepled his hands on the desk in front of him. "I'm pleased to report that he has finally been successful. As of now, the Russian President is on board." He grinned widely, obviously very pleased with himself.

"Excellent!" Amati said. "That was the last piece of the puzzle. With Lazarenko backing the plan, the Alliance cannot be stopped."

"That is correct," Petrovich said. "And on a related matter, my purchases of gold bullion continue on schedule. How about yours, Vincento?"

Amati nodded. "Yes. I am on track on that as well."

Inez cleared her throat. "I have looked into Hector's accounts and he too has been buying gold as agreed. I will continue that, starting today."

"Very good," Amati said, "It appears our plan is proceeding quite well on both your ends. However, I need to bring you up to date on my own situation. The good news is that my distribution of the fake currency is continuing without a hitch. And, as you see in the newscasts from around the world, the inflationary result from our efforts has been dramatic. The financial markets are in a near panic and the central banks in America, Europe and Asia are in crisis mode."

Amati paused, then said, "And now, to the not-so-good news. The FBI indictment against me still stands, and the U.S. is actively trying to extradite me. I have appealed to Prime Minister Bertoli to prevent that from happening. However, I have not heard back."

Petrovich leaned forward in his seat, his face grim. "What do you plan to do, if Bertoli does not block the extradition? You are a key part of this operation."

"Do not worry, Dimitri," Amati said, with more confidence than he felt. "I have several contingencies should that occur. Trust me, the Alliance will succeed."

The oil man nodded, but the worried look on his face remained.

"So," Amati said, "unless either of you has anything else, I'd like to conclude our meeting. Dimitri? Inez?"

The other two shook their heads and Amati said, "Very good. Goodbye, my friends. We'll talk soon."

He turned off the video screen and leaned back in the seat, relieved the call was over.

Pouring himself a double of Glenlivet, he tossed back the scotch in one long gulp.

He picked up the phone and dialed a number, desperately hoping for positive news.

Chapter 26

Moscow, Russia

Dimitri Petrovich was in the back seat of his Mercedes limo, as it cruised on the MKAD highway. Surprisingly, he mused, it wasn't snowing today, although the sky had that dark, somber look that promised it would later on. Sitting next to him on the leather seat was his secretary, Karina.

"Read me the last part of the letter," Petrovich said to the young woman.

Karina did so. Afterward, she looked up at him.

"Good. That'll be fine," he said.

"Is there anything else, Mr. Petrovich?"

"Yes. But you can put your notebook away." He pressed a button on the armrest and the opaque glass partition that separated the front and back part of the limo buzzed closed. He pressed a second button and the car's back area privacy panels slid into place, covering all the windows and providing complete seclusion.

Leaning back on the plush, leather seat, he unzipped his pants.

Karina, having been his secretary for a long time, knew exactly what was expected of her.

Silently, she took off her jacket and put it aside. Without taking off her silk blouse or short skirt, she slid off the seat and knelt on the floor in front of him.

Then she began to work on him, her deft hands as adept as her luscious mouth.

As he relished the delicious minutes of her expertise, he recalled the pleasure this woman had given him over the years. It was a pity this would be the last time.

But those thoughts receded as he she continued her actions. Soon he felt the familiar sensation of ecstatic pleasure and he exploded in one long rush.

Afterwards, Karina sat next to him and reapplied her makeup. That done, she combed her hair and turned towards him. "Was that good for you, Mr. Petrovich?"

"Excellent as usual, Karina."

"I'm glad."

Petrovich pressed the armrest button and the privacy panels slid away from the windows.

A somber sky stared back at him, the mid-day traffic lighter on this part of the highway. They were well north of the city, and the oil man knew his driver would be taking an exit off the freeway soon, per his earlier instructions.

Glancing at his watch, Petrovich estimated he had about ten minutes before they reached their destination.

"You've disappointed me," the oil man said, his voice sad.

Karina's eyebrows shot up. "But you just said...."

"Not that. The sex was very good. It's something else." Turning away from her, he scanned the dull scenery, a blur of farmhouses and patches of cultivated land.

The Mercedes slowed, got in the right-hand lane and took an exit off the highway. Using a two-lane road, the limo headed northwest. They were far from the city centre, the densely populated industrial areas gone, replaced by farmland.

"What is it?" Karina said, apprehension in her voice.

Petrovich faced her. "You betrayed me."

"Sir, I would never do that!"

He shook his head. "Don't try to deny it. I have proof. You're Chernov's spy."

The woman's face turned ashen, and she went quiet.

The Mercedes got off the paved street and took a desolate gravel road bordered on both sides by farmland. There was no traffic here and he spotted only a few farmhouses in the far distance.

"I'm sure you had your reasons, Karina. They don't matter now. The point is, you betrayed me."

Her eyes went wide. "What...what are you going to do? Kill me?"

Petrovich didn't answer, but rather pressed a button and the glass divider buzzed down.

"Stop the car," he told the driver.

The limo slowed and came to a halt.

"You're fired, Karina," Petrovich said. "Get out of the car. You'll have to walk back to Moscow."

Obviously having feared much worse, her face visibly relaxed. "Yes, sir. Of course, sir."

She yanked the door handle, and without looking back, quickly climbed out, closing the door behind her.

He watched as the woman took off her high-heeled shoes and began trudging barefoot on the gravel road, heading in the direction of the city.

Petrovich waited a few minutes, then said to the driver, "Do it now."

The Mercedes turned around on the road and began to accelerate toward Karina.

She must have heard the crunching of the gravel because she turned back at the last moment, right before the limousine struck her at speed. All at once Petrovich heard a loud thump, felt the car shudder, and saw her body hurtle in the air.

The car slowed and stopped.

Petrovich sighed, and with the same sad voice as earlier, said, "Go check. Make sure she's dead."

Chapter 27

Atlanta, Georgia

Markov was very relieved when the plane touched down at Hartsfield-Jackson.

The Aeroflot flight from Moscow had been long, tiring, and noisy, full of screaming kids and coughing old people. To make it worse, the food had been stomach-turning. He'd poked at the mystery meat as it swam in a rancid-tasting brown sauce, but had only been able to swallow a couple of bites.

The 747 taxied to the gate and began to unload the passengers. Gathering his belongings, he pushed his way out of the plane and got in line for customs.

An hour later, after renting a Chevrolet Impala from Hertz, he drove out of the airport and headed north on the busy highway.

Markov had been to the U.S. several times before on assignments, but never to this city. The skyline didn't look much different than Los Angeles or New York, just smaller. But Atlanta's blue sky was a welcome change from Moscow's dreary grayness. And the temperature was much warmer, he thought. Opening the windows, he let in the crisp air. Although the locals he'd seen so far were bundled in heavy coats, he hadn't needed anything more than a windbreaker.

Markov entered the address on the car's navigation system and looked at the digital map. The man he was meeting was northeast of his current location. Glancing back up to the road, he began scrutinizing the signs for the right exit.

***

The Impala pulled into the driveway of the shabby-looking home, a single-story place with a carport. Must be a crime-ridden neighborhood, he thought, because the house, like the other ones around it, had burglar-bars on all the windows. A dented Corolla sat in the carport, its bald tires and faded green paint speaking volumes about the owner's financial condition.

The Russian got out of the Impala and walked to the front door. He pressed the ringer, but it didn't work, so he knocked loudly.

A short, wiry man opened it a moment later. He was wearing what Markov knew Americans referred to as a "wife-beater" T-shirt and a pair of dirty jeans. It looked like he hadn't shaved in several days.

"Yeah?" the American said, his pock-marked face in a scowl. "Whatever you're selling, I'm not buying."

"I'm Tom," Markov said, using the cover name he had used when he contacted the man previously. "You must be Mr. Lanier. I trust you received my initial payment?" Markov's English was good, but he had a strong Russian accent.

Lanier's face changed from a scowl to a crooked smile. Opening the door wide, he said, "Sure did, Tom. Come on in. Have a seat."

Markov went inside, scanned the filthy room. Empty beer cans and other trash littered the floor. Porno magazines were stacked haphazardly on the sagging couch and the place smelled of stale beer and cigarettes. Ignoring the couch, the Russian remained standing.

He stared at Lanier, who had been juror number 5. A greedy and unethical man – he was perfect for Markov's purposes. "I'm glad you got the money, Mr. Lanier," Markov said.

"Would you like a cold one?" Lanier asked. "I've got Schlitz and Miller Lite."

"No. I'm fine. Is there anyone else in the house?"

"Just me," Lanier said with a snort. "My wife left me last year."

"Sorry to hear that. You ready to conclude our business?"

"You bet. You got the rest of the money?"

Markov reached into his pocket, pulled out a wad of $100 bills. He handed it to the other man. "Here."

The American grabbed it, counted it carefully. He looked up.

"Well, Tom, you're a man of your word."

Markov nodded. "Put it in a safe place – looks like this area sees its share of crime."

"That's a fact. But don't worry. I've got a .44 Magnum. That baby scares off the riff-raff we got around here."

"Now that we've got the money part out of the way, tell me about the court testimony."

"Sure, no problem." Lanier picked up a can of Miller Lite and took a slug. He burped, then said, "The witness in the grand jury was named John T. Ryan. He's a private investigator, does work for the FBI and the Secret Service."

"Good. Describe what he looks like."

Lanier gave him a detailed description.

"Very good. Can you tell me anything else about him?"

"He said he lives in Atlanta, and has an office in mid-town."

Markov nodded. "You've been very helpful."

Lanier took another sip of beer.

"Glad to do it. I hate the police." He grinned. "And I need the money too."

"I'm sure you do." Markov forced a smile. "I wouldn't mind having a beer before I go. Watching you drink made me thirsty."

"Sure, Tom. I'll go get it."

As Lanier turned toward the kitchen, the Russian punched him savagely in the neck, knocking the man off his feet.

Lanier screamed and landed on his back on the floor. Markov straddled him and using both of his beefy hands, grabbed the American by the throat.

His eyes wide, Lanier tried to punch the other man off, but his scrawny arms were no match for the Russian's muscular build.

Markov squeezed harder. The man's face turned bright red and he let out choking noises. The Russian kept at it until Lanier's eyes rolled white and his body sagged.

Continuing the pressure for another minute, Markov finally let him go and checked the man's pulse. He was dead.

Reaching into Lanier's pocket, he removed the wad of $100s. Markov stood, went into the bedroom.

Like the rest of the house, the room was a mess. Empty Pizza Hut cartons were on the floor, and the ashtray on the nightstand was overflowing.

Searching the drawers of the nightstand, he found what he was looking for. A Rossi .44 caliber Magnum revolver, and a box of ammunition.

There was no way Markov could have gotten a gun through airport security. Finding this one saved him the step of buying one on the black market.

After checking the load in the .44, he stuck the gun under his waistband, in the small of his back. Picking up the box of ammo, he stuffed it in his jacket pocket.

He went to the kitchen, took a Schlitz from the refrigerator and headed out of the house.

Back in the car, the Russian did a Google search on his cell phone. He looked up private investigators in the city and after scrolling for a minute, found the phone number and address. The wonders of modern technology, Markov thought with a smile.

He dialed the number and luckily reached the man. Using a phony name and pretext, he made an appointment for early the next morning.

An hour later he found Ryan's office building and scouted the area thoroughly. Then he grabbed a meal, bought some supplies, and checked into a Holiday Inn right off the interstate. He wanted to wait until nightfall to make his move.

***

The office building had an underground parking lot and he drove into one of the many empty slots. It was past 7 p.m. and most, but not all of the office workers had gone home for the day. Or so Markov hoped, as he climbed out of the car and walked to the locked door leading to the elevators. You needed a card key to get in and he leaned against the wall and waited.

He was rewarded ten minutes later when a middle-aged woman wearing a business suit came out. Giving her a broad smile, he stood to one side and held the door open. As she walked to her car, he slipped inside the elevator corridor.

Taking the lift to the right floor, he stepped out, looked both ways. The corridor was deserted.

He made his way down the hallway, looking for the right unit. He found it soon after, the door marked with a non-descript typeface. *J.T. Ryan, Private Investigator* it read.

Knocking, he waited. There was no response so he knocked again.

After another minute he knelt down and studied the lock. It was basic, intended to keep honest people out.

Taking a lock-pick tool set from his pocket, he worked on the lock. He'd bought the set earlier in the day, figuring it might come in handy.

Hearing a click, he pulled the revolver from his waistband, turned the knob, and looked inside.

The office was dark, so he felt around the wall, found the light switch and turned it on.

The room was small, unoccupied and simply furnished. A metal desk, a row of filing cabinets and several upholstered chairs. Gray industrial carpet covered the floor.

There was a small bathroom on one side of the room, with a closet next to that. He checked the closet and pushed some boxes out of the way. Then he turned off the office lights, relocked the door, returned to the closet and closed the closet door behind him. He sat on the floor, his back against the wall. Placing the gun by his side, the assassin closed his eyes to wait.

***

Markov awoke at 5 a.m., a full hour before the scheduled meeting. He was stiff and hungry, but he ignored that, and instead focused on his plan.

Picking up the Magnum, he checked the load again.

He leaned back against the wall and stared at the back of the closed closet door.

Half an hour later he heard noises coming from the office – a door opening and lights being switched on.

Quickly coming to his feet, he trained the gun in front of him and held his breath.

Hearing a toilet flush, he opened the closet door and lunged out, holding the .44 with both hands.

To his surprise, no one was in the office. He went in the bathroom, and it also was empty.

"Drop the gun!" he heard from behind.

Markov whirled around to find a large, muscular man pointing a gun at his face. He was sure the man was Ryan – he fit the description. The Russian now realized Ryan must have sensed something wrong when he came in and hid behind his desk.

With his heart pounding, Markov froze in his tracks.

"I said, drop the gun now," Ryan repeated.

Markov's thoughts raced. He had two options – open fire and probably get shot himself. Or comply and wait for the other man to make a mistake.

He chose the latter. "Don't shoot. I'm dropping it." He lowered the .44 and slowly put it on the floor. Then he held his hands in the air.

"Who the hell are you?" the American said.

"I...was going to rob you. Take your computer and whatever else I could find."

"What are you, European? By your accent I can tell you're not from around here."

"I'm German."

"Whatever. Don't move a muscle or you're dead meat."

Markov narrowed his gaze, studying the man carefully, waiting for Ryan to relax his guard.

"No problem," the Russian said. "I don't want to get shot over a lousy computer. Call the cops. I know the drill – I'll be out on bail in a couple of days."

"We'll see about that, smartass. Using a gun in a robbery is a serious offense in Georgia."

Ryan pulled a cell phone from his pocket, and keeping an eye on Markov, punched in some numbers.

But in that split-second that Ryan was distracted by the call, the assassin lunged at him. He hit the American full-force and both men tumbled to the floor, the gun and phone flying in the air.

They grappled each other and Markov realized the other man was just as strong as himself. They wrestled on the floor, each trying to get the upper hand.

Adrenaline pumping, he punched Ryan in the face several times, drawing blood.

But the American fought back fiercely, using his fists, elbows, and feet.

Markov grunted from a painful blow to his stomach, but spotted the revolver on the floor. Grabbing it, he tried pointing it at Ryan.

But the man was on him in an instant, also clutching the weapon.

As the two fought for control of the .44, their eyes locked on each other, both gasping for air.

Markov heard a deafening blast, saw Ryan flinch.

The revolver went off again and everything went black.

Chapter 28

Rome, Italy

Vincento Amati was having breakfast at his estate when his wife Livia entered the immense dining room. Her face was ashen and her eyes were red, as if she'd been crying.

Putting down the fork, he said, "What is it, Livia? What's wrong?"

His wife motioned for the maid to leave the room, and sat down across from him.

"Father just called," she said, her voice breaking. "He's been talking with Prime Minister Bertoli on your behalf." She stopped, covered his hand with hers. "I'm sorry. Father has begged him, but Bertoli won't budge. He's refused to block your extradition."

Amati's heart sank when he heard the words. Having Livia's father intercede was his last hope. Amati's own calls to the prime minister had not been returned.

"What will you do, Vincento?"

Amati pushed his plate aside, his appetite gone. He said nothing, his mind churning over his limited options. Rubbing his temple, he leaned forward in the seat. "The only thing I can do. Call the Cardinal."

She nodded, but her frown remained, knowing, as he did, that their lives would be much different from now on.

Amati stood, in a hurry to call the Vatican. Now that the extradition was unobstructed, the Americans would demand his immediate deportation.

But she continued to hold his hand, her moist eyes looking up at him, as if pleading with him not to go. "I love you, Vincento."

He caressed her face. "I love you too."

Then he turned and quickly left the room.

From his home office he dialed the Cardinal's private line, which was answered by Father Ignatius. The priest was Cardinal Fiori's personal assistant.

***

Amati was shown into Fiori's office, a lavish room with 20-foot ceilings and intricate marble decorations on the walls. A slight scent of incense pervaded the room.

Located in a "working part" of the Vatican, the office was well away from the tourist areas of the Piazza San Pietro and the historic museums. Amati had been here many times before.

As he waited, he stepped onto the balcony, which overlooked a courtyard with gardens and fountains. Although it was late January, the weather was unusually warm today and he relished the fresh air, a welcome distraction to his worries.

"Vincento!" he heard from behind him. He turned, saw a smiling Cardinal Fiori. A long-time veteran at the Vatican, Fiori had the Pope's ear, just as he'd been a confidant of the previous pope. With a shock of white hair, ruddy cheeks, a large nose and a sturdy build, the tall man cut an imposing figure in his cardinal's red robes.

Fiori held out his hand and Amati gave him a slight bow and kissed his ring.

"Thank you, Cardinal, for granting me an audience on such short notice."

Fiori waved a hand in the air. "We are old friends, you and I. It is never an imposition. Let's go inside, shall we?"

The two men walked back into the office and Amati stood, waited while the cardinal went around his huge desk and sat down. The ornately carved desk was made of highly-polished teak and probably dated back to the mid 16th century.

Amati sat on one of the wingback visitor's chairs and waited for the other man to speak first.

"So, Vincento. How are your children? And your wife, Livia?"

"Fine, Your Excellency."

"Good. Father Ignatius said you needed to speak to me about an urgent matter?"

"Yes, Cardinal. That is correct."

The religious leader steepled his hands on the desk. "Please, go ahead."

"Sir, serious allegations have been made against me, utterly false of course, by the American authorities. They claim that I was involved in a plot to kill an FBI agent and that I'm involved in a money counterfeiting scheme. As I said, these charges are spurious, but nevertheless, they are threatening to prosecute me. They've issued a subpoena for my arrest."

The cardinal's eyebrows shut up. "That's preposterous. You're a well-respected businessman and a large benefactor to the Church. Why would they suspect such a thing?"

Amati shook his head slowly. "Who can understand the Americans? It is insane, yet there it is. They are in the process of trying to extradite me to the U.S."

The cardinal's eyes narrowed. "So. I assume you will fight this?"

"Of course. I have good lawyers. Unfortunately, Prime Minister Bertoli and I have never been on good terms and ultimately it is up to him to grant the extradition."

"And his response?"

"He has not been helpful, Your Excellency. He has refused to block it."

Fiori placed his hands flat on the desk. "I see. Bertoli is a shallow, callous man. A political animal, in the truest sense of the word. He's never been a friend of the Church, either."

"That's true, Cardinal."

"So, Vincento, how can I help?"

Amati leaned forward in the chair. "Your Excellency, I need to disappear."

"Disappear?"

"Yes, sir. I'm sure that within days the Italian government will allow the Americans to take me back to the U.S. to face trial. I can't allow that to happen. I have to go to a safe place, a place the Americans can't find me."

Fiori frowned. "I don't understand."

Amati waved a hand in the air. "I have to hide here, in Vatican City. A sovereign state. The safest place in the world."

The cardinal's face flushed red. "You want us to protect you?"

"That's exactly what I want. Sanctuary."

Fiori rubbed his jaw. "I don't know. This could make real problems for the Church."

"No one has to know. It would be a secret. All I need is an office and a bedroom in some remote part of the Vatican. And it's only temporary, until my lawyers can figure out another solution."

The cardinal looked skeptical. "Still. You are asking for a great deal. If it were to get out that the Vatican was hiding a fugitive, it would greatly damage the reputation of the Holy See."

"Sir, I've been a stalwart supporter of the Church for decades. I've run many positive news articles on the clergy, in spite of all the sex-abuse scandals. Not to mention my generous monetary contributions."

"Of course, Vincento. You have been a true friend of the Catholic Church."

"All I ask, Your Excellency, is for your help now, when I really need it."

Fiori went quiet, and Amati realized the cardinal was not willing to risk his career to help him. Knowing he had no choice, Amati decided to play his last card. Pulling an envelope from his suit jacket, he placed it on the desk.

Fiori stared at the envelope. "What's that?"

"My security people are very good, sir. They've been monitoring your financial activities for years. We know all about your secret bank accounts in Zurich and the Caymans. Accounts worth tens of millions of dollars. Money that I'm sure the Pope or the Curia is not aware of. I don't know where the money came from, and I don't care. What's important is that I have proof that it exists."

Fiori's face went white. He picked up the envelope and quickly read the contents. His hands shaking slightly, he dropped the papers on the desk.

"I don't...know what to say," the cardinal whispered.

Amati picked up the papers and put them back in his pocket. "No one has to know, Your Excellency. About the bank accounts, nor about my residence here." He gave the man a thin smile. "It will be our secret."

Fiori, his face still ashen, nodded his agreement.

Chapter 29

Atlanta, Georgia

Ryan heard murmurs from somewhere far away.

He opened his eyes, saw hazy lights overhead and felt a pressure on his hand. The lights and sounds spun away and he closed his eyes. Let me sleep, he thought groggily, as he drifted off again.

"Wake up, J.T.," he heard. A faint voice, a woman's voice. "It's me, Lauren."

Opening his eyes, he saw a blurry form leaning over him. "Go away, damn it," he blurted out.

"Wake up, hon...."

Suddenly his vision cleared and Lauren's pretty face came into focus. "Oh, it's you," he said, trying for a smile, but his face felt numb, as did his arms and legs.

A worried look was on her face.

He glanced around the small room, at its antiseptic white walls and beeping monitors. "Where the hell am I?"

"Don't you remember, J.T.? Grady Memorial. You've been here three days."

The fog in his brain lifted somewhat. "My office. The fight. I remember a gunshot."

Lauren squeezed his hand. "That's right. You suffered a concussion. The bullet grazed the back of your skull. The doctor said you were very lucky."

"I don't feel lucky. I feel like crap." His head was throbbing from a blinding headache. "Can you get me some aspirin? I feel like my head's going to explode."

"I'll go get the nurse." She turned to leave, almost ran into Erin Welch as the agent came in the room.

"What are you doing here?" Lauren said to the other woman, her tone icy.

"Just came to see how he's doing," Erin replied.

Lauren folded her arms across her chest. "He's recuperating. Leave him alone, will you?"

"It's okay," Ryan said as he pushed himself up into a sitting position. Propping the pillow behind him, he leaned against the headboard.

Lauren glanced back at him, then stalked out of the room.

"How are you feeling?" Erin asked him.

"I'll live." He touched the bandages on the back of his head and looked down at himself. He was wearing one of those ridiculous hospital gowns that tie in the back. He shrugged, pulled the sheet over himself, and looked back at the agent. "I'm kind of groggy. What happened?"

"You were in a fight at your office. Two shots were fired. One grazed you, the other round blew the other guy's brains out."

He let out a low whistle. "Guess I am lucky."

"That's a fact."

His head still throbbing, he said, "Who was he?"

Erin pulled a chair by his bed and sat down. "A Russian. Name of Markov."

"Never heard of him. Russian, huh? That makes no sense."

Erin nodded. "We're trying to sort that out. Do you have any other cases you're working on that have a Russian connection?"

"No."

"This Markov lived in Moscow, had a criminal record. He was part of the *grupperovka,* the Russian mob."

Ryan tried to process that. "He said he was there to rob the place."

"Fat chance. From his record, it looks like he was a hired killer. We're working with the Moscow police, see if we can piece together who hired him. But the Russian cops aren't the most cooperative people in the world."

Ryan nodded. "Imagine that. You think this is connected to sigma?"

"I suspect it, but I'm not sure how the Russians fit into this whole thing. It's only been Italians and Mexicans up to now."

Ryan shifted his body, trying to get into a comfortable position. "How soon before I can go home?"

Erin shook her head. "Don't know. I want you back on the case, but I want you healed first."

She stood. "I've posted an agent outside. You'll have a security detail protecting you 24/7 until you get out of the hospital. Longer, if you want it."

He frowned. "I don't need a babysitter."

"You've got one, J.T., whether you want it or not."

Ryan rolled his eyes. "Great."

Lauren came back in the room, with a stern-faced nurse in tow.

He closed his eyes, wishing the pounding in his head would go away.

Chapter 30

Hart Senate Office Building
Washington, D.C.

There was a knock on his office door and Senator Dean Cage looked up from his infuriating iPad. The senator was a balding seventy-year old man with poor eyesight. He found new technology frustrating.

His assistant poked her head around the door.

"Senator, the Banking committee meeting is in fifteen minutes. But Mr. Amati is calling on the secure line. I have him on hold."

"Thank you, Marge. I'll take Vincento's call. Tell the committee I'm running behind schedule, have them start without me."

"Yes, sir," she replied and closed the door.

Putting the iPad aside, he picked up the receiver and pushed a button on the console. "Vincento, how are you?"

"I'm well, and you Senator?" the Italian said in his heavily-accented English.

"I can't complain too much. My knees ache and my back's a bitch, but I'm alive," Cage said with a chortle.

Amati laughed, but it sounded strained.

Cage sensed the man wasn't in his usual cheerful mood. "You received the latest shipment of the sigma machines I sent you?"

"Yes, Senator."

"Good. We're making excellent progress, don't you think?"

"Yes, sir. In fact, that's the reason I was calling. I wanted to bring you up to date on a couple of things."

Cage was momentarily distracted by a truck pulling into the parking lot of the building. His third-floor office overlooked the lot and through his window he had a clear view of the near-by Capitol Building and the rest of D.C. in the distance. "Go ahead, Vincento."

"There's been two developments. First, due to some unforeseen circumstances, I've...had to change my location. I know this is a secure line, but I'd rather not get too specific. I'm now working out of a new office."

"I see. I hope you've addressed your problems. We're getting too close for any screw-ups."

"Don't worry, Senator. It's nothing I can't handle."

"That's good to hear." Cage pushed his glasses up the bridge of his nose and jotted a note on a legal pad. A reminder to check on his partner's new "circumstances". Amati wasn't being very forthcoming.

"I also have some excellent news," Amati continued. "Our Russian connection has achieved a breakthrough. President Lazarenko has finally agreed to back our plan."

"That's good news. Very good news."

"Yes, Senator. It won't be long now before we can pull the trigger."

Cage's hopes soared. Soon he'd be able to retire from public office, leave this dreary city and retire to lavish comfort in the mansion he planned to buy in the Bahamas. "You've truly made my day."

The senator leaned back in the executive chair, his thoughts swirling with visions of white-sand beaches and crystal-clear, aquamarine waters. "Is there anything else, Vincento?"

"No. I'll call you next week, give you another progress report."

"Excellent. Goodbye." He replaced the receiver and pressed the intercom button. "Marge, come in here a minute."

His assistant came in the room and sat on one of the visitor's chairs. The prim, dour-looking woman was dressed in her usual attire, a somber black business suit. "Yes, Senator?"

Picking up the iPad from his desk, he handed it to her. "Get rid of this. I'll never be able to figure out the damn thing."

"Yes, sir."

"Marge, I want you to call my broker. Have him purchase an additional $500,000 of the gold mutual fund. I'll wire him the money later today."

"Yes, sir. Anything else?"

Cage glanced out the window again. A gray, overcast sky stared back at him.

Looking back to her, he said, "I want you to find me a realtor that specializes in Bahamian properties. I'm only interested in waterfront homes."

The woman cocked a brow. "Sounds expensive, Senator."

Cage smiled. "A man can dream, can't he?"

***

Sitting behind the podium of the Senate Hearing Room, Dean Cage listened with rapt attention. As Chairman of the Banking Committee, and a Washington power broker for decades, Senator Cage had sat through hundreds of similar hearings. But today's was different. The hearing was standing room only, packed with media and spectators.

"... and the current financial crisis," Federal Reserve President Stevens said, continuing with his testimony, "has worsened considerably. The inflation rate in the U.S., like in other countries, is at an all-time high."

Cage waved a hand in the air to interrupt. "We know all that, Mr. Stevens. The food riots in American cities are front-page news. The question is, what are you doing about it?"

Stevens grimaced. "We've tried many things already, Mr. Chairman. We don't have that many bullets left."

"What about price controls?" Cage asked.

The Fed president shook his head. "Nixon tried that in the 1970s and it didn't work. Every country in the world that has tried price controls and they have all failed."

"I see," Cage said. "What about going back to the gold standard? Having the U.S. dollar be backed by gold?"

"We thought of that, sir. But worldwide gold supplies are in short supply. There's not much gold left on the open market. As you're probably aware, the price of gold bullion has soared over the last year. And anyway, it wouldn't be feasible for us to go back to the gold standard. The U.S. runs such a large deficit that we couldn't buy enough gold to back the dollar."

Cage nodded. "So. It appears to me we are in an extreme crisis. What's your next step, Mr. Stevens?"

"I'm meeting with the European central bank presidents next week. We hope to come up with a coordinated solution."

"And if that doesn't work?"

Stevens rubbed his forehead and didn't respond at first. Then he leaned forward in his chair. "God help us then, Mr. Chairman."

Chapter 31

Atlanta, Georgia

Ryan was reclining in bed, surfing channels, trying to find something interesting to watch among the vast wasteland of daytime TV.

Bored, he turned off the set and picked up a book from the nightstand. This was his third day out of the hospital and Lauren had insisted he recuperate at her house. He had agreed, although he was beginning to have second thoughts. She had taken time off from work to nurse him back to health, and her strict adherence to the doctor's instructions was getting on his nerves. Left on his own, he knew he'd already be back working on his pending cases.

Leaning back against the headboard, he cracked the book and began reading. It was a mystery novel. He had read the first few chapters and was intrigued by the lead character, a P.I. like himself.

Lauren came in the room and sat on the bed. She was holding a glass and a bottle of pills. Today she wore a pink polo shirt and Levis, her auburn hair pulled into a ponytail.

"It's noon," she said. "Time for your medicine."

"Again?"

"Yes, again."

He swallowed the pills, washed them down with the water.

Lauren smiled. "I'll make you some lunch. What would you like?"

"You," he said, reaching over to caress her face.

She stood up and wagged her finger at him. "The doctor said no sex for a week."

"What does he know?"

"He's the one with the medical degree."

Ryan shrugged, then smiled. "All right. You win. For now."

She shook her head slowly. "You're too much, J.T."

"Better than being not enough," he replied with a chuckle.

This made her smile and she sat on the bed again. Glancing at the open book in his lap, she said, "What are you reading?"

"A book."

"I can see that, silly. What's it about?"

"A private investigator who's solving cases, which is what I should be doing right now."

Lauren frowned. "The doctor said...."

He put the book aside. "I know, I know."

"I'm trying to help you. Make sure you heal. You had a bad concussion. You were practically in a coma for three days."

Ryan held up his palms. "I hear you, hon."

"So. What do you want for lunch?"

He thought about that for a moment, but before he could answer, his cell phone rang.

She picked it up from the nightstand, held it to her ear and said hello. She made a face, handed him the phone.

"It's what's her name," Lauren said frostily, before she turned and left the room.

"This is Ryan. Who's this?"

"Erin Welch."

"Erin, good to hear from you."

"I don't think your girlfriend likes me very much."

"She's great, but some people rub her the wrong way. You know women, how they can be...."

"I'm a woman."

He laughed. "You got issues too."

Ignoring his remark , she said, "How're you feeling?"

"I'm bored out of my skull. But my headaches are gone. A couple of more days and I'll be good to go. By the way, you got something new on the case?"

"That's why I'm calling. No progress yet on the Russian guy. The Moscow cops aren't giving us anything. Those bastards have clammed-up. My guess is they're on the take."

"Damn. We've got to out figure how the Russians are connected to sigma."

"I haven't given up on it, J.T. We're putting pressure on our State Department – maybe they'll be able to get the Moscow police to open up."

"Okay. Anything else?"

"Some bad news," Erin replied, "about Vincento Amati. Remember we got his extradition approved by the Italian government?"

"Sure, I remember."

"The Italian police and the FBI went to arrest him yesterday. He's gone, and nobody knows where he is."

Chapter 32

Vatican City
Rome, Italy

Vincento Amati took the food tray from the silent monk with the shaved head and closed the door of his austere, one-room apartment. Amati had tried communicating with the brown-robed monk for a week to no avail. The man was either mute or sworn to a religious vow of silence. In any case, the monk was punctual, delivering the meals at exactly the same time each day.

Amati placed the tray on the simple wood table and glanced around the cramped, cell-like room, deep in the bowels of Vatican City. Located in a remote part of the cavernous, multi-level basement of the Vatican complex, the room had concrete walls that gave off a damp, musty smell. The room was basic – it consisted of a tiny kitchen, a cot, a small bathroom and a desk area.

Amati had wondered idly who else lived in the warren of rooms in the basement, and guessed they housed low-level priests and monks. It didn't matter anyway, as the room was still far better than a federal prison in the U.S. And, hopefully, only a temporary solution.

As he picked at the overcooked chicken dish, he fiddled with the dial of his portable radio, trying to find pleasing music. Finally settling on a classical station, he chewed the food and washed it down with weak coffee. His mind wandered, at first to the hot young starlet he'd been bedding until recently, then to his wife Livia. He was starting to realize that he had under-appreciated his wife for years. Amati resolved to change that, once the extradition problem was resolved.

Draining the rest of the coffee, he picked up the empty dishes and placed them in the small sink. Turning off the radio, he sat behind the wooden desk. A state-of-the-art console computer was on the desk, and for this Amati was grateful to Cardinal Fiori. With the computer and its encrypted high-speed internet connection, Amati was able to manage his business affairs.

He turned it on, read through his emails and responded. Most were routine, dealing with his media company. One was from his girlfriend, asking about the acting role he'd promised her. He didn't reply to that one, knowing he had more pressing matters to attend to.

Consulting his watch, he closed his email account. The video conference call was due to start soon.

Typing in a long sequence of numbers, he waited for the call to come up. A moment later the computer's screen image split in two. On his right was Dimitri Petrovich and to his left was the striking face of Inez Sanchez.

"Dimitri and Inez, good to see you both again," Amati said, his voice more cheerful than he felt.

The Russian and Mexican responded in kind and Amati decided not to wait, but rather plunge into his new circumstances.

"I wanted to bring you up-to-date," Amati said somberly, "on the indictment against me. Unfortunately, the Italian government has decided to cooperate with the Americans. I was almost arrested. Luckily, I've been able to relocate to a safe place."

"From what I can see of your new place," Petrovich stated with a cynical smile, "it's not up to your usual luxurious standards."

Amati shrugged. "Only temporary, my friend. And the important thing, I still control my business affairs from here. On a positive note, I can tell you that my counterfeiting operation continues without any problems."

"That's good to hear," Petrovich said. "I have some news on that as well." He paused, spread his hands flat on the desk in front of him. "As I told you recently, President Lazarenko has agreed to our plan. He will be holding a televised press conference soon, to announce the details." Petrovich smiled. "In anticipation, I have increased my purchases of gold bullion. I suggest you two do likewise. Remember, there is only a finite quantity of the ore, and only a few countries such as Russia have large mining deposits."

Amati leaned forward in the chair. "That's great news about Lazarenko. I look forward to watching the press conference. Let me know the date and time and I'll make sure my news stations run it, here in Europe and elsewhere. In fact, I can build up anticipation for it by promoting it in advance as a major worldwide event."

"Good thinking, Vincento," Petrovich said. "I know I can always count on your marketing savvy."

Now that the Russian had shared his news, Amati turned toward Mrs. Sanchez. He noticed the woman had shed her funereal black clothes and was now attired in a bold print dress. "Inez, would you tell us about your progress?"

"Thank you, Vincento," she said, playing with the large diamond brooch that dangled from her neck. "Since we last spoke, I've taken total control over my husband's business. The drug and fake money aspects of the enterprise are continuing. I have a few loose ends to take care of, but otherwise, everything is running smoothly."

"Very good," Amati said, admiring the way the woman filled out her dress. "I look forward to working with you in the future."

Inez gave him an enigmatic smile. "And I you, Vincento."

Amati looked at Dimitri, and back at Inez. "Is there anything else?"

Neither responded and Amati said, "Very well. Let's conclude the call. I'll talk with you soon."

The Italian turned off the computer.

He stood, walked to the nearby cot and lay down. Staring at the low ceiling, he tried to get comfortable on the lumpy mattress.

On the wall hung a small wooden crucifix, much different than the priceless, bejeweled one in his office. Nevertheless, he closed his eyes and prayed to it. With God's help, he was sure the Alliance plan would succeed.

And maybe, just maybe, after the operation was complete he could turn his life around. Put the greed behind him and devote himself to doing God's work.

For a moment a vision of his nude girlfriend filled his thoughts.

But he pushed those thoughts aside, and focused on his wife and the crucifix on the wall.

He closed his eyes and prayed again.

After tossing and turning on the narrow, uncomfortable bed for hours, he finally fell asleep.

Chapter 33

Mexico City, Mexico

Inez Sanchez picked up her bedroom phone, dialed her driver and told him to bring the Bentley to the front of the estate.

Then she turned to the full-length mirror and studied her appearance. She had chosen a sensible, business-like pants suit with flat shoes. Satisfied, she slung the overnight bag over her shoulder and headed out of the room.

A few minutes later she stepped out of the house and got in the back seat of the luxury automobile. Lowering the glass partition, she told the driver, "The Rodriguez warehouse in Juarez."

Closing the glass, she leaned back against the plush leather and settled in for the long drive.

***

The Bentley pulled into the parking lot in front of the sprawling warehouse.

Grabbing the tote bag, Inez exited the car. She noticed the truck bays along the side of the building were all taken, the tractor-trailers being loaded by workers on fork-lifts. Business was booming, she thought, as she approached the entrance.

Two guards holding AK-47s stopped her from entering the building.

"I'll have to search you first," one of the men said.

She rolled her eyes. "They did that already at the gate entrance."

"I'm sorry, *señora*. Just following orders."

Inez nodded, handed the guard her bag. He inspected it thoroughly.

"Please hold out your arms," the man said.

Grudgingly she complied, and allowed herself to be patted down by the other guard.

She went into the building, where she was escorted by a young woman into an empty conference room.

Minutes later a tall, slender man with slicked-back hair entered the room. Manuel Rodriguez. They had met once, briefly, at a business dinner her husband had hosted. He was dressed in a corduroy shirt and jeans.

"*Señora* Sanchez," Rodriguez said with a phony grin. "You honor me with your visit." He extended his hand and the two shook.

He motioned to the conference table. "Why don't we sit? Would you like coffee? Or tequila, perhaps?"

Inez sat across from him. "No," she said curtly.

"I'd like extend my sincere condolences on your husband's passing," the man said. "A tragic thing."

She nodded, but didn't reply.

Rodriguez propped his feet up on the table and she noticed he was wearing hand-tooled, silver-toed boots. "So, *señora*, may I ask why you are here?"

She leaned forward. "You gave me no choice, you bastard. You didn't return any of my calls."

He shrugged. "I've been very busy. You know how it is...."

Inez slapped her hand across the table, knocking the man's feet to the floor.

"You need to treat me with respect, Rodriguez. Starting right now."

His face flushed red and he gripped his chair's armrests.

"You're lucky you're a woman. Otherwise I'd kill you for doing that."

Inez let out a harsh laugh. "You don't have the *cojones*."

A puzzled look crossed his face. It was clear he was only used to dealing with pliable women.

"How long have you been a distributor for my husband's business?" she asked, her voice cold.

"Eight, nine years."

"Didn't Hector treat you fairly in all that time?"

"Yes, of course. Your husband was a man of his word."

She placed her hands flat on the table. "I also keep my word, and I've taken over his business."

"A woman?" he said with a crooked grin.

"Yes, a woman."

"I don't know, *señora*. This is a tough business."

She slapped him hard across the face.

Startled, he pulled back from her. He cocked his fist to strike back, but stopped himself.

"Where do you get your product, Rodriguez?"

"From your company," he said, rubbing the red mark on his cheek.

"Accept it. You work for me."

Rodriguez eyes were full of hate, but he said nothing, obviously trying to process the situation.

Inez leaned back in the chair. "Why don't we start over? I'm a reasonable woman. You show me respect and I'll show you the same."

He studied her closely for along moment. Nodding, he said, "I agree. I need you and you need me."

"Good, *Señor* Rodriguez. And let's drop the formality. Call me Inez from now on."

"Of course, Inez."

She played with the diamond brooch on her neck.

"How are things going, Manuel? I saw your loading bays are full of trucks."

"My business is strong, *señora*. The *gringos* across the border have an insatiable appetite for the coke and fentanyl."

"Excellent. You're an important part of my business. Out of my fifteen distributors, you're one of my largest. How is the counterfeit money operation going?"

He smiled. "Very profitable."

"Good. Very good."

Rodriguez glanced at his watch.

"I have to check on an important shipment, Inez. But I would be honored if could stay for dinner at my *hacienda* tonight. We could discuss business and get to know each other better. In fact, I have many guestrooms. You would be more than welcome to stay, and start your trip back tomorrow. How does that sound?"

She mulled that over and realized the idea fit into her plans.

"What a lovely gesture, Manuel. I accept."

***

"Would you like more cognac?" Rodriguez asked, holding up the bottle of Courvoisier.

"Of course," Inez replied and he poured them another round.

After an elaborate, six-course dinner, Rodriguez had suggested an after-dinner drink in his lavish study. Floor-to-ceiling book cases lined every wall, and they were full of old and she suspected very rare books.

Although it was not a cold night, nevertheless the massive fireplace was burning, giving off comforting warmth.

Rodriguez opened a silver box, took a cigar out and offered it to her.

She shook her head and he lit up, began puffing.

"There is nothing better than a Cuban cigar," he said between puffs.

Inez took a sip of cognac. "Hector used to say the same thing."

"I miss him, Inez. He was my mentor in many ways. Taught me a lot about the drug trade."

"I miss him too, as do the children."

"His death was so sudden. I always thought he was such a healthy man."

She shook her head slowly. "Life is fragile. But let's not dwell on the past. Let's focus on what lies ahead."

He lifted his glass. "To the future!"

"To the future," she repeated, taking another sip of the Courvoisier. Putting it down, she lifted the bottle and refilled his glass.

Rodriguez gave her a contrite smile. "I'd like to apologize for my rude behavior earlier today. I was way out of line. But, I'm sure you realize, like Hector did, that running a large, complex operation such as yours is no easy task. But if you had someone you could trust, really trust, to partner with you, it would make your life easier."

"What are you suggesting, Manuel?"

His eyes sparkled with intensity, and his intention was quite clear. "A much closer relationship between us."

"Hector just died. The thought of another man sharing my bed is...difficult."

Rodriguez puffed on the cigar and blew out the smoke. He covered her hand with his. "Think of it as a partnership. You are a woman alone. Your children need a father figure. I could give you the companionship you need. I could help you run your business." He rubbed her hand slowly. "You are a beautiful woman. An intelligent woman. You just need a man to share your life with."

She sipped the cognac.

"You're a persuasive man. I can see why my husband trusted you."

Rodriguez smiled. "You can trust me also."

She placed the glass on the side table. "I believe I can."

"I take that as a yes?" he asked, anticipation in his voice.

Inez nodded.

"Would you like another drink, *señora*?"

"No, I think I've had enough."

He stood and held out his hand.

"In that case, Inez, why don't we seal the deal?"

***

189

Inez lay on the king-size bed, hating herself for what she'd just done.

Next to her on the bed was Rodriguez, sound asleep, his nude body tangled in the sheets. The bedroom was dimly lit, but even so, she thought the pig had a self-satisfied smirk on his face, and she hated herself even more.

Rodriguez was snoring and he smelled of sex and booze and cigar smoke. She couldn't wait for it to be all over so she could take a long, hot shower to wash off his stink.

Slowly, she pushed the sheet off of her, and as quietly as possible, got off the bed. The room was cool and goose-bumps rose on her naked skin. But instead of donning her negligee, she rummaged through her overnight bag which lay on the floor at the foot of the bed. Finding her leather gloves, she put them on. Then she searched the bag for a second item.

Imbedded in the inner lining of the bag she found what she was looking for. A long, thin metal wire.

Although she had never learned to play the Steinway grand piano Hector had bought for her years ago, the damn thing was finally good for something.

Stretching the piano wire taut between her hands, she padded back to Rodriguez's side of the bed. Still snoring, the man's filthy scent repulsed her.

On the nightstand was the empty bottle of Courvoisier. Before the sex, she'd made sure he drank all of it, urging him to finish it, appealing to his macho male pride. She had known it would make her job easier, later on.

Crouching on her knees, she slowly looped the wire behind his neck. She crossed the wire at the front, by his Adam's apple, and with all her strength, jerked the wire tight against his throat.

His blood-shot eyes snapped open, his hands reaching for his throat.

Inez pulled tighter, the wire cutting into his skin, drawing blood. His eyes bulged and his feet kicked against the bed. He tried to push her away, but he'd had too much to drink, making his efforts weak and uncoordinated.

Her arm muscles stretched to the breaking point, she persisted, pulling the wire even tighter.

Rodriguez let out a sick, grunting noise and his body sagged. But instead of letting go, she kept up the pressure.

Ignoring the pain in her arms, she relished the death of the pig in front of her.

Eventually she released the piano wire and slumped to the floor. She lay on the thick carpet, staring at the ceiling and trying to catch her breath.

After a minute she sat up and stared at the corpse.

"You bastard," she spit out. "I could have never trusted you. Never in a million years."

Standing, she went to the bathroom to take a shower.

Afterward she dressed, put on her makeup, and plucked her cell phone from her bag. Scrolling through the stored numbers, she selected the one for Oscar Cruz, the President of Mexico.

"This is Inez Sanchez," she told the president's personal assistant. "Tell Oscar I need his help now. I need a military escort to pick me up at this location." She read off Rodriguez's address in Juarez.

"*Si, señora*," the young man responded. "Is there anything else?"

"Yes, one other thing. Also send a morgue wagon. There's been a tragic accident."

"*Si, señora.*"

Chapter 34

Atlanta, Georgia

"Enough already!" Ryan said.

Lauren stood by the bed, her hands outstretched with the pill bottle and a glass of water. "The doctor said —"

"Screw that. I've had enough of this crap."

"Please, J.T. It's only for a few more days."

He flung off the covers and got up from the bed. "No. That's it."

"J.T.," she pleaded. "It's too soon."

"I'm going crazy, Lauren. I've got to get back to work."

She put the glass and bottle on the nightstand and folded her arms across her chest.

"No you're not. I won't allow it."

"Who are you, my mother?"

"Please, J.T."

He tried to walk around her to get to the closet, but she moved to block his way.

Shaking his head slowly, he said, "My mind's made up, okay?"

She frowned, her shoulders slumped and she stepped aside.

Ryan went to the walk-in closet and put on a button-down shirt, dress slacks and his navy blazer. Grabbing his holstered S & W pistol from the top shelf, he clipped it to his belt.

When he came out Lauren was sitting on the bed, hands folded on her lap, her eyes moist.

"I'm sorry," he said. He turned and left the bedroom.

***

He drove the Acura to downtown Atlanta and parked in the lot of the Secret Service office building. When he climbed out, he inspected his badly-dented and scratched car. He hadn't had time to get it fixed after his run-in with the Range Rover. Luckily, the thing still ran, although some of the dash warning lights were glowing red.

After going through the layers of security in the building, he was escorted by a male agent to Erin Welch's corner office. It was a sunny, clear day, and sunlight spilled into the well-appointed room.

Erin looked up from her desk.

"J.T. ... didn't think I'd see you back so soon."

They shook hands and he sat across from her.

"I'm feeling great," he lied. Actually he felt weak and a little disoriented, but he wasn't about to admit it.

"Good to hear." She closed the lid on her laptop and pushed it aside on the desk.

"What's new on the case, Erin?"

She shrugged. "Not much. The Moscow cops are still giving us the runaround. The State Department's been leaning on them, but so far, we got nothing."

"Crap. I'd love to know the Russian connection to this damn thing."

"You and me both."

He glanced out the window, saw a few commercial flights circling overhead, no doubt waiting to land at the world's busiest airport a few miles south of the city.

"Can you get the Director of the Secret Service involved?" he asked. "Have him try to get the information from the police in Moscow?"

"Did that already. We're hitting a brick wall."

He rubbed his jaw. "This smells bad. Something's going on, that's for sure."

"I agree."

193

"What's the situation on Amati, Erin?"

The agent's face scrunched, as if she'd swollen a bitter lemon. "The *carabinieri* have been looking for him for over a week. He's vanished."

"Jesus. Nabbing him would be the big break we need."

She nodded. "The Italian cops and the FBI have searched his home and office. They've questioned his wife and the people at his company. Nothing."

Ryan stood, began pacing the office. "I can't sit around and wait for something to happen. I've got to make it happen."

"Like what?"

He stopped, looked down at her.

"Go over there. Find the son-of-a-bitch."

"You think that's a good idea? You just got out of the hospital."

"Got a better idea?" he asked.

Erin didn't respond, and a moment later shook her head.

He sat on the chair, leaned forward. "Call Paul Adams in Rome – tell him I'm coming over."

Chapter 35

Moscow, Russia

Dimitri Petrovich sat tensely in the back seat of the S-Class Mercedes, as it made its way through heavy traffic on the way to the Kremlin. His thoughts churned on the upcoming press conference. So much was riding on it.

As usual it was a dreary, gray day, with a heavy snow falling. The plow trucks were out in full-force, pushing the dirty snow unto the sidewalks, impeding pedestrians as they scurried to work. The clanging of the trucks echoed loudly, filtering into the limousine.

"You finished the report we talked about yesterday?" he asked Olga, his new assistant, who sat next to him in the car. The dowdy, overweight Ukrainian woman was a far cry from Karina, but she would do for now. After the press conference, he would have time to find a more suitable replacement.

Olga shuffled through her notes. "Almost, Mr. Petrovich. It'll be done by the end of the day."

He gave her an irritated look. "See that it is."

The car slowed and Petrovich looked out the window. They were just outside the Kremlin's looming, red-brick walls. Built in the 15th century, the massive 50-foot high walls with the intricate turrets gave the gray city a historical flair that it otherwise lacked. Or so thought Petrovich, a history buff since childhood.

Their car approached the front gate and waited behind a long row of similar black limos. They were all there, he was sure, for the much anticipated conference. Amati had done a good job of marketing it in advance. It had been the top news item for a week.

Finally their car reached the gate and the driver handed the armed guard their invitation, authorized by Prime Minister Chernov. The guard read it carefully, scanned it with a hand-held wand, and waved them to the security staging area. Here the cars were inspected for explosives and the occupants searched for weapons. Bothersome to say the least, the security measures were necessary, the oil man knew, because of ever-present terrorists threats.

Finally done, the car drove through the Kremlin grounds and up to the Presidential Palace, its white and gold arches and green roof covered with a coating of the grayish snow. They went down into the underground parking area and parked.

Petrovich turned to Olga.

"You'll have to wait for me here. Only VIPs are allowed into the conference."

"Yes, sir," she replied.

"Put the time to good use," he said icily. "Finish the report."

"Yes, Mr. Petrovich."

He climbed out and made his way to the elevators, where Russian Army soldiers once again checked the IDs of the incoming guests.

***

The massive auditorium was filled to capacity. It was the largest room at the Palace, with seating for over five thousand. The crowd consisted of high-level Russian government officials, elected congressmen, military officers, business leaders, and media from around the world. At the front, brightly lit by numerous TV camera lights, was the podium and a table behind which the speakers were already seated.

It was noisy in the crowded room, and hot from the lights. Petrovich tugged at his tie and loosened the top button of his shirt. He was seated in the twentieth row of the auditorium, well back from camera range. His involvement in the plan would remain secret, as he and Chernov had always intended. The limelight belonged to others. The oil man only wanted the money. And to be a power behind the scenes.

From his vantage point he could clearly make out Ivan Chernov, sitting next to President Lazarenko. Chernov's balding, gray hair and weathered Slavic features were a stark contrast to the president's youthful appearance. The thirty-five year old Lazarenko, with his stylish Seville Row suit, closely-cropped blond hair and blue eyes, looked more like a movie actor than a politician. An empty suit, Petrovich had always thought. But a dangerous one, because the president believed he was always the smartest man in the room, when in fact he was a Moscow University drop-out with an average IQ.

Petrovich scanned the news cameras that were trained on the podium. Among the cluster of Russian news crews, he also spotted three cameras with Amati's company logo. That alone would guarantee worldwide coverage of the event.

The Chairman of the State Duma was standing on stage behind the podium, speaking at length about the current state of the Russian economy. As head of the Russian parliament, his function today was to simply introduce the president. But the chairman, a long-winded and wily politician, was taking the opportunity to campaign for the never-ending cycle of future elections. Petrovich ignored the man, impatient for Lazarenko's speech to begin.

Eventually, the chairman concluded his remarks and introduced the president.

Lazarenko stood quickly and grabbed the microphone, obviously tired of the other man's bluster.

The president smiled widely, showing off his perfectly-capped teeth.

The crowd clapped and cheered.

To Petrovich's consternation, Lazarenko was hugely popular.

"Fellow citizens and guests from around the world," the president began. "As you know from the news reports, I am here to make a major announcement regarding the financial state of our country. And in fact, this announcement will impact not just Russia, but other nations in Europe, the Americas and Asia. But before I do that, I'd like take this opportunity to give you some background on the financial crisis that has plagued our economy, and the world's economy, for over a year." He went on to describe, in detail, the high rate of inflation and its negative impact on the economy.

Petrovich noticed the speech was extremely well written, beyond the capacity of the president. A clever writer well-versed in economics must have created it, the oil man thought. The speech was transcribed to the teleprompter screens in front of Lazarenko, making it easy for the president to read. Nevertheless, Petrovich had to give the man credit. Lazarenko's verbal delivery was authoritative and flawless, a likely reason for the man's popularity.

"The present financial crisis must be corrected," Lazarenko continued, "and we must do it now, before the world plunges into a depression as deep as was experienced during the 1930s. As you know, the central banks and governments of the leading economic powers have tried to deal with this issue for a long time." He paused, obviously for effect. "But they have failed. We are no better off now than we were six months ago. In fact, the food riots that we see routinely have spread to cities across the world, including here in Russia." He paused again and frowned. "This cannot be tolerated. This cannot continue. The future of our country, the future of the world depends on bold, decisive action."

Petrovich leaned forward in his seat and the crowd grew silent, anticipating the importance of the president's next words.

Lazarenko smiled and spread out his palms in front of him.

"My friends, I have devised such an action. I have developed a plan which will solve the current financial crisis. My administration's proposal, once ratified by the Russian Duma, will eliminate the horrific ravages of rampant inflation."

He lowered his hands and continued.

"The Russian government will discard the ruble as its monetary unit. We will establish a new currency, a currency that our country will use, and one that other countries around the world can also adopt. The name of this new currency is the Gold-Dollar. And what makes this new paper currency unique is that unlike the ruble, the U.S. dollar, or other world currencies, the Gold-Dollar will be backed by gold."

A hushed silence fell over the crowd, but a moment later the audience began to clap their approval, building to a thunderous roar.

When the clapping subsided, Lazarenko continued. "As you know, Russia is a major producer of gold bullion; in fact our ore reserves are the second largest in the world. Because of this, we, unlike other countries, have the capacity to create this new currency. And what makes the Gold-Dollar unique is that unlike the U.S. dollar, it will always have an intrinsic value. With U.S. dollars and other currencies, more and more is printed every day, with nothing to back them up, creating massive inflation."

The president paused and smiled. "I would like to extend an invitation to all the governments from around the world. Join us. Adopt the Gold-Dollar for your currency. You will see a dramatic reduction in inflation. Your citizens will once again be able to lead productive lives and not fear they won't be able to afford bread, and milk, and gasoline."

The clapping began again, and the crowd rose to its feet.

Lazarenko smiled widely.

When the applause subsided, he said, "I'll be glad to take your questions, now." He pointed to the CBS reporter on the first row. "John, you can be first."

As the questions began, Petrovich leaned back in the seat, relaxing for the first time of the day. The president had presented the Alliance's secret plan flawlessly, he mused.

Petrovich's thoughts turned to his own future. With the announcement now made, the price of gold on the open market would skyrocket. The value of his personal holdings would grow exponentially, and continue to grow after the Gold-Dollar became fully established. Before this, he had been a rich man – now, he would be worth billions. He savored the moment, knowing his life had changed forever.

Chapter 36

Rome, Italy

Ryan stared out the window of the Fiat and zipped up his windbreaker. It was a cold day in Rome and the car's heater didn't work.

He turned toward FBI agent Paul Adams, who was driving the car. "You should trade-in this beater. Get a decent car."

"I told you before," Adams said, as he down-shifted the manual drive transmission into third gear. "This city's an expensive place to live. I'm on a ramen noodle diet as it is."

Ryan nodded, stared out again. They were on the Via Giulia, headed north. The traffic-choked avenue followed the Tiber River as it weaved its way through the Trastevere district. He noticed the level of the river was much lower than when he'd been here last – they must be having a dry winter.

"Erin filled me in on Amati," Ryan said. "Said he's gone aground."

Just then a motorcycle cut in front of them.

Adams slammed on the brakes and leaned on the horn. "Damn Italians!" he snapped. He sped up and shifted into second. "Yeah. Vincento Amati is gone. I went with the *carabinieri* to pick him up, but he wasn't at home and no one knows where he is."

"You questioned his family?"

"Of course, J.T. You don't think I know how to do my job?"

Ryan chuckled good-humoredly. "I won't answer that, on the grounds it'll piss you off."

Adams shook his head slowly. "Enough with the jokes. You're getting on my nerves."

"Okay. You go to his place of business?"

Adams slowed the car as it approached an intersection. "Yeah. He runs a media company. I interviewed his employees — the managers and other staff — nobody's seen him or heard from him in weeks."

"They telling the truth?"

"No way to know for sure. But from what I've learned, they're highly paid. They have a lot to lose if Amati goes to prison."

Ryan tried to get comfortable on the thinly-padded seat. "What's your next step?"

"We got the green light from the Italian government to tap his phone at home and work. Apparently they want to catch him as much as we do. Anyway, the taps are in place now. If he makes contact, we hope to trace it back to his location."

"You think he's in Italy?"

Adams frowned. "No telling. Amati's a rich man. He could be anywhere."

"So, basically, you don't have any leads."

The agent didn't reply, his eyes focused on the heavy traffic. He took a left onto Via Cicerone.

"That's about it, J.T. We wait for Amati to make a slip and call in."

"Not much of a plan," Ryan said with a wry grin.

A moment later they reached the Givani Hotel and Adams double-parked by the front entrance.

Ryan grabbed his bag from the back seat. "Thanks for the lift."

The agent nodded. "What are you going to do now?"

"Check in and grab a good meal. Alitalia serves crap food on their flights."

"Then?"

"I'll let you know, Paul. But I'm not big on waiting."

***

Ryan started up the Hertz rental car and cranked up the heater. The VW Jetta was as plain as a brown paper bag, but at least the heater worked.

Easing the car out of the hotel parking lot, he found the Via Nomentana and took it to the outskirts of the city. He'd gotten directions to Amati's estate from Adams, and as he wound his way through the exclusive neighborhood, he admired the sprawling Mediterranean-style homes that lined the wide streets.

Amati's wall-enclosed estate was set well back from the road, with a paved drive leading to the gated entrance. He stopped the car by the speaker box mounted to the side of the ornate, wrought-iron gate.

Pressing the button, he said in Italian, "I'm John Ryan. The Italian police made an appointment for me to see *Signora* Amati."

"Let me check," came back the response. A moment later he heard a click and the gate slowly opened with a whirring sound.

He drove through, passing elaborate gardens and fountains. A tennis court, an Olympic-size pool, and several outlying buildings also lined the winding road.

Stopping in the semi-circular driveway in front of the massive, three-story Mediterranean-style estate, Ryan turned off the VW. Climbing out, he walked up the steps to the portico and pressed the bell.

A young, pretty woman in a maid's uniform opened the front door.

"This way," she said. She led him through the lavish home, her low heels clicking on the marble floors.

He was shown to a spacious room filled with 17th century Baroque furniture. All the pieces were gilt-trimmed wood with overstuffed brocade fabric. She asked him to wait and left.

Gilt framed oil paintings hung on the walls, depicting historical scenes of King Emmanuel in a variety of battle scenes. Ryan remembered Emmanuel was the person who had unified Italy from a cluster of fiefdoms into a country.

"*Signore* Ryan," he heard a woman's voice from behind him.

Turning, he saw a thin, unattractive woman with a pinched face approach, her hand extended.

"*Signora* Amati," he replied, and they shook. Her hands felt cold and bony.

She waved them to the couches. "Please, sit."

Ryan nodded, and sank onto the thickly-padded sofa. "Thank you for seeing me."

She had hooded eyes and a hooked nose and was dressed in a simple black dress that covered her from her neck to her ankles.

"As if I had a choice," she said curtly. "The police insisted."

Ryan smiled. "That may be so, but I still appreciate it." He leaned back in the couch, sinking deeper on the upholstery. "You have a lovely home."

She sniffed. "Get on with it. I don't have time for small talk."

Ryan realized charm wouldn't work on this woman. She was cold as ice and twice as hard.

He leaned forward in the seat. "Your husband has been missing for weeks. Do you know where he is?"

"I told the *carabinieri*. He left. I haven't heard from him since."

Ryan studied her face for a sign of a tell that she was lying. But he didn't spot one. "How long have been married?"

"Thirty years."

"Don't you find it odd – that he left without saying a word?"

She grimaced, said nothing.

"I think you're lying, *signora*."

Her face turned red.

"Tell me the truth, or I'll have the police arrest you."

Her face went from flush to ashen and she stood. "That's enough. Leave now. If you have any more questions, contact our attorneys."

Ryan got up from the sofa. "I'm going to catch him. And when I do, he's going to prison. And if you keep quiet, you're going with him."

She crossed her bony arms across her flat chest. "Out! Out of my house."

"Fine. But this isn't over."

The woman's lips pressed into a thin line, and she turned and stalked out of the room.

A moment later the maid came back.

"*Signorina*," Ryan said to her with a wide smile. "You're very pretty. I'm sure you like *Signore* Amati and that he liked you. A lot, I bet. He's still in Italy, isn't he? In fact, I think he's still here in Rome."

The maid smiled shyly. Then her face went blank, as if realizing she'd made a mistake.

"This way, *Signore* Ryan," she said, pointing to the hallway.

He followed her out, knowing he knew a lot more now than before coming here.

***

Ryan was having dinner at his hotel's restaurant when his cell phone buzzed. Grabbing the phone from the table, he held it to his ear. "This is Ryan."

"J.T., it's Adams."

"My favorite FBI agent."

"Wiseass. Listen, we may have a lead on Amati. He made a cryptic call to his home ten minutes ago. Talked to his wife. Spoke with her for a couple of minutes."

Ryan's adrenaline started pumping. "Where did the call originate?"

"Don't know yet, we're still trying to sort that out."

"Focus on Rome, Paul. He's here somewhere."

"How the hell do you know that?"

"When I went to his house today – just a feeling I got."

"A feeling?"

"Yeah, Paul. Trust me."

There was silence on the line and Ryan said, "You there?"

"Yes, I'm still here. Okay, we'll focus on Rome."

"Good. Call me if you get anything."

"Will do."

The line went dead and he put the phone on the table.

The middle-aged waitress walked up and picked up the empty bottle of Peroni.

"Another beer?" she asked.

"Yes, another one," he replied, picking up his knife and fork and digging into the veal piccata.

Glancing at his watch, he realized it was too late to visit the media company. He'd get a fresh start the next day.

***

Ryan had just returned to the VW in the company parking lot when his cell phone buzzed. Plucking it from his pocket, he leaned against the car.

"Ryan," he said.

"It's Adams. Where you at now?"

"Just finished interviewing Amati's employees."

"Anything?"

"That's a dead end, for now."

"I have a lead," he heard Adams say. "But it's bizarre."

"What is it, Paul?"

"You were right about one thing. Amati called from Rome. But you'll never guess where the call originated."

"You're right, I can't guess."

"Amati called from somewhere in the Vatican."

Ryan pressed the phone tighter against his ear to make sure he was hearing the agent correctly. "The Vatican?"

"Told you it was strange, J.T."

"What the hell would he be doing there?"

"Don't know. I've got a couple of my agents working on that now, trying to figure out a connection."

"Did you get a specific location?"

"No. The Vatican is a huge place — it's not just one building but a whole complex. We haven't been able to pinpoint his location."

Ryan unlocked his car and got in. "Okay. I'll call Erin. She's got a lot of resources at the Secret Service. Maybe she can help."

"Good idea. But listen, no matter where he is there, the place is off-limits."

"What are you talking about?"

"The Holy See is located in Vatican City. It's a sovereign country, not part of Italy. The Italian government has no jurisdiction there. And obviously, neither does the Bureau."

"So the *carabinieri* can't arrest him?"

"No way."

Ryan drummed his fingers on the wheel. "You got to give that bastard Amati credit. He's really thought this through."

"Yeah, he did."

"Okay, Paul. I've got to sort this out. Figure a way to outfox Amati. Let's talk later."

"Later," Adams said and disconnected the call.

Ryan scrolled the stored numbers on his cell and pressed one of them. It rang for a long time and eventually a female voice came on the line.

"It's Ryan," he said. "Rise and shine."

"J.T.," Erin Welch said groggily, "you know what time it is?"

"It's 6 p.m. local time, so it's midnight in Atlanta."

"You better have a damn good reason to wake me up again!" she snapped, irritation in her voice.

"Got a good lead on the case."

"You do?"

"We found where Amati is."

"Hold on," she said, her voice excited now. "I've got to sit up and take some notes." She came back on a moment later. "Shoot."

"Adams traced a call Amati made to his wife. The call originated in Vatican City."

"You're kidding."

"No, it's true. That's why I'm calling. I know the Service has pretty sophisticated equipment. I need you to help Adams pinpoint Amati's location."

"I can do that. I can also lean on the CIA – I've got a contact there – he may be able to help."

"Good. Thanks, Erin."

"But even if we do find out, we can't just barge into the Vatican and arrest him. Even Hitler didn't do that during World War II."

"Yeah, Adams told me all about that."

"What are you planning to do, J.T.?"

"Don't know yet."

"Listen, don't start an international incident."

"I'm a private citizen," he said. "I'm not part of the U.S. Federal government."

"You still work for me," she barked. "If you get caught breaking the law and this thing blows up, it's my ass that's on the line."

"And it's a cute ass, too."

"Damn it, J.T.! Get serious. I'm giving you a direct order. Don't try to arrest Amati in the Vatican. That place is a fortress. They have an army of Swiss Guards protecting the Pope, not to mention private security. I want Amati as much as you do, and I'm going to find a legal way to get him. I'll get the State Department involved. I just need some time."

Ryan's thoughts churned. He wanted Amati badly. The Italian was most likely the mastermind of the sigma operation, and the man ultimately responsible for Steve Nichols's death. And Vatican City was only ten miles from the media company parking lot. So close.

But at the same time, he knew he needed Erin's help.

He didn't want to burn that bridge.

"Okay, Erin. I agree."

"You're not going to shoot your way into the Vatican?"

"That's right, I'm not," he said, his mind beginning to formulate a plan.

"Good. I'll call you later today when I have more information."

The call went dead and he put the phone away.

He sat in the car another ten minutes, fleshing out his plan.

A smile crossed his lips. He'd told Erin what he wouldn't do – but not what he would.

Cranking up the VW, he eased out of the parking lot and merged with the traffic.

Chapter 37

Vatican City
Rome, Italy

Vincento Amati was in his one-room apartment in the bowels of Vatican City, finishing his meager lunch. Today the silent monk had brought a sparse meal consisting of a tuna sandwich and tepid potato soup. He was weary of the food and the place, but knowing it was temporary made it palatable.

Finished, he put the dirty dishes in the sink and sat behind the wooden desk. Turning on the console computer, he tapped in the long series of numbers, now memorized.

The video screen came to life, and as he anticipated, his two partners were already on the video conference call.

As usual, Dimitri Petrovich's face filled the right side of the screen and Inez Sanchez was on the left.

"Dimitri and Inez," Amati said, "good to see you both."

After they exchanged greetings, Amati stated, "Dimitri, I saw President Lazarenko's press conference. You are to be congratulated. The announcement went even better than I had anticipated. It was flawless. The Alliance plan is well on its way to fruition."

Petrovich beamed. "Thank you, Vincento. I agree. Our young president presented the Gold-Dollar in a very convincing manner. Even if he is a moron, he's our moron!" The man guffawed, and was joined by his two partners.

"As you've probably seen on the news," Petrovich added, "the Gold-Dollar concept is being very well received. Key economists in Europe and elsewhere around the world are saying it's a good solution to the financial crisis."

"I agree," Amati said. "The plan is getting good support. I've been working with my media people and, starting today, we will begin running positive news stories about the Gold-Dollar. The news feeds for TV, radio, and internet will be saturated with our coverage in a matter of weeks."

"Excellent," Petrovich replied. "The Russian Duma is beginning to debate its approval, but because Lazarenko is so popular, its acceptance is guaranteed. I expect the Gold-Dollar will be a reality in thirty days, maybe less."

"Good," Amati said. "And on a side note, I'm sure the two of you are aware that gold bullion prices have skyrocketed since the announcement. The three of us are now rich, super-rich. Once the Gold-Dollar is adopted by Russia and its usage spreads, the three of us will become some of the richest people in the world."

Inez Sanchez, who had been fairly quiet since the conference began, spoke up. "I also have good news." She smiled and ran a hand through her long hair. "Since we last talked, I've been able to consolidate my control over my husband's drug cartel. The business is now unquestionably mine and mine alone."

"Very good, Inez," Amati said.

"And I have other positive news," she continued. "I have talked at length to my friend, Oscar Cruz, the President of Mexico. He has agreed to support the Gold-Dollar. In fact, he will be holding a press conference later today, in which he will announce that Mexico will adopt this new currency, replacing the peso." She smiled broadly and both men congratulated her.

"So it appears," Amati said, "that everything is going according to plan. Is there anything else we need to discuss?"

"I see, Vincento," Petrovich said, "that you are still in the same dreary room. What are your plans now?"

Amati leaned forward in his seat. "Do not worry, Dimitri. I have been working on that. In fact, by the end of this week, I hope to be in my new location."

Petrovich nodded. "Somewhere pleasant, I hope."

"For security reasons I won't discuss where it is," Amati replied. "But trust me. It's a very, very nice place."

Chapter 38

Rome, Italy

Ryan was on the Via Pastini, not far from the Pantheon, when his cell phone buzzed. Not wanting to get into a car accident on the busy road, he pulled the VW to the shoulder and stopped the car. An Alfa Romeo sedan blasted its horn as it zoomed around him.

"Ryan," he said, answering the phone.

"It's Erin," he heard the agent say. "Got some info on Amati."

He turned off the car, pressed the phone to his ear. Her voice sounded tinny, the result of the city's notoriously bad cell phone reception.

"Go ahead, Erin."

"My friend at the CIA worked his magic. They were able to trace the phone call to a specific location. It confirms what Adams's people found out earlier. Amati is at the Vatican complex. Building 6. Apparently that building is a dormitory for Vatican City. It houses priests. He's in room 42, which is in a sub-basement of the building."

"Good work, Erin."

The call kicked out for a second, then her voice came back on. "I've got some other information, but it's not good."

"Let's hear it."

"I've been working with the State Department. They've been in contact with the Vatican. The Holy See is neither admitting nor denying that Amati is there. They said they are looking into it, would get back to us."

"Sounds like a stall."

"I think so too, J.T."

"So, what's next?"

"We keep the pressure on. We gave them a deadline of this Friday to respond. Told them it was urgent. That Amati is a known fugitive, wanted not only by us, but by the Italian government."

"What was their response?" Ryan asked.

"They said they would get back to us. They reminded us that the Roman Catholic Church has been around for over two-thousand years. The implication was that it will take them some time to respond."

"I don't know if we can wait, Erin. Amati might find out we're pressuring the Vatican and decide to flee. He'll vanish again. With his kind of money, he could go anywhere."

"I realize that. But I don't want you going in there, guns blazing. I don't want you doing a Rambo and killing a dozen priests, or nuns, or whatever. I don't need that kind of crap on my record. They'll get rid of me so fast I won't know what hit me. Let's give it until next week – that should be enough time for the Holy See to respond."

Ryan thought about this and shook his head slowly. "Frankly, I think we should move now."

"I know you do. But it's my case and I'm in charge. Wait until you hear from me."

"Jesus, Erin," Ryan said. "That bastard's going to get away."

"No he won't. I've been doing this a long time. I won't let Amati gives us the slip."

Ryan thought the woman was being naive, but said nothing.

"Okay, J.T. I'll call you as soon as I hear back from State. In the mean time keep working your other leads."

"Sure," Ryan said, knowing full well there were no other leads. "Talk to you soon."

She hung up and he put the phone away.

Drumming his fingers on the wheel, he watched as a stream of cars and motorcycles whizzed by on the busy road.

It was a sunny day, and bright sunlight streamed into the VW. But his mood was far from sunny.

Amati was going to get away – he was sure of it. The man was too bright not to smell it coming. He probably had eyes and ears all over the Vatican.

Regardless of what he had told Erin, he had to act. Now. Not a week or a month from now, after it was too late. Making a final decision, he turned on the car. Easing back into traffic, he sped away, eager to put his plan in play.

***

Ryan spent a full day doing online research on the Vatican complex.

Finally, his eyes bleary from staring at his laptop screen, he felt as ready as he was going to get.

Glancing at his watch, he knew it was time. It was 7 p.m. and darkness had descended on the city.

Going into his hotel room's bathroom, he stared at his reflection in the mirror.

A black-robed man stared back. The priest's cassock fit him tightly, especially around his large shoulders, but he had no choice. He'd bought the garment from a uniform supply store yesterday, and it was the largest size they had. He tried adjusting the white clerical collar on his neck – it fit snugly, and he tried to loosen it, to no avail. Picking up the small Ruger revolver from the sink countertop, he stuffed it in the cassock's pocket. Next, he grabbed the small bottle, a handkerchief, and pieces of rope, and put them in the other pocket.

Finally, he shrugged on his windbreaker and zipped it up to his neck, which disguised his appearance. He didn't want the hotel staff seeing him dressed as a priest. During his stay at the hotel, he had always worn business clothes.

He headed out of the room, and made his way to the lobby and out to the parking lot.

Finding the black cargo van he'd rented earlier, he opened the door at the back. The cargo bay was empty, save for an industrial, wheeled clothes hamper, covered with a tarp. Satisfied, he slammed the door shut and got in the van. Firing up the engine, he left the area and began his short trip to the Holy See.

Ten minutes later he was in Vatican City.

Driving by the Piazza San Pietro, he noticed St. Peter's towering cupola was well lit. Tourists still milled in the large piazza.

To his right was the Papal Palace, the building where the Pope resided. This area, he knew, was incredibly well protected by an army of Swiss Guards.

Bypassing all that, he took the Via Corridori to the Via Plauto, past a row of historical-looking buildings. He slowed, looking closely at the buildings, remembering the pictures he'd studied online. These buildings were much too ornate to be the modern-looking structures that served as dormitories. At the end of the street, he took a left, and finally found what he was looking for – four drab-looking buildings, five stories each, clustered around a central, grassy courtyard. The courtyard was well-lit by street lamps and men dressed in clerical robes bustled about, obviously in a hurry to get to their destination.

Ryan drove around the street that bordered the courtyard, studying the buildings. All four looked identical, but small placards by the entrances identified them. Finding the right one, he drove to the back of the building using a service road, and parked by the back entrance. There was a parking lot there, with three cars parked in it. Lighting came from streetlamps on black metal poles.

He inspected the back entrance area. Besides a truck loading bay, there was a regular size door, with an ID reader box mounted next to it.

The area was deserted and he knew he could be in for a wait.

He took off his windbreaker and climbed out of the van. After unloading the wheeled clothes hamper, he pushed it slowly toward the regular size door. He stopped five feet from it and leaned on the hamper to wait.

Ryan was rewarded fifteen minutes later, when an elderly, tall priest dressed in black came out of the door, his ID card dangling on a lanyard from his neck. The ID card was the one thing the detective lacked, and he had to improvise.

"Please, father," Ryan called out as he began pushing the cart toward the entrance. "Can you hold the door for me? My hands are full."

The priest gave him a kindly smile and held the door open.

"Thank you, father," Ryan said as he passed the priest and entered the building.

"No problem," the man replied.

Ryan quickly scanned the wide hallway both ways.

There was no one about. He spotted a bank of elevators at the center of the corridor.

Pushing the cart, he made his way there, but his heart sank when he reached them. There was another ID reader by the elevator doors, something he hadn't expected.

"Christ," he uttered in a low voice. Now he had no choice but wait again for someone else to show up.

Pushing the cart to one side of the hallway, he leaned against the wall to wait.

Finally, after what seemed like hours but was only ten minutes, he heard the rumble of the elevator as it made its way down from an upper floor.

He got behind the cart and when he heard the *thunk* of the elevator reach his floor, he began pushing toward the door. As the elevator door slid open, he rolled the cart in, almost hitting a rotund man in brown robes as he tried to step out.

"I'm sorry, brother," Ryan said, recognizing the man was a monk by his brown tunic.

"No problem, father," the monk replied, who looked surprised to see a priest pushing a cart. Ryan had learned during his research that most of the grunt work at the Vatican was done by monks, as opposed to priests, but the uniform supply places he'd visited hadn't carried any monk's tunics. And in any case, being disguised as a priest could also be an advantage, because of the Catholic Church's pecking order. Priests served as supervisors to monks, nuns, and lay people.

Ryan pressed the elevator floor button and the doors slowly slid shut.

As the unit descended to the basement level, Ryan's heart began pounding. He ran a checklist through his mind, visualizing the next five minutes.

He had one chance to get this right. One wrong move and alarms would be sounded, guards would be called. Most likely he'd have to shoot his way out. Something he desperately wanted to avoid. It was one thing to capture a bastard like Amati, but something else entirely to kill or wound innocent men.

The door slid open.

Slowly, he pushed the cart forward, hoping the corridor was empty.

But it wasn't.

Two priests, talking loudly, were coming his way.

Lowering his head, he took a left on the hallway, moving away from them.

But the priests were in deep conversation, an argument actually, talking about some obscure religious artifact, something well beyond Ryan's knowledge.

In any case, the men ignored him as they continued their ardent discussion. He glanced back, saw them board the elevator.

As soon as the elevator doors closed, he turned the cart and pushed it the other way, the direction to room 42. Moving past the closed doors of the other apartments, the dinginess of the place sunk in. The walls were plain gray concrete, the corridor floors the same. Fluorescent light strips cast a harsh pallor over the area, and it smelled damp and musty. Obviously, the priests resided in a very basic environment. Idly he wondered if bishops or cardinals lived in similar apartments, but deep down knew that probably wasn't the case.

The room numbers were painted on the metal doors in simple script and he tensed the closer he got to the right number.

Then he saw it, just ahead on the right.

He pushed the final three feet and rapped on the door.

"Yes?" a muffled voice said through the door.

"Towel and linen change," Ryan replied.

The door swung partially open and a man stood there dressed in a bathrobe. Ryan had studied the photos carefully and recognized the man immediately. Vincento Amati.

"The monk changed my linens earlier today," Amati said in a tired voice.

Ryan shrugged. "Must be some mix-up. I brought you fresh ones."

"Come in," Amati said, opening the door all the way. "But hurry, I'm busy."

Rolling the cart in, Ryan scanned the small room quickly. "I'll be done in a minute, *signore*. Go ahead with your work. Don't mind me."

Amati went to a desk and sat down to face a large computer. He had an email account open, and was in the process of writing one.

Ryan closed the door to the room and went into the tiny bathroom. But instead of collecting the damp towels, he pulled the bottle and handkerchief from his cassock's pocket. Opening the bottle, he poured the chloroform on the cloth and closed the lid. Stuffing both items back in his pockets, he went back into the room.

Amati was still at his desk, but in the process of turning off the computer.

Ryan quickly approached from behind, wrapped one arm around the man's throat. Amati let out a choked-off scream and, his arms flailing, tried to push off the detective.

Ryan squeezed the struggling man harder, and with his free hand, pulled the handkerchief from the pocket. But before he could slap it on the man's face, Amati elbowed him in the gut.

Ryan grunted and stepped back, trying to recover from the blow.

But in that split-second before the detective could attack again, Amati bolted out of the chair and, grabbing the stand-alone computer keyboard, flung it at Ryan.

Ryan, his heart racing, ducked and went into a martial-arts side stance. He hit Amati with a powerful side kick, the blow sending the other man reeling to the floor. The kick had landed on the Italian's face, drawing blood from his mouth and nose.

He rushed Amati and before the groaning man could recover, pressed the handkerchief to his bleeding nose. Moments later the man's body slumped and he went quiet.

After catching his breath, Ryan tied Amati's hands and feet with the rope.

The detective stood, looked around the room. An ID card lay on the wooden table and he picked it up and slid it in his pocket.

Next he turned to the computer. It could be a treasure-trove of information, and he turned it on. But it was password protected. Glancing at his watch, he realized he had to get moving, get out of there before he was found out. He picked up the computer console and disconnected the stand-alone monitor. Lifting the console, he carried it to the linen cart in the center of the room.

Taking the tarp off the cart, he removed the towels and linens he had purchased yesterday, and placed the console into the cart.

Dragging Amati's inert body over, he awkwardly lifted the man and pushed him into the cart. Finally, he threw the sheets and towels over him and pulled on the tarp.

Opening the door, he rolled the hamper into the corridor and reclosed the door.

A group of priests had just gotten off the elevator and were coming his way.

With one hand in his pocket holding the revolver, he lowered his head and began pushing toward the elevators.

The men passed him, their conversation loud. Something about the high price of the restaurant meal they'd just had. Luckily they ignored him and he continued down the corridor.

Pulling out Amati's ID card, he used it to board the elevator.

He rode up to the ground floor and made his way out of the building.

Moments later he was by the van.

The area was still deserted, but he spotted a uniformed guard on the sidewalk, heading toward the back of the building. Although it was a dark night, the streetlights provided good illumination and Ryan noticed the guard was armed.

Quickly opening the cargo doors, he lifted the front end of the now much-heavier cart to the cargo floor. Then he got behind the hamper and lifted the back-end with a groan.

He shoved the cart in, slammed the doors shut.

Racing to the driver's side door, he began to open it, but not before the guard approached him.

"Stop," the guard said, holding up his flashlight. His other hand was touching his holstered automatic. He was a heavy-set man, his uniform stretched tightly across his abdomen.

Ryan held his breath.

"You don't look familiar, father," the guard said. "And I know almost all of the priests that live here."

Ryan smiled widely. "Just delivering linens, my son."

The guard shined the flashlight on the unmarked van. "A priest making deliveries?"

His thoughts racing, Ryan said, "Brother Roberto is sick today – I'm just covering for him."

The guard nodded, but he looked unconvinced. "May I see your ID, father?"

"Of course," the detective replied, reaching into his pocket. He handed it the other man.

As the guard studied the ID with his light, Ryan leapt at him, knocking him off his feet. Ryan landed on top of him, punched him with a left jab to his gut, followed by a wicked uppercut to his jaw.

Pulling the handkerchief from his pocket, he slapped it to the man's face.

The guard struggled, but a moment later went limp.

Ryan glanced around, saw car's headlights approaching from the front of the building.

Dragging the body to the back of the van, he reopened the doors and awkwardly lifted the unconscious guard into the vehicle.

He closed the door, just as an Alfa Romeo pulled into the parking lot, a few cars over.

Climbing in the van, he fired it up and made his way out of the lot.

His adrenaline still pumping, he drove slowly through the Vatican City streets, not wanting to get pulled over for speeding.

But once he saw St. Peter's towering cupola recede in the rear-view mirror, he breathed a sigh of relief and stepped on the gas.

Holding the wheel with one hand, he plucked his cell phone from his pocket and pressed a number. When the call was answered, he said, "It's Ryan. I got him. You ready?"

"Yes," came back the response and he turned off the phone.

He took a right, and a left, and headed out of the city.

A half-hour later he was on the outskirts of Rome, driving north on the A12. Traffic was light on the highway, mostly passenger cars and a few trucks.

He spotted the sign for the private airfield and took the next exit.

The airfield was visible from the service road, and it didn't look like much. Just a long, asphalt airstrip and a row of planes enclosed by a tall fence. There was a small airport tower, but it was dark. The only illumination came from the airstrip lights and some security lamps on the fence. The place seemed deserted, but as he got closer he noticed an armed guard patrolling the fenced-in area.

Ryan slowed the van and approached the runway. Sitting on the tarmac was a silver-color Gulfstream G500 with no markings except for the tail number. Not far from the plane he noticed a parked Fiat.

The Gulfstream was situated on the far side of the airstrip and he drove toward it.

As soon as he pulled up next to the plane, its lights came on and its twin jet engines whirred on to a high-pitched whistle.

Ryan turned off the van and got out.

The plane's side door slid open and a metal staircase unfolded to the ground. A man he didn't recognize climbed down, and stood at the foot of the staircase. He studied Ryan closely and spoke into his ear-piece.

A moment later FBI agent Paul Adams climbed down from the plane, a grin on his face.

"Got to hand it to you, J.T. Never thought you'd be able to pull it off."

Ryan extended his hand and the two shook. "Ye of little faith," he said with a chuckle.

Adams nodded. "Let's see him."

The detective opened the van's cargo doors and climbed in. Adams followed.

"Who's that?" Adams said, pointing to the unconscious guard sprawled next to the cart.

"A casualty of war," Ryan said. "But don't worry – he's just knocked out. He'll be awake in an hour."

Ryan pulled the tarp off the cart and removed some of the towels. Amati was there, still unconscious, the blood on his face now dry.

"So this is the great Vincento Amati," the agent said.

Ryan grinned. "He's doesn't look so great now." He pulled the rest of the linens off the man, and grabbed him by the shoulders. "Help me carry him to the plane," he said.

Adams picked up the Italian by his bound feet and together they lifted the body out. With the agent grunting, they carried Amati to the jet, up the steps and into the plane.

They sat him on one of the leather buckets in the passenger compartment and buckled the seatbelt.

Ryan glanced around the plush cabin. "Nice bird. What's a Gulfstream like this run? It can't be cheap."

"Your tax dollars at work, my friend."

Ryan nodded and slumped into the seat across from Amati.

"What do I do with the other guy?" the agent asked.

"I'm sure there's some bottles of booze on this plane. Take one with you. On your way back to Rome, lay him out in an out-of-the-way place. Pour the booze on him. He'll wake up, confused as all hell. But he'll stink of liquor and may not even report what happened."

Adams gave him a wry smile. "Funny, I would have never thought of doing that."

"Listen. There's something else. In the laundry cart, there's a computer. Amati's. It's password protected, but maybe your people can break through. I'm sure there's important info on it."

Adams nodded. "Got it."

"Do me a favor, will you? Return my rental vehicles – the van and the VW – back to Hertz. And check me out of the hotel. You can send me my things later."

"No problem, J.T.," the agent said. "The pilot will fly you direct to Atlanta."

"Thanks, Paul."

The two men shook hands again and the agent turned and went to the cockpit. He left the plane soon after.

The whine of the jet engines grew into a muffled roar. Ryan buckled his seatbelt and stared out the oval window.

The jet rolled forward on the airstrip, picking up speed. Soon it was hurtling down the runway, and a moment later shuddered as it took off.

Ryan was pressed into his seat as the powerful engines angled the plane up into a steep climb.

In the distance, the lights of the city glowed brightly, but soon after they receded into tiny points.

He closed his eyes, eager to get home.

Chapter 39

Atlanta, Georgia

Sunlight streamed into Erin Welch's downtown office, as the agent paced the room.

Ryan leaned back in one of the visitor's chairs.

"Relax, Erin," he said. "He'll talk. Eventually."

"I don't know, J.T. We've had Amati in custody for almost a week and still nothing."

He studied the blonde as she kept retracing her steps.

"I saw the article in the paper," he said. "You got some major kudos for bringing in Amati. Catching the man responsible for the death of two FBI agents is a big deal. I'd be surprised if you didn't get a promotion out of this."

She stopped pacing, faced him. "You're the one who caught him."

"Yeah," he said with a smile. "But the press doesn't know that. And that's fine with me. I don't want the publicity. I just want to solve this case."

Erin nodded. "Me too. But we've got to get Amati to open up. The FBI guys have questioned him several times, as have I."

"You ought to let me have a crack at him."

She shook her head. "This is the U.S. He's in Federal custody. You can't just go in there and kick him in the balls, or water-board him, or whatever else you do."

Ryan smiled. "Don't worry. I'll play nice."

"Bullshit!"

Just then Ryan's cell phone buzzed and he answered it. He heard static from the other end. A man's voice broke through, sounding tinny and faraway.

"It's Paul Adams," he heard the FBI agent say.

"Hey, Paul. How are things in Italy?"

"Could be better, J.T. Remember the computer Amati had?"

"Sure."

"Our tech guys have been working on it, trying to break through the password protection and access the files."

"Tell me you have good news."

"Afraid not," the agent said. "We got it turned on, but the computer must have had some high-tech security software program installed. After we tried a series of passwords to get into the files, the hard-drive crashed. The passwords we used were obviously wrong, triggering the crash. They've tried everything to recover the data, but the thing is fried."

"So you got nothing."

"That's right, J.T. We got nothing."

Ryan's heart sank.

He looked up at Erin, who was going around her desk to sit down.

"Okay," Ryan said. "If you're able to salvage anything, let me know. We have a lot riding on that."

"Don't get your hopes up," Adams replied before he hung up.

Ryan put his phone away. "That was Adams."

"Bad news, I gather," Erin said.

"Yeah. Amati's computer fried itself. Some built-in security program."

Erin grimaced. "We're screwed."

"We are. Now we need to break Amati more than ever."

She placed her hands flat on the desk. "I'm going over to the jail later today," she said. "I'll take another run at him."

"Good luck. Remember, if you need help, you've got my number."

She nodded. "I'll keep that in mind. By the way, there's something else we need to talk about."

"You're giving me a raise?"

"No," she replied, her voice stern. "You signed a contract. You're fee is set."

He laughed. "Yeah, I know. Just thought I'd lighten the mood."

"This is serious."

He held up his palms. "Sorry."

"You remember Markov?" she asked. "The Russian guy?"

"Sure. I'll never forget that bastard."

"We never got the Moscow police to cooperate on him, and I've got a pretty good hunch why."

Ryan raised an eyebrow.

"I assume you've been watching the news, J.T.?"

He nodded.

"You've probably seen what happened in Russia," she said. "Their president announced the creation of a new paper currency. The Gold-Dollar, which will be backed by gold."

"I heard."

"Well, I think Markov's attempt to take you out and President Lazarenko's new currency may be linked. Somehow the sigma conspiracy, the counterfeit money, Amati, and Lazarenko are all connected."

He mulled that over a moment. "It makes sense. I also saw that Mexico was the first country to announce they would be adopting the Gold-Dollar when it's issued. There's probably a connection back to Sanchez."

"I agree. The Mexicans are knee-deep in this thing."

"Okay," he said. "Now we have a pretty good idea what sigma is all about."

She tucked her long hair behind her ears. "Yes. The conspiracy pumped billions of counterfeit U.S. dollars and other currencies into the world markets. Inflation soared. These currencies are becoming worthless. We have a worldwide financial panic. Enter the Gold-Dollar. Backed by gold. Lazarenko said they'll start issuing the new money in a matter of weeks. We've already seen Mexico, and several European and Asian countries say they'll switch to it also. The Gold-Dollar is getting very good press, in Europe and here in the States. The damn thing is building momentum."

"You'll have to excuse me, Erin, but I'm no economics expert. What's the big deal if that happens? Couldn't the U.S. adopt it also?"

The agent frowned. "It's not as simple as it sounds. If we switched to the Gold-Dollar, the U.S. economy would be at the mercy of the Russians. If the Russians control the currency markets, they could dictate the world's economy. Oil, metals, raw material, food, would all be priced in Gold-Dollars."

"So why don't we be back the U.S. dollar with gold?"

She shook her head. "The Russians have one of the world's largest gold reserves. They are the second largest producer. And now there's a shortage of gold, worldwide. We couldn't get our hands on that much if we wanted to. I've been watching the Congressional hearings in Washington on the crisis. From what was said, the U.S. is running such a massive budget deficit that it wouldn't be feasible anyway."

"Sounds bad."

"It is."

Ryan rubbed his jaw. "And if the U.S. does nothing?"

"The crisis gets worse," she answered. "Counterfeit dollars are still flooding into the States. We're getting reports from our field offices every day. The more fake money that comes in, the less value the real currency has. Inflation is spiraling out of control."

Ryan went quiet, his mind processing everything the agent had told him. Finally he said, "So what do we do?"

"I don't know, J.T. I just don't know."

Chapter 40

Atlanta, Georgia

Ryan was at the Varsity restaurant having lunch when his cell phone buzzed. Putting down his chili dog, he took the call. "Ryan."

"It's Erin Welch," he heard her say.

He was sitting at a window table that overlooked I-75. Heavy mid-day traffic whizzed past on the freeway below. "Some good news, I hope?"

"I'm afraid not, J.T. The Bureau guys and I just finished talking with Amati again. He's not budging. Won't say a word. It's not looking good."

"How long have you been at it?"

"Two weeks," Erin said.

"Listen, you've got to let me at him. I swear I won't torture him. I just need you to find out some information for me."

"Against my better judgment, I'm going to let you. We're running out of time. The Russians are getting a lot of support for the Gold-Dollar. More and more countries are jumping on board. If the trend continues, the U.S. may not have a choice. We may have to adopt it." There was a pause on the other end, then she said, "What information do you need?"

Ryan took a sip of his Coke. "The Italian government was very cooperative with us. It seemed like they were eager to catch Amati. I need to find out why."

"Okay. I'll do research. Anything else?"

"Yeah. Get as much info as you can about Amati's wife. Her background, what kind of relationship she had with Vincento, that kind of thing."

"I'll get it."

"Good. Call me later?"

"Will do," Erin said. She ended the call and he put the phone away.

He went back to eating his chili dog and fried onion rings.

As usual, the food was greasy, but also delicious. He'd worry about the heartburn later.

***

Ryan was on the 400, driving north in his rented Toyota Camry, listening to music on the radio. He missed his Acura, which was still in the body shop – it wouldn't be ready for another week.

His cell phone buzzed and he picked it up and took the call.

"It's Erin," he heard her say. "Where are you now?"

"On the road," he replied, his eyes focused on the stream of traffic all around him. "Heading up to Lauren's place."

"Give her my regards," the agent said, her voice dripping with sarcasm.

He grinned. "I will. What's up?"

"I got the info you were looking for."

"Shoot." He pressed the phone to his hear to block out the road noise.

She talked for the next five minutes and he listened carefully, committing everything she said to memory.

When she was done, he said, "Thanks. That's exactly what I needed."

"One more thing, J.T. I made arrangements with the FBI. You can talk to Amati tomorrow at 11 a.m. He's being held at their high-security detention center. It's in the basement of their downtown office."

"I know the place."

"Hopefully, you were doing the questioning, not being questioned."

He laughed. "Now who's the comedian?"

"Turnaround is fair play."

"Touché, Erin."

He hung up and began to look for the right exit off the freeway.

***

"So what happens next?" Lauren said, as she sipped chardonnay from a long-stemmed glass.

"The Feds have tried everything." Ryan replied. "But Amati's clammed up. They're giving me a shot at him tomorrow."

They were sitting next to each other on the sofa in her living room, Lauren resting her head on his shoulder. Smooth jazz was playing in the background.

"What do you plan to do?" she asked.

"I'll play it by ear. Welch got me some interesting info on Amati. I'll have to see how he responds." He lifted his mug of Sam Adams and drank.

She caressed his shoulder with her palm. "I'm just glad you're back."

"Me too."

They stayed like that for a long time, enjoying each other's company.

Eventually his thoughts turned to what tomorrow would bring, and the next day after that. He was hopeful things would turn out well for his country, and for Lauren and himself.

But he knew, maybe better than most, that life was very unpredictable.

Chapter 41

FBI Building
Atlanta, Georgia

Ryan was led into the interview room of the detection center and told to wait by a stone-faced FBI agent. The detective had been here once before, years ago, with Steve Nichols. They had questioned a suspect in a high-profile kidnapping case.

He sat on one of the chairs by the metal table, and took stock of the place. Not much had changed in the drab, windowless room. The same gray walls, the same glary overhead lighting. The place was dank and smelled of strong cleaning solvents. Mounted on the ceiling were two video cameras – Ryan knew the interview was being closely monitored, and taped, by Bureau agents.

Five minutes later Vincento Amati was led into the room by two agents carrying Mac-10s. Amati wore a baggy orange jumpsuit and his hands and feet were shackled.

The agents pushed the Italian onto a chair on the opposite side of Ryan and wordlessly left the room.

He studied Amati closely – the man had aged in the two weeks he had been here. His eyes were sunken, his hair unkempt, and he had a scraggly beard, as if he hadn't shaved in a while.

"*Signore* Amati," Ryan said in Italian. "You remember me?"

Amati stared at him, his face not registering recognition.

"Last time you saw me, *signore*, I was wearing a priest's cassock."

Amati's face lit up with indignation. "You bastard!"

Ryan smiled. "Come, come. You should thank me. I liberated you from that grimy Vatican basement." He waved a hand in the air. "To this much nicer place. I suspect the food is better here."

Amati scowled. He spat at Ryan, the wad of spittle landing on his cheek.

The detective took out a handkerchief and wiped it off. "All right, I was hoping you'd be grateful, but I guess I was wrong."

"What do you want?" Amati snapped, switching from Italian to English. "I've already told the others I'm not talking."

"So I've heard. So I've heard. Well, we'll see about that."

Ryan went quiet and Amati stared at him, his black eyes trying to bore through his skull.

Ryan stared back, his face blank, not saying a word.

As the silence stretched from seconds to minutes, Amati began shifting in his chair, his face perplexed.

In his years in Special Forces Ryan had been taught several interrogation techniques, and he was employing one of them now. The silent treatment. Silence made people uncomfortable, and eventually forced them to say something, anything, to break it.

"What do you want?" Amati blurted out.

Ryan glanced at his watch, counting off the minutes, but said nothing.

"I know my rights!" the Italian shouted.

Ryan yawned.

"I want my lawyer." Amati said. The man kept fidgeting in his chair, his manacled hands tapping on the table.

Still Ryan said nothing.

"What is it? What is it you want?" the Italian pleaded.

After a full ten minutes, Ryan finally spoke. "It's not what I want, Amati. It's what you want."

Amati frowned. "What do you mean?"

"I found out some interesting information about you. Obviously you are a very wealthy and powerful man, back in Italy. But, as you can see from your incarceration here, that isn't helping you right now. Now you're just a common criminal, charged with very serious crimes. Conspiracy to murder two American agents. Counterfeiting, plus a host of other crimes." Ryan knew all this for a fact. "And in addition to that, you will be charged under the Patriot Act for terrorist activities." This last was pure conjecture on Ryan's part, but he felt the added pressure would only help. "You know what that means, Amati? It means you'll be tried in a military court as an enemy combatant. All those fancy lawyers won't help you there."

A deep frown crossed the Italian's face. It was clear he'd heard of the Patriot Act.

Ryan leaned forward in his chair. "The U.S. government will seek the death penalty in your case. And, since you'll be tried in a military court, there's a high probability." He paused for effect. "In fact, it's more than a probability. It's a certainty. Your sentence will be death."

Amati's face turned ashen.

"But that's not your only problem," Ryan added, his voice low.

"No?" the Italian whispered.

Ryan slapped his hand on the table, startling the other man. "No! You have other things to worry about."

"What?" Amati asked, his voice quavering.

"As I told you earlier, I uncovered some interesting things about you. One is that you and the prime minister of Italy don't get along. In fact, Prime Minister Bertoli has hated your guts ever since you opposed his rise in politics. That's why he was so agreeable to having you deported."

Amati looked perplexed, obviously confused where the conversation was going.

"I'm sure you're asking yourself," Ryan continued, "what can Bertoli do now? He's already helped us getting you out of Italy and into our custody. What more could he do?"

Ryan's hand formed into a fist and he pounded the table.

Amati pulled away, his eyes wide.

"Bertoli can do plenty. And he will. Our State Department," Ryan lied, "has had several discussions with him and he is planning on taking further measures against you."

Ryan folded his arms across his chest. "How long have you been married to your wife Livia?"

"What? What does she have to do with it?"

The detective pounded the table again. "How long?"

"Over...thirty years...." Amati muttered.

"Thirty-two years and ten months, to be exact."

"Yes. Leave her out of this. She's a good woman."

Ryan nodded. "She is a good woman. Better than you deserve, my friend. You're always whoring around with your starlets, if you can call them that. But they're whores really. Livia is a devoted wife. You should have treated her with more respect all those years."

Amati didn't reply, his face clouded in fear.

"If you tell us what we want to know," Ryan said, "we'll talk Bertoli out of what he's planning to do."

"What's that?"

"First, he's going to seize all of your assets," Ryan continued. He was fabricating all this, but it sounded very convincing. "The Italian government will take over your media company, your mansions, your bank accounts. You'll be penniless. You won't be able to retain your expensive lawyers. You'll have to make do with a pathetically overworked and underpaid public defender. And Bertoli is going to do something else, something you're not going to like one bit."

"What? Tell me!"

"Bertoli is going to have your wife arrested, brought up on charges of conspiracy to commit murder. I know a little about the Italian justice system. And I know about Italian jails. More like filthy dungeons. She'll be lucky to get out in thirty years, if she lasts that long."

"Livia...he can't do that. She had no part in this."

Ryan pounded his fist on the table again. "He can and he will. Unless you talk, of course. If you talk, we'll convince Bertoli to leave your wife alone."

Amati's shoulders slumped. "What do you want to know?"

"Tell me everything. Sigma. The conspiracy. The counterfeiting. Who else is involved, your partners. I know in general about the Mexican connection and the Russian link, this new Gold-Dollar. But I want specifics: names, locations, everything." Ryan leaned forward again, and his voice turned gentle. "Tell me everything and we'll take the death penalty off the table for you. You'll go to prison of course, but our prisons are a hell of lot better than the Italian kind. And your wife will be spared. Livia will continue to live in your villa in Rome."

Amati's face showed a range of emotions – fear and anger of course, but something else. Compassion for his wife, maybe? Ryan hoped so. A lot was riding on the man's confession.

Amati said nothing as Ryan waited.

Chapter 42

FBI Building
Atlanta, Georgia

Vincento Amati's thoughts raced as he weighed his options. He leaned back in the uncomfortable metal chair and shifted his hands on the table. The heavy metal bracelets that shackled his hands and feet were tight, so tight they almost cut his skin.

But as he stared at the big American man across from him, the physical discomfort was the least of his worries. Amati had expected to face some jail time in the U.S., but since he had hired the best, most expensive lawyers, he estimated he would only do a few years at some minimum-security place. But this business about the Patriot Act scared him. And what Bertoli was planning scared him even more. The Prime Minister despised him and would stop at nothing to have his revenge. Taking over his assets and arresting Livia was something he would do. Without a doubt.

The American kept staring at him, waiting for his response.

Sweat rolled off Amati's forehead. *Could he betray Livia?* The woman had been loyal to him for a lifetime. He visualized her in tattered prison garb, forgotten in some filthy, crowded Italian penitentiary for thirty years.

No, he decided. He couldn't subject her to that.

"I want it in writing," Amati said. "Write down the terms and I'll talk."

The American reached into his briefcase and pulled out a pre-printed form. Then he began filling it in. Afterwards, he signed it. The American pushed the form across the table, along with a pen.

"Sign it," the American said.

Amati read through the document, which looked official. The terms were exactly what the man had described. He awkwardly grabbed the pen and scrawled his name at the bottom.

"Now talk," the American said, picking up the document and putting it in his briefcase. He pulled out a tape recorder and turned it on.

Amati nodded. He began talking, leaving nothing out.

When he was done thirty minutes later, his mouth was parched.

"So," the American said, "this Dimitri Petrovich and Prime Minister Chernov and President Lazarenko are all in on it?"

"Yes."

"And the counterfeit currency was intended to increase inflation and create a need for a gold-based currency like the Gold-Dollar?"

"Yes," Amati replied. "It was all part of the Alliance plan. My plan, and that of my silent partner."

"Who is that?"

"He's an American. His name is Dean Cage."

"The Senator?"

"Yes. That's him."

The American let out a low whistle. "Jesus. Cage is an institution in Washington. Has been a senator as long as I can remember. How was he involved?"

"He has a high-tech company that manufactured the sigma machines," Amati said.

"But what would Cage have to gain?"

"Money. More money than he could ever imagine. The Alliance has made all the partners billionaires."

"Greed," the American said, shaking his head slowly. "It all comes down to greed."

Amati nodded. "Yes."

The American turned off the tape recorder and put it away. The man stood.

"Remember," Amati said, "you guaranteed that Livia will not be arrested."

"Don't worry. She won't. I'm a man of my word."

Amati nodded, relief washing over him.

Chapter 43

Atlanta, Georgia

Ryan turned off the tape recorder and waited for a reaction from Erin Welch.

They were sitting in her office and she had sat silently in rapt attention as she heard Amati's voice describe the sigma operation in detail.

She leaned back in the executive chair. "It's incredible. Lazarenko, Chernov, Petrovich, Cardinal Fiori, Sanchez, Markov. Incredible. And Senator Cage. The audacity of their plan blows my mind."

"Me too," Ryan said.

"You did a hell of job getting that confession."

Ryan smiled. "I told you I was good."

"Don't let it go your head. We still have to figure a way out of this mess. We know a lot, but we still have to figure out a way to stop it."

The detective nodded. "I've been thinking about that."

"By the way, J.T. How'd you get Amati to confess? He's been mute for two weeks."

Ryan reached into his briefcase and pulled out the document Amati had signed. He slid it across the desk and she read through it quickly.

Erin scowled. "What the hell is this? I've never seen this before. The letterhead on this is printed with the FBI logo and address. Who authorized this?"

"Yeah, about that. I had the form printed at one of those quick-print places."

"God, J.T. I give you an inch and you take a mile!"

"It got the job done, didn't it?"

She pursed her lips and scrutinized the form some more. "You signed this. You don't have the authority. You're a contractor! You can't make promises you can't deliver."

Ryan's voice went hard. "I got him to talk. It's up to you to sell it up the chain of command."

Erin frowned, but he could tell her mind was already thinking of a way to do it.

With a finger she stabbed one particular section of the document. "What about this thing with Prime Minister Bertoli. The State Department hasn't made a deal with him."

"You're right, they haven't. I made all that up. Bertoli had no plans to arrest Amati's wife. But I guessed the idea of her arrest would seal the deal with Amati."

She grunted. "Okay, okay. At least I don't have to deal with that." She placed the document on the desk. "I'll work on getting the District Attorney to agree to this thing. And based on what you got in return, he'll probably go for it. For your sake, I hope so."

"Good."

"But we still have a bigger problem. How do we to stop the Alliance plan from taking effect. The Gold-Dollar is going to be adopted by Russia and a host of other countries in a matter of weeks. It's being supported by the World Bank and the IMF. I'm sure the U.N. will back it, once it rolls out. The momentum is building."

Ryan rubbed his jaw. "Like I said before, I've been thinking about that. I've got an idea."

She looked at him skeptically. "Am I going to like it or hate it?"

He smiled. "If it goes well, you'll love it. If it goes south, we're both in deep weeds."

She sighed. "Okay. Let's hear it."

Chapter 44

Atlanta, Georgia

Ryan took a deep breath. Everything hinged on Erin going along with his plan.

"Like you said," Ryan began, "there's only weeks before the Russians come out with the Gold-Dollar. A lot of countries are ready to adopt it. The U.S. may be backed into a corner. We may have to join the new currency, whether we like it or not."

Erin nodded. "I'm with you so far."

"So. We have to act fast. Very fast. We can't wait for the State Department, or the U.N., to act. We have to take matters into our own hands."

"I'm listening, J.T."

"You're probably asking yourself, what can we do?"

"Enough preamble. Get on with it."

"Okay, Erin. We do the only thing we can do. We shine the spotlight of worldwide media coverage on this. Expose the sigma conspiracy. Expose the Alliance. Name names. Lazarenko, Amati, Sanchez, Petrovich, all of them. We have to discredit the Gold-Dollar. We have to discredit the whole financial crisis. The crisis is phony because it was created by the flood of counterfeit money the Alliance produced."

She frowned. "You're saying don't go through the legal channels and try to indict and prosecute the people responsible?"

"That's exactly right. We can do that later, after we've discredited the conspirators."

"Sounds risky, J.T. We'd be going against procedure and protocol."

"Fuck protocol! We've got to fix this, stop it in its tracks. And we only have one shot at it."

The agent folded her arms across her chest, and she went quiet, obviously deep in thought. A minute later she said, "Alright, for arguments sake, let's say we do this. How would we go about it?"

He leaned forward in the chair. "We have to go to the press. Give interviews. Hold a press conference. Invite the media – TV, radio, internet, all of them. Have multiple press conferences. State the facts. Get the word out. When people hear what's been happening for the last year, the basis of the crisis, the Gold-Dollar will be discredited. Countries are going to be livid they were duped into going along with it. Remember, once the flow of counterfeit money stops, the inflation levels will go back to normal, over time. It might take a year or two, but it'll happen."

Erin nodded. "Okay. It's possible it may work."

His voice went hard. "It will work. Trust me."

She tucked her hair behind her ears and went quiet for another minute. "Alright. I'll grant you there's a good a probability that it would derail this new currency. It'll probably work. The problem is, I have to sell this plan it to my superiors, and they'd have to convince the Directors of the Secret Service and the FBI."

Ryan breathed a sigh of relief – Erin was buying into his plan.

But convincing her of the next part was going to be even harder.

"We don't have time for that," he continued. "If we try running this up the flagpole, it'll get tied up in knots. The top people won't want to take risks without studying this for weeks, probably months."

"So what are you suggesting, J.T.?"

"There's only one person who can sell this to the media."

"You, J.T.? I didn't think you liked publicity."

"You're right. I don't. I'm a better doer than a talker. Have been my whole life. It's got to be you. You're perfect for the job. You know more about this conspiracy than anyone else. You could answer any question."

Her mouth fell open. "Me?"

"Sure. You're smart. Intelligent. A good speaker. And you're a beautiful woman. The media will love you."

She shook her head. "I don't know. I'd be taking a hell of a risk. My bosses would kick my ass for going around them."

He smiled. "I've told you before – it's a cute ass."

Her hands formed into fists. "Damn it, J.T.! Stay serious, will you? Jesus!"

"Okay. No more jokes." He leaned back in the chair. "Look at this on the positive side. If it works, you'll get that big promotion you wanted. Your career will skyrocket." He paused for effect. "I could see you being FBI Director one day."

"Really?"

"Sure. You've got the brains and the looks to make it to the top."

The agent went quiet as she thought about it all.

"And there's one last thing to consider, Erin. An important thing. We owe it to the two dead agents to expose this conspiracy. We owe it to Steve Nichols."

Erin said nothing for a long moment. Eventually she nodded. "Okay. I know I'll probably regret it. But okay. I'll go along with your plan."

"Great. Now let me fill you in on the details."

Chapter 45

Atlanta, Georgia

The headquarters of ZNN are downtown, right across the street from Centennial Olympic Park. Ryan had been to the news network several times before, mostly to have lunch with his reporter friend Gary Harris. Gary and Ryan's friendship went way back to their college days. Both had graduated from Georgia State. They had also gone through ROTC together and had received their Army officer's commission at the same time. After that their lives took different paths, Ryan going into active duty, and Gary going into the reserves and the life of a reporter.

Ryan sat tensely in the back of the almost empty studio and watched as Gary interviewed Erin Welch. It was her first interview with the press, and probably the most important. Gary had promised him that if it went well, ZNN would broadcast the story worldwide.

The TV lights bathed the stage, and even from where he was sitting Ryan could make out the details of Erin's face, the slight worried look there and but also the determination in her eyes.

Both she and the reporter were seated in armchairs on the small stage. Off to one side, a producer looked on. Two video cameras were trained on the interview, their operators hunched behind the bulky units.

It was hot in the room, and beads of sweat broke out on Ryan's forehead. He brushed it aside, focused on what was being said.

So far, it had gone well. But the detective held his breath, wanting this to go as smoothly as he had visualized it.

He studied the agent, listened closely to every word. She was wearing a stylish black suit with a light gray silk shirt. She looked and sounded professional.

But Gary was a thorough reporter, and although he was Ryan's friend, didn't feed her softballs. He asked tough questions, prying out every detail.

When the interview was complete an hour later the camera lights dimmed and Gary and Erin stood. They shook hands and the reporter walked away to consult with the producer.

The agent picked up her purse and slung it over her shoulder, then walked off the stage to where Ryan was sitting.

"How'd I do?" she asked, her voice tired. She looked worn out and she slumped unto the auditorium seat next to his.

"You did fine, Erin. Better than fine. You're a natural."

"I was nervous."

"You didn't show it."

"I thought that guy was your friend, J.T. He put me through the ringer. Asked tough questions, and he repeated them, like he was trying to catch me lying or something."

"He's a good reporter. He was just checking the facts. This is a big story. Explosive, involving a lot of important people."

She rubbed her eyes with her hands. "Damn lights. And the heat in here. Jesus."

Ryan patted her on the shoulder. "You did great, Erin. I'm really proud of you."

She smiled. "Thanks. What happens next?"

"I told Gary I'd give him an interview also, but off camera." He stood. "Why don't you wait here, while I do that."

"Sure."

Ryan walked up to the stage. Gary had just finished with the producer and met Ryan by the armchairs. The reporter was a tall, lean man with sandy hair and ruddy cheeks.

"How'd she do?" Ryan asked.

"Perfect," the reporter responded. "She's a tough cookie. I couldn't break her, though I tried. It's a hell of a story. Thanks for bringing it to me first, J.T."

"It's good we can help each other out."

"I talked with my producer," Gary said. "After I interview you, we'll edit her video, and it'll run tonight. In fact, it'll be our lead story on the 6 o'clock news."

Ryan took in a deep breath, relaxing for the first time today. "Good. The sooner the story breaks, the better."

The reporter pointed to the chairs. "Let's sit over there and finish this up."

Ryan sat in the padded chair and settled back.

He glanced around the auditorium. The cameramen and the producer were already gone. The only person left was Erin. Her eyes were closed and it looked like she was asleep.

There was a tape recorder on the table between them and Gary turned it on.

"This is Gary Harris," the reporter began, "with ZNN News. With me today is John Taylor Ryan...."

Chapter 46

Atlanta, Georgia

Ryan leaned back on the sofa in his apartment, surfing the TV channels.

He sipped coffee and finally settled on Fox News. They were rebroadcasting Erin's interview, which had aired on ZNN two days ago.

Ryan had already seen it replayed on CBS, ABC, and NBC.

The story had gone viral on the internet, reaching a worldwide audience.

He shook his head slowly, amazed how fast the report had spread. Erin Welch, an unknown Secret Service agent until this, was now one of the most talked about people on television. News outlets from across the country and overseas were clamoring for more interviews. She was being hailed as a genuine hero.

But it wasn't all positive. She had been branded a liar by the Russian and Mexican governments, the Vatican, Senator Cage, and others.

But the effect of the news had been dramatic. The Gold-Dollar's widespread adoption was now in question. The United Nations and the World Bank were asking tough questions. The new currency's momentum had been stopped.

He finished his coffee and put the empty cup on the side table.

Ryan watched the end of the news segment, and with his eyes bleary, turned off the set.

He didn't know what tomorrow would bring, but the last several days had been a hell of a start.

Chapter 47

Mexico City, Mexico

Inez Sanchez was swimming laps in the Olympic size pool of her estate when she heard the maid calling her name. Inez swam to the edge of the pool and propped her arms on the tiled rim.

"*Señora* Sanchez," the maid said, "there are soldiers at the door. They need to see you immediately."

"What about?" she asked the young woman, irritation in her voice. She hated to have her morning routine disrupted.

"They wouldn't say, *señora*. But said it was urgent."

"Alright. Show them in. And bring me another drink."

The maid nodded and turned to walk back to the mansion.

Hoisting herself out of the pool, Inez grabbed a towel and dried herself off. After donning sunglasses, she put on a plush terry robe over her one-piece swimsuit.

Finishing her mojito, she glanced up at the brilliant blue sky. It was a perfect March day, warm and sunny. A perfect day for sunning herself, and later for a horseback ride at her ranch.

A moment later, a squad of heavily armed soldiers strode up, led by an officer. By their uniforms and insignias she could tell they were part of Mexico's elite Special Forces unit, usually used in protection details for the president of the country.

Her stomach began to churn, apprehensive about their sudden visit.

The officer stopped in front of her. "I'm Captain Torrez. You are Inez Sanchez?"

She held her head up high. "Yes, I am. What do you want?"

"I am here to inform you that you have been charged with treason against Mexico. A military trial has been conducted and you have been found guilty."

"What trial? What the hell are you talking about, Torrez?"

"The judge has decided on the sentence, *señora*."

"What? Are you insane? I'm a personal friend of President Oscar Cruz."

"You have been sentenced to death."

She picked up her cell phone and began to dial.

The officer brusquely grabbed the phone away from her. "I have my orders, *señora*."

A sinking feeling settled in the pit of her stomach. "Orders from whom?"

"I report directly to President Cruz. He has given the order."

"No! It can't be. Please," she said, her voice breaking.

Captain Torrez moved off to one side and motioned to his men.

The squad lifted their assault rifles.

In a split-second, she saw the muzzle flashes, heard the roar of the blasts, and felt a blinding, burning pain as the hail of bullets shredded her body.

She crumpled to her knees and everything went black.

Chapter 48

Vatican City
Rome, Italy

It was a large and elaborate garden, filled with rows and rows of roses, lilies, violets, oleanders, bougainvilleas, and geraniums. Located in a remote part of Vatican City, it was Cardinal Fiori's private escape from the machinations of church life. And better yet, it was all his, a gift to the cardinal from the previous pope. He tended the garden twice a week, sometimes more, depending on his schedule.

Today he was working on his beloved roses, pruning the dead leaves and removing the dried petals.

He hummed as he worked. In the background he could hear the chirping of birds, the tinkling of a nearby fountain, and in the distant background, the hum of traffic from Rome. As usual, he was wearing a gardener's apron over a simple black tunic, not wanting to soil his regal cardinal robes.

"Cardinal," he heard from behind him.

Fiori was kneeling on the lush grass as he worked, and turned to see Father Ignatius standing there.

"Yes? You know I don't like being disturbed when I'm here."

"Of course," the priest said. "But something's come up."

"It better be good, Ignatius."

"Yes, Your Excellency."

"Well, spit it out."

"The reporters are still calling, Cardinal. What should I tell them?"

Fiori grunted. "The Vatican has already issued an official statement. That damn American agent, whatever her name is, is lying."

"Agent Erin Welch."

"Whatever," Fiori snapped. "We've issued the statement and we stand by it. Amati was never hidden at the Vatican. The woman is a liar."

"Yes, Your Excellency. But the press keeps calling, wanting to interview you. What do I say?"

Fiori shook his head slowly. "Say I'm not available. Just keep repeating our statement to whoever calls. Understood?"

"Yes, Cardinal."

"Don't worry, Ignatius. This will die down soon. You'll see. There'll be another hot story, another scandal around the world, and the media will forget all about this Amati situation." He paused, smiled gently at the young priest. "Remember, the Church has been around for twenty centuries. This is only a tiny blip in the annals of time."

"Yes, Cardinal." The priest bowed his head slightly and walked away.

Fiori turned back to his roses and took in a deep breath, savoring the pleasing scent of the flowers. He began humming again and continued with the pruning.

He became so engrossed that five minutes later he had forgotten all about the conversation with Father Ignatius and the sordid topic of Amati.

Chapter 49

Washington, D.C.

The headline on the front page of the Washington Post glared at him in extra bold print: *Criminal probe of Senator Cage widens.*

Senator Dean Cage had stared at the headline and the accompanying article for the last ten minutes, hoping by some miracle it was a bad dream, a nightmare. But it wasn't.

The endless calls from the media for the last several weeks attested to that. The bloodsucking reporters had hounded him and his staff mercilessly. His denials of involvement, accepted at first, had become hollow as the Senate Ethics committee and the Justice Department became involved. The currency counterfeiting, a key driver behind the financial panic gripping the country, had made him a *persona non grata.*

His inside-the-beltway cronies had deserted him. His influence, built from twenty years as Washington power-broker, had evaporated.

As he sat at the dining table of his high-rise condo, he reflected on how everything had gone so terribly wrong. His secret association with the Alliance, once his ticket to a life of luxury and unparalleled wealth, had turned into the worst mistake of his life.

Silently, he cursed that damn Amati for coming up with the plan to begin with. But he was just as culpable, the senator realized. It was Cage's high-tech machines that made the sigma operation a reality.

He pushed aside the toxic newspaper, and stared numbly out the window to the small terrace and beyond. It was an overcast day, full of angry dark clouds, matching his mood.

His cell phone rang but he ignored it. Another bastard reporter. He let it go to voice mail, along with the other hundreds of calls.

What now? he thought. An ugly trial, a probable conviction. *Prison?* He was sure of it.

At seventy, did he want to spend his remaining years in an orange jumpsuit and a ten-by-ten cell? He'd heard horror stories about prisons – rapes, shivs in the back, beatings by other inmates. All true, he was certain.

The senator stood and looked down at himself. He was still in his sleepwear and bathrobe, though it was three in the afternoon. It didn't matter. Not anymore.

On bare feet, he padded to the glass slider that led to the balcony and opened it. He stepped outside, approached the railing and stared down to the street below, 14 floors down. It was windy and the gusts buffeted him. He grabbed the railing to steady himself. He suffered from vertigo and just being out here made him dizzy.

Cage had always been afraid of heights. But as he stood there, he tried to get past that and visualize what it would be like. Simple really. One leg over the railing, then the other. Let go and it would be all over.

Another wave of nausea hit him and he stepped back, retreated into the condo.

He sat at the table again, his thoughts racing.

Finally, he made his decision.

Standing, he forced himself to walk into the bedroom.

Sitting on the bed, he opened the bottom drawer of his nightstand.

The Smith & Wesson .357 handgun rested inside, its black finish gleaming dully.

He'd bought it for protection years ago, fired it a few times at a gun range.

Protection. How ironic. Now he would protect himself from something he feared more than death. Shame. Being hated by the country he'd served his whole life.

Picking up the revolver, he realized it would be an extremely painful way to die. But mercifully quick.

He cocked the hammer. Then, holding the heavy gun with both hands, he inserted the barrel into his mouth. The metal felt cold and tasted greasy. The smell of gun oil filled his nostrils.

As he sat there with the barrel in his mouth, the senator was glad he'd never had a wife, never had children. The shame at what had happened would even be worse.

Cage stared at the blank wall of the bedroom, trying to steady his nerves. His heart was pounding, his stomach churning.

But it will be quick, his mind kept repeating.

It will be all over soon.

Very soon.

Now.

He pulled the trigger.

Chapter 50

ADX Florence, Maximum Security Facility
U.S. Penitentiary (a Federal Supermax prison)
Florence, Colorado

Vincento Amati pressed the phone receiver to his ear, to drown out the noise of the other prisoners talking on nearby phones.

"How are you, Livia?" he asked for the second time.

"I'm alright," his wife replied, her voice breaking. She'd been crying from the beginning of the call.

He was in a bunker-like room, subdivided into small cubicles that resembled animal cages. Metal bars and heavy-wire mesh separated each cubicle from the others.

Called the 'communication room' by the prison guards, the place was used by inmates to call loved ones and friends on the outside. Each cubicle consisted of a black phone, a small table and a chair. Heavy metal hooks bolted on the floor were used to connect the inmate's shackles, allowing only a few inches of movement. Amati's own manacled feet had been secured this way as soon as he'd stepped into the cubicle.

Outside the row of partitioned spaces stood a group of correctional officers, armed with Mossberg heavy-duty shotguns.

The long-distance connection to Italy was full of static and Amati strained to hear his wife's voice. "I'm fine," she repeated. "I'm just worried about you, Vincento."

Amati shifted in the metal chair, trying to get into a comfortable position. "Don't worry, Livia. It's bearable here. Three meals a day and an hour of exercise in the yard. It's the best I can hope for. For now."

She began crying again and he waited for her to regain her composure.

"It's you I was concerned about, Livia. Tell me the truth. Have you been harassed? Has Prime Minister Bertoli threatened you with arrest?"

"No. Nothing like that."

He breathed a deep sigh of relief. The American, John Ryan, had kept his word.

"I'm lonely without you, Vincento. I miss you."

"I miss you also. I love you."

Livia broke down again, her sobs punctuated by the static of the phone connection.

"When do you think you will get out?" she asked a moment later.

"It will be a long time, Livia."

"How long?"

He clutched the receiver tightly. "Possibly the rest of my life."

"What do your lawyers say?"

"They're working on it."

"Stay hopeful," she said. "You may get out of prison in a few years."

"I am hopeful," he lied.

Amati heard a rap on the metal bars behind him and he turned his head. One of the prison guards was there.

"Time's up," the guard said.

Amati nodded, and turned back to the phone. "I'll call you next week, Livia. I love you."

He heard her begin to weep again and he hung up the call.

Chapter 51

Moscow, Russia

Dimitri Petrovich groaned with pleasure.

He was sitting in the back seat of his Mercedes limo, being serviced by his latest find, Elena. A striking blonde from Kiev, his new secretary was a huge improvement from the last.

Elena, her dress hiked up above her waist, sat on his lap and rocked back and forth in a steady rhythm.

In a matter of minutes, she brought him to an extremely rewarding conclusion.

As she pulled away and sat across from him on the facing seat, he zipped up his pants.

He took another moment to savor the experience, then pressed a button on the armrest. The privacy panels covering the windows accordioned open, letting in weak sunlight.

The view outside was unchanged. A mostly cloudy sky hung over the four-lane highway. They were well north of the city now, and the crush of traffic was gone, replaced with an occasional truck or van from the surrounding farms.

He was on his way to his *dacha* in Khovrino, looking forward to spending the weekend with the attractive and talented Elena. The horrific setbacks the Alliance suffered had put him in a foul mood. A few days of vodka and sex, he hoped, would give him the respite he needed.

While the young woman straightened her clothes and worked on her makeup, he stared out the side window.

He frowned as the recent events flashed across his mind. The Gold-Dollar was doomed, he knew. His relationship with Prime Minister Ivan Chernov was badly damaged – the man wouldn't even return his calls. And Petrovich's huge investment in gold bullion had backfired. The price of gold on the open market had crashed, once news of the sigma counterfeiting scheme was revealed.

Luckily, he still had his oil business to fall back on. Although he was no longer a billionaire, he was still rich.

Glancing back to the blonde, he watched as the woman brushed her long hair. She gave him a suggestive smile and a thrill ran through him, as he anticipated the weekend.

He still had plenty of money to afford her, he mused, and more like her in the future. That thought brought a smile to his face.

Life would go on, despite the fiasco of the sigma operation. He would regroup and focus on his oil company. He would forget about Chernov, and Amati, and Sanchez, and get on with the rest of his life. Only 51, he was at the prime of his life.

The Mercedes slowed down and slid into the exit lane. Petrovich saw the sign for Khovrino. They were only a half-hour from the *dacha*.

He pressed another button on the armrest and the opaque divider glass to the front of the car whirred down.

"Call the maid at the house," he told the driver. "Tell her we'll be arriving soon and to have lunch ready."

"Yes, Mr. Petrovich," the driver replied.

The oil man closed the divider and turned to the blonde. "Would you like a drink, Elena?"

"Yes, of course."

Sliding open a side panel, he took out a bottle of vodka and two tumblers. He filled the glasses and handed one of them to the woman.

"To the future," he toasted, lifting his own tumbler in the air.

"To the future," she replied, clinking the glasses.

A short while later the limo pulled into the long gravel driveway of the two-story, stone-front *dacha*. Although modest compared to Petrovich's palatial home in Moscow, this country retreat had one big advantage. His wife never came here, and in fact, didn't even know it existed.

The Mercedes drove up to the front of the house and stopped.

The driver climbed out of the car, but instead of opening Petrovich's door as usual, the man walked quickly away.

Puzzled, the oil man pulled the door latch to exit.

But the car door was locked. Frowning, he pressed the controls on the armrest and tried opening it again. To his amazement, the door wouldn't budge.

"What's wrong?" Elena asked.

"An electric malfunction," he replied, hoping that's all it was.

He tried the door on the other side, but it too was locked.

Next he tried to lower the divider glass, but here again the controls seemed frozen.

Beads of sweat broke out on his forehead and he brushed them away. Picking up the car phone, he tried dialing out, but the line was dead.

He kicked at the door, trying to jar it open, but all he managed to do was to hurt his foot.

His thoughts raced. What the hell was going on? Glancing outside, he saw the driver nowhere around. Pulling out his cell phone, he dialed the number for the *dacha*. He'd tell the maid to call a mechanic.

But the line rang endlessly – for some reason, she wasn't picking up.

Petrovich's heart pounded as he tried to figure a way out.

"What's happening?" Elena said, alarm in her voice.

"Shut up, bitch!" he snapped. "Let me think."

Remembering something about a manual override for the car windows, he opened another side panel. He saw the small hand crank for the left-side window.

With a sigh of relief, he reached for the lever and began turning, but nothing happened. It appeared the mechanism had been disconnected.

He gasped for air as he desperately tried to figure a way out. Since his driver doubled as his bodyguard, Petrovich was not armed. He realized now that was huge mistake – he wouldn't be able to shatter the window with a gunshot.

Elena, her eyes wide, cringed in the corner of the seat and said nothing.

Then he heard it. A loud click, from somewhere underneath the car.

And in that split-second, he knew. Chernov. Petrovich had become a liability, and the prime minister was cutting his losses.

The car bomb went off a second later.

The twenty pounds of Semtex plastic explosive vaporized the Mercedes into a flaming cloud of metal, plastic, and human fragments.

3 Months Later

Chapter 52

Atlanta, Georgia

Ryan was in his mid-town office, sipping coffee and doing paperwork, when he heard a rap at the door.

Looking up, he saw Erin Welch standing there. The woman was dressed in a stylish navy suit with a white blouse.

"Have a seat," he said with a grin. "You want coffee? I just brewed a fresh pot."

The agent made a face. "No coffee – I want to live."

Ryan chuckled, and pushed aside the file he was reading.

She sat on one of the visitors chairs and reached into her jacket pocket. Pulling out an envelope, she slid it across his desk.

"What's that?" he asked.

"A bonus."

He picked it up, slipped out a check. It was made out to him for a large amount.

"What's this for?" Ryan asked.

"A bonus, for a job well done."

"Thanks, Erin."

"What are you going to do with it?"

He thought about that a moment. "I promised Lauren a vacation. To Paris. This'll cover it."

She grimaced. "Her. When you and I first met, I figured you for a player. Thought you'd be the type to prowl Buckhead nightclubs, looking for 20-year olds with boobs out to here."

"No," he said with a smile. "Lauren's the one."

She shrugged. "I should be so lucky."

"Don't worry, Erin. You'll find the right guy. It just takes time."

"Yeah."

"So," he said, "what's happening with the sigma case? I've moved on to my other work and haven't been following it that closely."

Her face brightened. "Very well, actually. I'm sure you remember the Russian connection?"

"Sure."

"Well, Dimitri Petrovich was murdered with a car bomb a while back. And they just found Prime Minister Chernov's body in a Moscow gutter. Two shots to the head. No suspects. It looks like President Lazarenko is covering his tracks." She paused a moment. "On a related front, Hector Sanchez is dead, and his wife, who took over his business, is also dead. And Amati is at a Supermax prison, facing a life sentence."

He nodded. "And the Gold-Dollar?"

"Going nowhere. It's been discredited. No country will adopt it now."

"Good. What about the inflation problem?"

Erin smiled. "We've been monitoring the counterfeit money situation closely. The inflows into the U.S. have stopped. Interpol tells us they've seen the same thing in Europe and Asia. Inflation in the U.S. has stabilized. In fact, I read this morning in the paper that it appears to be trending down."

"That's good to hear."

"The worldwide financial crisis," she added, "is improving. At this rate, in another year or two, things will be back to normal."

Ryan was relieved, and glad he'd made a contribution. He took another sip of coffee.

"That's the big picture," he said. "But how are you doing?"

She tucked her long hair behind her ears. "My boss at the Secret Service hates me. Can't stand the fact I went around his back and went public to expose the conspiracy."

"You did the right thing."

"Yeah," she said with an enigmatic smile. "But there's a bright side. The Director of the FBI called me. Wants me to head up their Atlanta office."

"That's great, Erin. What did you say?"

She looked pensive. "I told him I'd let him know. I've been with the Service for ten years. But it would be a big promotion for me."

"Go for it," he said, genuinely happy for her. "It's the brass ring you've been looking for."

The agent said nothing for a moment. "You're probably right, J.T."

Erin stood.

"Thanks, again," she said.

"For what?"

"For solving the sigma case."

"I couldn't have done it without you," he said. "It was a team effort."

Erin nodded and smiled. Then she turned and left the office.

He went back to doing paperwork.

Taking a sip of coffee, he picked up a manila folder. His next case.

Opening the folder, he began reading. Five minutes later he finished reading and closed the folder. He was definitely excited about the new case, but at the same time apprehensive. He knew the investigation would be dangerous, for himself and possibly to others close to him.

Still, he'd never turned down a case and he wasn't about to do so now.

END

***
About the author

Lee Gimenez is the award-winning author of 15 novels, including his highly-acclaimed J.T. Ryan series. His novel FIREBALL, a J.T. Ryan Thriller, was a Finalist for the 2019 Author Academy Award. Many of his books were Featured Novels of the International Thriller Writers Association, among them CROSSFIRE, FIREBALL, The MEDIA MURDERS, FBI CODE RED, SKYFLASH, KILLING WEST, and The WASHINGTON ULTIMATUM. Lee is a multi-year nominee for the Georgia Author of the Year Award, and was a Finalist in the prestigious Terry Kay Prize for Fiction. Lee's books are available at Amazon and many other bookstores in the U.S. and Internationally.

For more information about him, please visit his website at: www.LeeGimenez.com. There you can sign up for his free newsletter. You can contact Lee at his email address: LG727@MSN.com. You can also join him on Facebook, Twitter, LinkedIn, and Goodreads.

***
Novels by Lee Gimenez

The Sigma Conspiracy
Crossfire
Fireball
FBI Code Red
The Media Murders
Skyflash
Killing West
The Washington Ultimatum
Blacksnow Zero
The Nanotech Murders
Death on Zanath
Virtual Thoughtstream
Azul 7
Terralus 4
The Tomorrow Solution

CROSSFIRE, a **J.T.** Ryan Thriller
is available at Amazon and many other bookstores in the
U.S. and Internationally.
In paperback, Kindle, and all other ebook versions.

FIREBALL, a J.T. Ryan Thriller
is available at Amazon and many other bookstores in the
U.S. and Internationally.
In paperback, Kindle, and all other ebook versions.

FBI CODE RED, a J.T. Ryan Thriller
is available at Amazon and many other bookstores in the
U.S. and Internationally.
In paperback, Kindle, and all other ebook versions.

THE MEDIA MURDERS, a **J.T.** Ryan Thriller
is available at Amazon and many other bookstores in the
U.S. and Internationally.
In paperback, Kindle, and all other ebook versions.

SKYFLASH, a J.T. Ryan Thriller
is available at Amazon and many other bookstores in the
U.S. and Internationally.
In paperback, Kindle, and all other ebook versions.

KILLING WEST, a Rachel West Thriller
is available at Amazon and many other bookstores in the
U.S. and Internationally.
In paperback, Kindle, and all other ebook versions.

THE WASHINGTON ULTIMATUM,
a J.T. Ryan Thriller
is available at Amazon and many other bookstores in the
U.S. and Internationally. In paperback, Kindle, and all other
ebook versions.

Lee Gimenez's other novels, including

- **The Nanotech Murders**
- **Death on Zanath**
- **Virtual Thoughtstream**
- **Azul 7**
- **Terralus 4**
- **The Tomorrow Solution**

are all available at Amazon and many other bookstores in the U.S. and Internationally.

Here's an excerpt from Lee Gimenez's award-winning novel, CROSSFIRE:

CROSSFIRE

a J.T. Ryan Thriller

A Novel
By
Lee Gimenez

Face-Look is the world's largest social media company. When that company's president is brutally murdered, the FBI investigates. As more people are killed, former Special Forces soldier John (J.T.) Ryan and FBI Assistant Director Erin Welch are assigned to the case. Ryan and Erin delve into the mystery and begin to uncover a vast criminal conspiracy behind the murders. A conspiracy involving not just Face-Look, but also the world's other social media and high-tech corporations. As more people are murdered, Ryan pursues the secret cabal of criminals across the USA, Japan, and Europe. The dangerous and harrowing journey takes him from the mansions of the super-rich to the gritty back streets of the criminal underworld. There he learns the ultimate goal of the secret group, known only as Viper. A goal so explosive it will cause the collapse of the American economy. Can John Ryan and Erin Welch capture the murderous criminals before they themselves are killed?

Chapter 1

Atlanta, Georgia

Feeling energized by the death that was about to happen, the sniper peered through his rifle's scope and adjusted the crosshairs. Although his target was in an office building a half-mile away, the custom-made scope allowed him to see clearly into the man's office on the tenth floor. The target, a tall, heavyset man was at his desk reading a report.

Using his laser finder and a small computer, the sniper made a few final adjustments to account for wind speed and direction. Then he slowed his breathing and slid his finger past the trigger guard until it rested on the trigger itself. He was using a Barrett M107, a high-precision, long-range rifle that was the weapon of choice for those in his profession.

He slowed his breathing even more, took another moment to zero in on the target, and gently pulled the trigger. The suppressed rifle coughed. A split-second later the armor-piercing round cracked the bullet-resistant window a half mile away.

The target's head exploded.

Then his lifeless body slumped forward on his desk and blood began to pool under his head.

Chapter 2

St. Croix
The U.S. Virgin Islands
the Caribbean

It was a sunny, cloudless sky, the temperature in the mid-seventies. The sky was a deep azure blue and the shoreline was crystal clear surf.

Another perfect day in paradise, John (J.T.) Ryan thought, as he exited the cottage and began walking toward the secluded beach. He noticed Rachel was already there, lounging on a chaise, sipping a drink. Ryan had booked the cottage for a week; the bungalow was part of a resort comprised of golf courses, tennis courts, several pools, restaurants, and miles-long beaches of sparkling sand.

Ryan almost reached the beach when his cell phone vibrated in his swim trunk pocket. Pulling it out, he answered the call.

"Ryan here."

"It's Erin," he heard the woman say.

"Erin," he replied with a chuckle. "My favorite ADIC." Erin was the Assistant Director in charge of the FBI's Atlanta office.

Erin sighed, used to his attempts at humor "How many ADICs do you know, J.T.?"

"Besides you? None."

"Then I guess the fact I'm your favorite isn't much of a compliment."

Ryan laughed. "You got me there. Why are you calling?"

"I'm working on a new case and I need your help."

Ryan was a former Special Forces soldier turned private investigator who did security work for law-enforcement agencies.

"My usual fee?" he asked.

There was no response and Ryan could visualize the FBI woman frowning. Finally she said, "Yes. Your usual fee. High as they are."

The PI grinned. "I'm worth it. Otherwise you wouldn't hire me."

"All right, smartass. Enough banter."

"What's the case about, Erin?"

"A high-profile murder. It happened yesterday. Here in Atlanta."

"Who's the DB?"

"The president of Face-Look. The big social media company located here in the city."

Ryan let out a low whistle. "That is high-profile. How was he killed?"

"He was assassinated. From what we've been able to piece together, he was shot by a sniper using a high-powered rifle."

"Any clues?"

"None so far, J.T. That's why I need you on this case. Your unorthodox methods are good at ferreting out information."

"Okay, I'll take the job. But I just got to St. Croix. I'm on vacation. I'll be back in Atlanta in a week."

"I need you here now," Erin said, her voice hard.

Ryan gazed toward the beach and saw Rachel waving at him. She looked delectable in her red bikini.

"No can do," he replied. "Like I said, I'm on vacation. I'll see you in a week."

"That's not good enough."

"Listen, Erin. I like working for you. And the FBI cases you've given me are some of the best work I've done as a PI. But Rachel and I have postponed this vacation too many times."

"I'm not going to change your mind, am I?," she said, a resigned tone in her voice.

"I'm afraid not. But don't worry, I'll be back next week. I'll come to your office the day I get back, okay?"

"All right, J.T."

He hung up the phone and slipped it in the pocket of his swim trunks. Then he strode the short distance to the beach, his bare feet sinking into the warm sand. He sat on a lounge chair next to Rachel's.

She rested her drink on a side table. "Who was that on the phone?"

"Erin from the FBI."

Rachel gave him a worried glance. "Does that mean ...."

"No, beautiful. I told Erin I wasn't going to cancel my vacation." He smiled. "I'll work on the case when I get back."

Her expression brightened and she returned the smile. "That's a relief." She caressed his arm and her smile turned mischievous. "We've got a lot of catching up to do, you and me."

Ryan gave her a long look, taking in her intoxicating beauty. She was a tall, lean, and curvaceous woman in her mid-thirties. With long blonde hair, sparkling blue eyes, and classic good looks, she resembled a model. Besides her looks, she also had a razor-sharp mind and a vivacious wit.

Ryan pointed toward her red bikini, which did little to conceal her curves. "Since you're a CIA operative, you must be working undercover. But looking at your swimsuit, you're barely undercover."

Rachel laughed. "You play your cards right and you may get to see a lot more."

He grinned and they held hands. Then they both looked out toward the rolling surf a few feet away. Ryan felt more at ease and content than he had in a long time.

The warm sun and light breeze lulled him into sleep.

He awoke with a start sometime later and heard the clatter of machinery in the distance. Looking around the secluded beach, he saw nothing except palm trees, rolling surf, and the white sandy beach.

As the sound grew louder, he got up from the lounge chair and shielded his eyes from the bright sun to get a better look.

"What is it?" Rachel asked. "What's that noise?"

Then he spotted it, a black helicopter flying low toward their location. He pointed. "Chopper. Could be military."

Rachel stood next to him as they watched the helicopter land on the relatively flat beach. The rotor wash sprayed sand in all directions.

As the craft powered down, Ryan noticed there were no markings on the chopper, which was a Sikorsky Black Hawk. Its bay door opened and three men climbed out and began trudging towards them, their boots sinking into the sand. All three were wearing U.S. Army fatigues, with Military Police markings on their uniforms. The PI noticed they also had holstered sidearms.

When they were a few feet away, one of the men approached Ryan. "I'm Lieutenant Holder," he said. "Are you John Taylor Ryan?"

"Yes. I'm J.T. Ryan. What's this about?"

"You need to come with us, sir."

"You haven't answered my question, Lieutenant. What's this about?"

"Sir, that will all be explained later. It's a matter of national security. You just need to come with us."

"I'm not going anywhere until I get some answers."

Ryan noticed the MP's hands moved and rested on the butts of their holstered pistols.

"We can do this the easy way," the lieutenant said, "or the hard way. It's totally up to you, sir."

Ryan glared at him, then glanced at Rachel who looked bewildered.

"This is not a request," the lieutenant added. "It's an order."

Angry and confused, Ryan balled his fists.

"You better go," Rachel said in a quiet voice. "You have no choice, J.T."

The PI took a deep breath and let it out slowly. "All right, damn it."

The MPs escorted him to the helicopter and they climbed inside.

The rotor blades spooled faster and the engines whined to a loud roar. The chopper lifted off and seconds later receded into the horizon.

Chapter 3

The Pentagon
U.S. Department of Defense
Washington, D.C.

After a five hour flight from St. Croix to D.C. on a military transport jet, J.T. Ryan had been escorted to the small conference room he was in now.

The three MPs who had put him in the helicopter were still with him, posted outside the conference room. On the flight he had been given food and a change of clothes, but none of his questions had been answered.

Ten minutes later the door to the conference room opened and an Army officer wearing his Class A blue uniform stepped inside. Closing the door behind him, he extended his hand to Ryan. "I'm General Keating."

As they shook hands, Keating said, "Please have a seat, Mr. Ryan."

They sat across from each other at the conference table and Ryan said, "Am I under arrest?"

The general gave him a wry smile. "Of course not." The man was tall and wiry, with close-cropped sandy hair, and looked to be in his mid-fifties. He was a brigadier, a one-star general, and from his military ribbons Ryan knew the man had been posted to a long list of duty stations.

"I'm sorry about the abrupt flight," Keating said. "But in light of recent events, we needed to brief you as soon as possible."

Ryan nodded, relieved he wasn't under arrest, but still confused why he was there. "In that case, General, I'd appreciate an explanation. The MP said it was a matter of national security?"

"That's correct, Ryan. It is." The man leaned forward in his chair. "Everything I'm going to tell you is classified Top Secret. Is that understood?"

"Yes, General."

"All right. Yesterday the president of Face-Look was murdered. Have you heard about this?"

"Actually yes. The FBI has already hired me to work on that, when I get back to Atlanta."

Keating gave him a hard look. "Have they now? Well, our investigation takes priority over that."

Ryan waved a hand in the air as if to encompass the whole room. "What's the Pentagon's interest in this murder?"

"I'll get to that in a moment. Are you familiar with the DIA?"

The PI nodded. "The Defense Intelligence Agency? Sure. The DIA is the military's version of the CIA."

"That's correct. I'm with the DIA. In fact, I'm second in command. And I'm heading up the Face-Look investigation."

"Sir, why is the DIA so interested in this? I would think the FBI would be the best organization to handle a case involving a private company."

"Under normal circumstances you would be correct, Ryan. But we've had Face-Look on our radar for quite some time. We've been monitoring them for years. Do you know much about them?"

"I know they're a large social media company."

Keating nodded. "Not just large, but the biggest. They're larger than Twitter, or Instagram, or Facebook."

"Okay, I'm with you so far. But I still don't see the military's interest."

"Face-Look," the general continued, "has a worldwide audience of 2.2 billion people. And all of these people give up much of their privacy when they join social media networks. They share personal details, photos, posts, friends lists, family names, etc. They take polls online, read news items, find products to buy, and message friends. And all of this vast amount of information is kept in Face-Look's computer databanks for practically forever."

"Face-Look," the general added, "has become the largest intelligence gathering organization in the world."

"I didn't realize how widespread and intrusive they were," Ryan said. "I'm not into social media very much myself. I'm too busy with my PI work."

Keating steepled his hands in front of him. "Normally this intelligence gathering is benign. They store the information about people and it is kept private. But we at the DIA have become concerned that if all of this data falls into the wrong hands, the results could be catastrophic. The potential for blackmail, corruption, and criminal activity is vast."

The general paused as Ryan realized the ominous implications of what the man had just said.

"And now that Face-Look's president has been murdered," Keating continued, "we've decided to become directly involved."

"I understand, sir. But why do you need me, General? I'm sure you have military people who can carry out the investigation."

"That's true. We do. But having you investigate this case has several advantages. First, you're based in Atlanta, where Face-Look's headquarters is located. So you know the area well. Second, we need a civilian face to head this up. The DIA is a secretive organization – we don't want it known that we're interested. And the third reason is obvious – you're former military – you're familiar with our ways."

Ryan nodded. "I can appreciate that, sir. But I've already committed to working on this for the FBI. I can't walk away from that."

Keating waved that away. "You can still keep them in the loop. As long as you understand you work for the DIA. We take priority."

"I don't know about this, General. My whole business as a PI is based on the work I do for the FBI, Homeland Security, and other law-enforcement agencies. I don't want to jeopardize that."

Keating grimaced. "You have no choice, Ryan. This is not a request. I'm giving you a direct order."

"What are you talking about, sir? I left the Army years ago."

The general pointed an index finger at him. "Don't force my hand. Accept this job or you will regret it."

Ryan's blood pressure rose and his hands balled into fists. "With all due respect, sir, what the hell does that mean?"

Keating had brought with him a thick file folder, which he opened now. "This is your U.S. Army service record, Ryan. Very impressive. You served as an Airborne Ranger, then a Green Beret, then finally in Delta Force, Tier 1. The most elite of the Special Forces, even more elite than the Navy SEALS. You received numerous commendations for valor in combat including a Purple Heart and a Silver Star. You were even awarded the Medal of Honor. Impressive stuff."

The general paused, then said, "You left the Army with the rank of Captain. But if you hadn't been such a smartass in the military, I'm sure you would have been promoted to Major or even Colonel."

Keating paused again and he removed a sheaf of papers from the file and slid them across the table toward the PI. "There's a clause in your Army enlistment contract, Ryan, which you signed years ago. The clause is in small print at the every back of contract. I'm sure you never read it – most people don't."

The general gave him a tight, hard grin. "The clause stipulates that in times of a national security need, the Army can re-activate you back into the military. All it takes is a General officer, such as myself, to invoke that national security need."

Ryan had been unaware of the clause in his contract. But as he quickly scanned the document, its meaning was now crystal clear.

General Keating's hard grin remained on his face. "Welcome back to the Army, Captain Ryan."

Chapter 4

Tokyo, Japan

The Asian woman picked up the handset of her desk phone and pressed the encryption button. Then she tapped in a phone number she had committed to memory long ago.

A man answered on the second ring. "Yes?"

"It's me," she said in flawless English. She was Japanese, but spoke five different languages. "The operation has begun. We took the first step in Atlanta."

"Excellent." The man paused a moment. "Is everything else on schedule?"

"Yes."

"Very good. Keep me informed as things progress."

"Of course." She disconnected the call and hung up.

Standing, she went to a corner of her large, luxuriously appointed office. She was an avid chess player and had installed a life-size chess set in that part of the room. The intricately carved ceramic pieces all resembled Samurai warriors from 17th century Japan. She pushed one of the smaller, but still heavy figurines forward two squares. That particular game opening move was called Pawn-to-King-four. She smiled. *It'll be awhile before I can claim Checkmate. The important thing is the game's begun.*

Then she went to a teak cabinet and poured herself a large tumbler of Chivas Regal scotch. Turning around, she faced the floor-to-ceiling windows of her office.

The room, located on the top floor of the skyscraper, gave her a panoramic view of Tokyo's ultra-modern skyline. It was nighttime and the rows and rows of high-rise buildings were lit up in a riot of neon light.

The woman sipped the scotch and mulled over her next steps.

Chapter 5

FBI Field Office
Atlanta, Georgia

Erin Welch heard a knock at her door and glanced up from her laptop.

J.T. Ryan was standing at her office entrance, a worried look on his handsome face. Erin closed the lid on her laptop.

"Come in, J.T. Have a seat."

The man took one of the visitor's chairs fronting her desk.

"Didn't expect you back until next week," she said.

Ryan frowned. "My vacation was cut short."

"What happened?"

"It's a long story."

Erin studied the tall, good-looking man in his late thirties. He was 6'4" and powerfully built, with a weightlifter's physique. He had close-cropped brown hair and brown eyes. As usual he was wearing a blue blazer, slacks, and a white, buttoned-down shirt. He looked tired, as if he hadn't had much sleep.

"What, no banter? No smartass comments?" she said, amazed he hadn't already cracked one of his lame jokes.

"Not today."

"Okay, J.T. You ready to work my case?"

Ryan nodded. "I am. But I need to tell you something before I start. I've got another boss on this besides you."

"What do you mean?"

"I've been reactivated back into the Army."

"How's that possible?"

Ryan grimaced. "Some bullshit clause in my enlistment contract. Like I said, it's a long story. I'm not happy about it, but it is what it is."

"Now I understand your sour mood. What's the military's interest in this case?"

"They've been monitoring Face-Look for some time. They're concerned with the immense data gathering capability of the social media company. When their top executive was murdered, they decided to get more involved."

Erin nodded. "All right."

She opened a desk drawer and took out a file which she handed to Ryan. "In here's the information we have on the murder. The FBI and police reports, the coroner's findings, and CSI information."

Ryan opened the folder and scanned the details. "Not much here."

"You're right, J.T. It was a professional hit. They left virtually no clues behind."

The man closed the folder and stood. "In that case, I'll get to work."

"What's your first stop?"

"The morgue."

Chapter 6

Fulton County Morgue
Atlanta, Georgia

J.T. Ryan drove his Ford Explorer out of the FBI building's underground lot and headed south. A short while later he pulled into the parking lot of the morgue on Pryor Street.

He went through the building's security checkpoint and was shown into the non-descript office of the Medical Examiner. As usual, the whole building smelled of strong antiseptic, the cleaning solvent masking, but not quite erasing the pungent stench of human decomp.

Ryan shook hands with the M.E. and took a chair facing his desk. Ryan had been here many times and knew the man well.

"So, J.T., what brings you here today?" Doctor Mallory asked. The M.E. was a gaunt-looking man with oval wire-rimmed eyeglasses and a pallid complexion.

Ryan leaned forward in the chair. "I'm investigating the murder of Matthew Ross, the CEO of Face-Look."

"Of course."

"You've completed the autopsy, doc?"

"I have." Mallory opened a desk drawer, took out a file, and opened it. "My findings are very straightforward. Ross died of a massive head wound. The bullet that shattered his skull came from a high-powered weapon."

"Could you determine the caliber of the round?"

"Not exactly. But I could give you an educated guess, considering we process an average of 2,500 deaths a year in this building."

Ryan nodded. "Go ahead. You've never steered me wrong before."

"The bullet cracked a shatter-proof window and then penetrated Ross's head. As you can imagine, all we found were the bullet's fragments. But my conclusion is that it was a .50 caliber round."

The PI rubbed his jaw. "That means a very-sophisticated, high-end rifle was used. The type used by professional snipers. No question this was a well-planned assassination."

"I agree, J.T." Doctor Mallory closed the file folder. "Anything else I can tell you?"

"I want to see the body."

"You sure? I know you've got a strong stomach, but this is gruesome."

"I'm sure. I may pick up some clues."

"All right. But I have to make this quick. I've got three more cadavers to process today."

"Don't worry, doc. Those folks aren't going anywhere."

Mallory frowned at Ryan's attempt at levity. He stood and said, "Follow me and I'll take you back there."

The M.E. led Ryan down a long, white-tiled corridor and moments later they entered what the building's employees referred to as the 'meat locker'. It was the storage area where cadavers were kept after autopsies. The room was kept at a frigid 36 degrees and Ryan shivered from the cold.

Mallory strode past a long row of stainless-steel freezer lockers and stopped in front of one of them. He opened the locker door and slid out the metal shelf. Then he removed the sheet covering the corpse and stood aside so that the PI could see.

Ryan had witnessed his share of death, while in combat and later in law-enforcement, but he still swallowed hard. The M.E. had been correct in his assessment – it was a gruesome sight. The dead man's head had literally been blown off. All that remained were bloody chunks of brain matter and skin tissue and cracked skull fragments. His neck resembled raw hamburger meat.

Ryan inspected the cadaver for another minute, then turned back to the M.E. "You can close it up."

Mallory nodded, covered the body with the sheet, and slid the metal tray into the wall.

They left the frigid room and Ryan exited the building, knowing the gruesome sight would haunt his dreams for several days.

Chapter 7

Downtown
Atlanta, Georgia

After reading the FBI report Erin had given him, Ryan pulled out a paper map from his SUV's glove box and studied it carefully. The map, which was a detailed diagram of the downtown area and its nearby surroundings, showed the avenues and all of the side streets. It also identified the numerous high-rises that comprised Atlanta's skyline.

A half-hour later he folded up the map, put it away, and fired up his Explorer. Then he spent the next three hours driving through the areas south of downtown, scouting out possible locations where the sniper had taken the shot. After stopping at multiple buildings to determine a likely sight line, he spotted an abandoned structure about a half-mile from the Face-Look skyscraper.

He parked at the curb, got out, and studied the fifteen-story building, which appeared to be an office complex. It was partially finished – no windows or doors were in place, its construction most likely halted years ago due to lack of financing.

Ryan took out a rucksack from his SUV's hatch and went inside the deserted, dim interior. Using a flashlight, he made his way around the first floor, which was covered with cobwebs and dust. He found a concrete staircase at one side of the space and began climbing the stairs to the tenth floor.

When he got there, he noticed it was a wide-open area, with only support beams in place. He headed toward the north part of it, and stopped just shy of where the glass windows would normally be installed. A light breeze was blowing, swirling dust into the room. He gazed out toward downtown Atlanta.

Taking out a pair of binoculars, he focused on the Face-Look headquarters building a half-mile away. The murdered man's office had been on the tenth floor and thru his binos the PI could clearly see the plywood that now covered the shattered window of his office.

It's a perfect sight line.

Realizing this was an excellent location for the sniper to take his shot, Ryan spent the next hour scouring the large, open space, looking for disturbed areas.

He found it eventually, a spot near the edge of the floor where the windows would normally be. Footprints and other fresh marks were evident on the otherwise dust-covered floor.

He looked for shell casings but found none. *The sniper was a pro. He cleaned up his brass after taking the shot.*

The PI had brought with him a small CSI kit, which he took out of his rucksack. Erin had given him the kit years ago. Although Ryan was not a crime scene expert, he knew enough to carry out several procedures.

Opening the kit, he took out fingerprint tape and DNA tools and started collecting samples from the disturbed area of the dusty floor. That done, he took photos of the footprints. Satisfied he'd collected as much evidence as he could, he packed up the CSI kit. He'd call Erin when he got back to his vehicle to schedule her techs to come out to the scene and do a more thorough job.

Then he made his way down the stairs and headed back to his SUV.

Chapter 8

Salt Lake City, Utah

The man was driving south on Interstate 15, away from the city. The car ahead of him, a gray Lexus sedan, was doing sixty.

The man realized the Lexus was pulling away from him and he floored the accelerator of the big rig he was driving, a Mack semi truck. The truck's large diesel engine growled, it's twin smokestacks spewed a burst of black dust, and the hulking vehicle surged forward.

The man peered into the distance ahead of him, then glanced at his rearview mirrors. There was no traffic on the mostly deserted interstate.

The timing's right. Almost perfect.

He cut the rig's steering wheel left and slid into the passing lane. He kept his foot jammed on the accelerator, the semi picking up speed. The speedometer ticked up. 65 mph. 70 mph, and he was alongside the Lexus.

The man eased off the accelerator and glanced down at the gray sedan, which was dwarfed by the massive truck. He cut the wheel to the right, the big rig edging closer to the car.

For a brief moment he caught the Lexus driver's wide-eyed look of panic, as he realized what was about to happen. The truck driver felt energized by the terrified look. He cut the wheel even further right and the two vehicles collided.

The scraping metal howled, the car's windshield exploded, and its tires shredded. The 5,000 pound Lexus was no match for the 80,000 pound truck and the car was thrown off the interstate, it spun 360 degrees, and crashed head-on into a rocky formation by the road, one of the many rock-strewn buttes that covered large parts of the mountainous state of Utah.

The semi, barely scathed from the collision, kept driving south.

The driver slowed the vehicle and glanced into the rearview just as the gas tank of the Lexus exploded, a ball of fire engulfing the crushed remains of the car.

He sped up again, wanting to quickly put distance between himself and the crash scene.

Half an hour later he pulled off the interstate, slowed the big rig, and stopped. Climbing out of the stolen truck, he started jogging away from it toward his own vehicle, which he'd hidden behind a butte. Ten minutes later he got in his Jeep. He took a swig of water from his canteen and pulled out his SAT cell phone. Turning it on, he pressed the encryption button and tapped in an international phone number.

When the woman answered, he said, "It's done."

"You've taken care of our Utah problem?" she asked in flawless English.

"Yes."

"Excellent."

"When can I expect payment?"

"I'll wire you the money today," she said.

"Good. Will you have other work for me?"

There was no answer for a moment, then the woman said, "I'm sure I will. I'll text you the details."

He heard a click on the line and realized she had hung up.

Chapter 9

Tokyo, Japan

The Asian woman hung up the call and placed the handset on the cradle of her desk phone. She smiled, pleased at the news she'd just heard. The operation was on track.

Standing, she went around her desk and strode to the life-size chess set in a corner of her massive, luxurious office. Going behind one of the intricately-carved ceramic pieces, she pushed it forward two spaces and then one space to the left. Each of the chess pieces resembled 17th century Japanese warriors. The one she had moved now, a white Knight, was her favorite chess piece because of its ability to penetrate deep into enemy lines.

Satisfied the board resembled the operation's current progress, she turned around and faced the far wall of the room. Attached to the wall was a huge flat-screen television. Picking up a remote, she turned on the TV and selected channel 13. On this channel she could monitor the activity at the businesses she owned.

Clicking the remote, she scrolled through multiple live images of industrial operations, finally settling on one. Displayed on the screen was a large room with hundreds of employees diligently working at their computer workstations.

The Asian woman zoomed in for a closer look at several of the employees. She finally stopped when she spotted one of her favorites. He was a strapping young man in his mid-twenties. He was good, very good in fact, at following directions and had given her much pleasure in bed. The operation was going so well that she had decided to give herself a special treat.

She zoomed in closer with the TV remote so she could read his employee ID number, which was stenciled below his name on his badge. Turning off the TV, she went to her desk and picked up the phone.

"Yes?" her young assistant answered on the first ring.

"Bring me employee number 38726," the Asian woman said in Japanese.

"Of course. When do you want me to do that?"

"Now!" the Asian woman snapped. "Now, you idiot. What did you think?"

"Yes, ma'am."

She slammed down the phone, irritated be her assistant's incompetence. Then she went to her teak cabinet and poured herself a large tumbler of scotch. Taking a sip of the liquor, her thoughts turned to the strapping young man from her factory.

Yes, she thought, a smile forming on her lips. *He will be a welcome diversion*. She had been putting in eighty hour weeks preparing for the operation and was looking forward to a few hours or relaxation.

Chapter 10

FBI Field Office
Atlanta, Georgia

"Good job on finding where the sniper took the shot," Erin Welch said. "My agents and Atlanta PD had been looking for that spot for days and came up empty."

J.T. Ryan grinned. "I told you I was good."

Erin rolled her eyes. "Don't let it go to your head. It's already too big as it is."

Ryan laughed. He had just come into her office and he approached her desk and placed a large manila envelope on top of it. "The evidence I collected at that building is in here."

"All right. I'll have my lab guys process it, along with anything else my CSI unit finds at the scene."

Ryan sat at one of the chairs fronting her desk. "So. Do I get a bonus?"

Erin frowned. "For what?"

He pointed to the envelope. "For getting that."

"Keep dreaming," the FBI woman said with a frown. "Your rates are too high as it is."

Ryan chuckled. "Just kidding."

She gave him a long, stern look, then her expression softened. "I should know you by now. You never stop joking around, do you?"

Ryan grinned again. "I do when there's a gun pointed at my face."

She moved aside the jacket she was wearing, revealing the Glock pistol holstered at her hip. She grinned back. "Don't tempt me, buster."

They both laughed and Ryan studied the attractive brunette, who as usual was dressed impeccably. She was wearing an expensive Ralph Lauren business suit, a dove-gray silk blouse, and Louboutin four inch heels.

The PI leaned forward in his chair and in a serious tone said, "So, what's next?"

"A few days ago I interviewed the man who's now in charge of Face-Look. He's the Executive Vice-President of the company. He seemed perplexed as to why the CEO was murdered. I didn't get anything of value from him. But I'd like you to take a run at him. Maybe you'll have better luck."

"Okay, Erin. Do you think he had any involvement in the killing?"

She shook her head. "I don't think so. But some people seem beyond reproach at first and turn out to be con-men or worse."

Ryan nodded.

She reached into a desk drawer, took out a sheaf of papers, and handed them to him. "Here are my notes and other info about this guy."

He took the sheets, scanned them, and rose. "I'll get going then."

"Okay. But a word of caution, J.T. This guy is a powerful man in the business world. He has a lot of contacts. Some, I'm sure, are high-up in government circles. Don't go in there and pull one of your Rambo stunts." She gave him an icy stare. "Don't rough him up. And don't pull your gun on him."

Ryan grinned. "Who me? When have I done something like that?"

"Go on, get out of here," she said with a sigh. "But remember. You've been warned."

The PI laughed, gave her a half-salute, and left her office.

He took the elevator down to the building's underground lot, got in his Ford Explorer and drove to Face-Look's headquarters, an ultra-modern, glass-and-steel structure that was one of downtown Atlanta's tallest buildings.

Ten minutes later he was shown into the large office of Tim Horvath, the Executive Vice-President of the company.

After introducing himself and showing the man his cred pack, Ryan took a seat in front of the executive's imposing desk.

"I already met with Ms Welch of the FBI," Horvath said, "and told her everything I know." He shrugged. "I'm not sure what more I can add."

Ryan nodded. "She told me you had been very cooperative. But, you never know, there may have been something you left out."

The man frowned. "I doubt it."

The PI studied the other man, who he knew was thirty-two, but looked much younger. He had a boyish look, with a slim build and a pale complexion. He was dressed casually in a black T-shirt and black jeans. Ryan knew the high-tech business world was run by very smart, very young people and Tim Horvath definitely fit the mold.

"You don't seem too broken up over Ross's murder," Ryan said.

"We were business partners. We were not close friends."

"Still. The killing of your CEO must have shaken you up."

Horvath shrugged. "Of course. But I saw it as more of a blow to our business plan. But now that I've had some time to process his death, I feel the company can move on."

"You're in charge of the firm now?"

"I am. Ross was the largest shareholder and my holdings were almost as large as his. That's why I'm now in control of the business."

"I see," the PI said.

"So, are we done here? I have a busy day today."

"No, we're not done here," Ryan said. "Let's start at the beginning. Tell me everything relevant about your business that happened in, say the last six months. Anything out of the ordinary. Anything that may have caused someone to want Matthew Ross dead."

Horvath glanced at his watch. "I'm a busy man. Is this really necessary? I told Erin Welch all this before."

Ryan smiled. "We can do this here. Or we can do this at the FBI office. Between driving over and back in Atlanta's heavy traffic, it might take a whole day."

Horvath let out a long breath. In an exasperated tone he said, "Fine. Where would you like me to start?"

"Tell me about Face-Look, your competitors, your overall business plan, anything that might shed light on your CEO's murder."

The executive nodded, and then spent the next forty minutes telling Ryan things he already knew from Erin's interview. Horvath began by describing how Face-Look had been able to surpass Facebook, its major competitor, and become the world's largest social media company. Then he proceeded to tell him about the rest of the industry. When Horvath was done, he said, "That's it. There's not much else I can add."

Ryan had learned nothing new, but sensed the company executive was holding something back. "Could I have some coffee?" the PI said, stalling for time. "I take it black."

Horvath glanced at his watch again. "I have a meeting soon."

Ryan grinned. "I'll drink it fast. Then I'll be on my way."

The executive scowled, but sensing the PI wasn't leaving, pressed a button on the intercom on his desk. "Mary," he said into the device, "could you bring a cup of black coffee for my visitor."

A woman's voice replied, "Of course, Mr. Horvath."

Five minutes later the door to the office opened and a woman came in holding a steaming mug, which she handed to Ryan. The woman was young and was wearing a tight, low-cut dress. Before leaving the office she flashed a warm smile at Horvath. Ryan glanced at the company executive and noticed the man blushed slightly.

After the secretary left, the PI slowly sipped the savory coffee while he gazed around the large office. On a credenza near the desk were a series of framed photographs. One of the photos was a family portrait. Horvath and a woman were in the picture, along with two young children. All of them were smiling brightly.

"You have a beautiful family," Ryan stated.

Horvath stared at the photo. "Thank you. My wife and I are blessed. We have two great kids."

Ryan took a shot in the dark. "I'm guessing your wife doesn't know you're screwing your secretary."

Horvath's face, which was pale to begin with, blanched. "I don't know ... what you're ... talking about ...." he stammered.

Ryan leaned forward. "You can deny it all you want, Horvath. But I know you're fucking her. Not that I blame you, she's a fine-looking woman."

The executive stood abruptly. "Get out of my office! I won't be insulted like this."

"Sit down," Ryan ordered. "I'm sure your secretary doesn't mind putting out to get a promotion, but I don't think she's willing to perjure herself with the FBI. What do you think?"

Horvath sank into his executive chair, a deflated look on his face. "What is this? Are you trying to blackmail me?"

Ryan shook his head. "No. Nothing like that. I'm trying to jar your memory. There's something you're holding back. Something pertinent to my investigation."

"All right." Horvath let out a long breath. "I guess there is something."

The PI drank more of the coffee and set the mug on the desk. "I'm listening."

"Three months ago, Matthew Ross had a visitor. An Asian woman. They met privately. I don't know what it was about. I asked Matt but he wouldn't talk about it. I sensed something was wrong."

"Okay. What else?"

"Last month," Horvath continued, "this woman came back and met with Matt again in private. From what I could gather, they disagreed about something. When I questioned him about it, he told me to stay out of it. He told me this woman was extremely well informed. Matt told me she could make trouble for me. She knew my secretary and I were, you know ...."

"And that's why you didn't say anything about this Asian woman before?"

"Yes, that's right. To protect my marriage."

"Okay. I understand now," Ryan said. "Who was the Asian woman? What's her name?"

Horvath shook his head. "Don't know."

"Was she alone?"

"No. She was always accompanied by a big Asian man. I assumed he was her bodyguard."

"Describe the woman."

"Striking looking – beautiful, but in a cold, hard way. Matt referred to her as the Ice Queen, probably because of her cold personality."

"How old was she?"

"Hard to say. She could have been in her thirties or older. She had a porcelain, doll-like face that many Asian women have – it makes them appear younger than they really are."

"Can you tell me anything else about her, Horvath?"

"She had long black hair and black eyes."

"Anything else?"

The man shook his head. "No."

"All right."

The company executive gave him a pleading look. "I've told you everything. Can you please keep quiet about me and Mary?"

"I won't tell anybody," Ryan said. Then he glanced at the framed photo of Horvath with his family. "But if you really are serious about protecting your marriage, I suggest you keep it in your pants from now on."

Horvath nodded, a dejected look on his face.

Ryan stood up and left the office.

www.ingramcontent.com/pod-product-compliance
Lightning Source LLC
Chambersburg PA
CBHW021459240626
47154CB00002B/443